Bittersweet Legacy

Jenna Ryan

Harlequin Books

TORONTO • NEW YORK • LONDON
AMSTERDAM • PARIS • SYDNEY • HAMBURG
STOCKHOLM • ATHENS • TOKYO • MILAN
MADRID • WARSAW • BUDAPEST • AUCKLAND

To Tom, who has gotten me through
many rough moments.
To Rowan, who will get me through many more.
And to Kathy, Bill, Kay and Alice.
You never let me down.

Harlequin Intrigue edition published April 1993

ISBN 0-373-22221-1

BITTERSWEET LEGACY

"My God, Damien. Look!"

But there was no time to look, or even think.

Directly in front of them, a powerful engine roared to life. Tires squealed on the wet pavement, and out of nowhere came a black car. It was on them before Damien could shove Melanie away. But just as it reached them, it stopped dead, as if it had run into an invisible wall.

The engine settled down to a low growl as the headlights snapped on. Then the door opened and a figure in black stepped out, an indistinct outline in the glare of the lights and the swirling fog.

"What do you want from us?" Damien asked.

"You'll find out," the figure promised. Then with deliberate care their unknown stalker slid back behind the wheel. A second later the headlights flared to bright. Damien heard the engine and in the next instant saw the car roll backward into the fog . . . and then the lights disappeared.

In silence Damien breathed the damp air into his lungs.

"He's going to kill us," Melanie said softly.

Damien pulled her close against him, pressing his face in her hair. "No, he won't," he promised. "But he's going to try."

ABOUT THE AUTHOR

Although Jenna Ryan worked in modeling and travel for several years, writing has always been her main career goal. She loves whodunits, thrillers, and old Alfred Hitchcock movies. She enjoys developing different characters, twisting the plot and creating a suspenseful atmosphere. Jenna feels that these three things heighten both the intrigue and the romance and give the reader a chance to use her imagination.

Books by Jenna Ryan

HARLEQUIN INTRIGUE

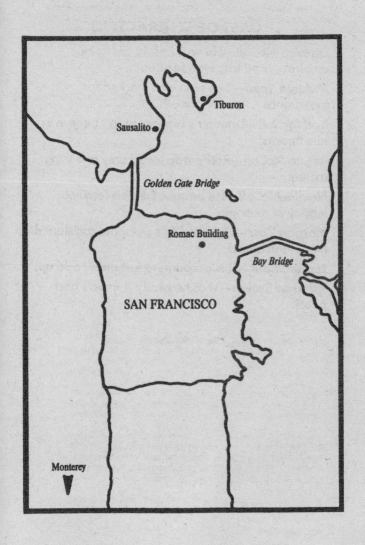

Tiburon

Sausalito

Golden Gate Bridge

Romac Building

Bay Bridge

SAN FRANCISCO

Monterey

CAST OF CHARACTERS

Damien McCall—He was heir to the Romac empire . . . and targeted for death.

Melanie Rossi—She was also marked for inheritance . . . and for death.

Rolf McCall—Damien's brother didn't believe in idle threats.

Regan McCall—Rolf's wife loved only one thing: money.

Neville McCall—He bequeathed his family a legacy of revenge.

Morgan Voss—Did Neville's personal assistant do more than assist?

Tucker Smith—This accountant just didn't add up.

Addison Brown—Was he really Romac's best pilot?

Prologue

Chicago, 1937

Tom Rossi's leather-shod feet dragged on the plush hotel carpet. It felt wrong what he and Nev had done. The way they lived, the deals they'd struck, everything they'd accomplished these past few years seemed so corrupt. And yet, deep in his guilty heart Tom knew he wouldn't change any of it. Only a fool would choose to sleep in a filthy doorway with yesterday's newspaper for a blanket, living on breadlines and praying for better times that never came. No, life and all its bitter circumstances had to be met and dealt with. The winners won and the losers lost. It was a simple matter of survival.

"You're shuffling, Tom. Conscience acting up again?"

Neville McCall's conscience never acted up. Self-made, self-possessed and Tom sometimes thought entirely self-serving, he strolled from the bedroom of his elegant hotel suite, the corners of his deep blue eyes crinkling as Tom poured himself a shot of whiskey.

"So, my friend, what news do you bring from our sullen partners?"

"Ex-partners." Tom bolted back his drink. "The Circle of Five has been dissolved." A humorless smile pulled on his lips as he stared into the empty glass. "They called us swindlers, swore to get even, then tossed me out on my ear."

Nev's chuckle was rich and throaty. "Swindlers, you say? Sounds to me like our former associates resent some of the deals we've made."

Tom's jet-black brows came together in a troubled frown. He drifted over to the window and pushed aside the velvet curtains, watching as a small group of hoboes scurried down a nearby alley. It had been snowing steadily for the past two hours. "I have a gut feeling about all of this, Nev. I can't explain it. I only know what I saw in their faces, and it wasn't good."

Laughing, Nev crossed to the window and clapped his partner soundly on the shoulder. "You let them get to you, my friend. What you need to do is pack up Isabelle and little Tommy and move out to the coast like I plan to do." He made a broad, sweeping gesture toward the western horizon. "We're going places, you and me. The Circle of Five is dead. It's just the two of us now, owners of a fledgling airline. We'll call it Romac Air, combination of our names. And when the economy improves, which it will, we'll be riding higher than ever."

Tom lowered his gaze to a man squatting on the corner of the street with a blank stare on his face. Maybe this Christmas would bring the man good luck. Tom, however, was unable to shed the sense of doom that had gripped him since his meeting with the other Circle members earlier that afternoon. Miracles were few and far between these days.

He glanced back at Nev's face, noting the self-assured expression. Scrooge and Marley, he reflected, and couldn't shake that sensation, either. "The higher we ride, Nev, the closer we'll have to watch our backs. Don't forget that. We've made our share of enemies these past few years. One of them might just decide to shoot us down."

"Not if we shoot first," Nev promised. "We outgunned the Circle of Five. Not even our enemies can stop us now."

Tom watched as the harmless-looking man squatting on the corner slowly drew a knife from inside his jacket and started up the street toward the bank. He sensed a sign of some sort in that, one of many he had come to ignore. He watched the snowflakes flutter and settle, a tainted Yuletide picture with only a few candied lights to proclaim the season.

Then he turned away from all of it. He couldn't allow himself to think this way. He and Nev were survivors. They did what was necessary. It was the only way to make it in this time of economic depression.

San Francisco, over fifty years later

RAIN TAPPED ON THE WINDOW of Neville McCall's private hospital room. To anyone who knew him, the man lying motionless on the bed would have seemed like a stranger, an imposter who bore only a passing resemblance to the great Romac Air mogul.

White hair framed a face that less than three hours ago had been the picture of health. Eighty-six years of experience had carved deep lines into features that now looked sallow and drawn. He was dying, and he knew it. That wasn't rain tapping at his window; it was Death, complete with pitchfork and horns and the pungent smell of brimstone.

Monitors beeped around him. Wires and tubes and needles protruded from his chest, arms, nose and mouth. His body felt numb; his mind was drifting into a semi-divine state. Soon he'd be with Tom again. Partners forever, they'd vowed in those lean, early years. On earth and ultimately in hell.

Nev's eyelids fluttered. He saw a shadowy movement in the chair beside the bed. His beloved Emily? No, she was gone. To heaven, he was sure. Who then? Rolf? Damien? Melanie?

He tried to make his mouth work, but no sound came from his throat. Above the tap-tap of October rain and the bleeping heart monitor, he heard a voice, soothing, but drowned out by something else. A memory. Angry words that flashed in his head, slicing through his grogginess.

An odd flapping sensation started up in his chest. The voice stopped speaking; the shadow left his side. But the words remained in his mind, sparking memories of a more desperate time. Pre-war, pre-prosperity for most, though he and Tom had never suffered. No, they'd survived the Crash and then some.

The scent of lilies and some kind of antiseptic wafted over him. But it was fall. Weren't the lilies dead?

There were two voices now, maybe more. They sounded concerned. Why couldn't he focus on them? Why did he keep seeing that horrible note and the eyes of the person who must have written it? He should have spotted the lie in those eyes a long, long time ago, should have recognized them from another time and place.

A sharp jolt of electricity shot through him. The flapping in his chest increased. The eyes of the person in his memory became disembodied entities that struck a note of terror in his strained heart. The person who'd written the hideous words wanted nothing from him. He was old, untouchable. He couldn't be broken. But there were others who could.

He struggled to speak, but it was a feeble sound that trickled out. *Dear Lord,* Nev groaned, his heart pumping madly while all around him people in white did their best to pull him back. What had he and Tom done? What kind of a monster had they created?

A steady, high-pitched hum filled his ears, and for an instant he felt almost euphoric. Then he saw Tom's face and behind that the scarred face of Death. They'd caused those scars. God help them, they'd destroyed the lives of people they loved most.

The words of the note seemed to float in the air above him. A strange numbness crept in. Nev felt himself beginning to drift away. Death had him within its grasp. Only the horror remained. And the message that would be his dying legacy.

Revenge is sweet, old man.
Bittersweet.

Chapter One

Flies droned against the dirty windows, a drowsy sound that Melanie Rossi remembered clearly from her childhood. She remembered the climate too, the sticky wet heat of the Venezuelan jungle that clung to her skin and made her cranky even though she'd promised herself that none of it would get to her. Not even the wearying hunt for a ride to this tiny village on the Orinoco.

She batted a bug from the table beside her then kicked her mother's cot with her foot. "Don't sleep," she said when it looked like the woman might doze off—or pass out, whichever came first. "I have to talk to you."

Cassandra Pascal Rossi lifted a cloudy glass to her lips. Rum, straight and high proof. "About what?"

"About you."

"There is no me. Only this." Cassandra held the tumbler up and laughed. "It's all I need, kid. Anyway, I still do my clay heads when the mood strikes." Flat on her back, she waved her fingers. "I'm perfectly fine, so why don't you fly off in whatever fancy silver bird brought you down here and leave me in peace."

Shoulders hunched, Melanie sat back. She folded her arms across her chest. "I can be a bitch too, Mother. I want you to listen to me."

"Go away."

"Not until you listen."

"Go or I'll sic Harry on you."

Suspicion narrowed Melanie's gray-green eyes. "Who's Harry?"

"My pet tarantula."

Melanie shuddered, and quickly scanned the floor. Nothing there but layers of grime and a small brown lizard. "I hate you," she muttered.

"Feeling's mutual. Go."

Melanie knew she should feel bad, or apologize or something, but it would be a lie. Well, half a lie. Of course she loved her mother, but only because she *was* her mother. As a person Cassandra was about as lovable as Harry, wherever he might be lurking. Again she checked the floor.

"You can sculpt just as well in San Francisco as you can here," Melanie pointed out. She rubbed her bare arms as something rustled beneath the cot. "Mother, don't you understand? Human beings weren't meant to live like this."

Cassandra mumbled a rude word in Spanish. "I'm happy," she said, then swirled her drink. "In another hour I'll be even happier." For a moment her eyes focused on Melanie's face. "My daughter, Romac Air executive. Elite Charter Division, right? But then you always were a mercenary little thing, greedy like your grandfather."

"I am not greedy."

Cassandra settled back with a rough laugh, her red-brown hair a mass of curls on the stained pillow. "The late, great Tom Rossi. What a crook. And Neville's no better. A swindle a day, that was their motto. It still is Nev's. The old coot. If I knew jungle voodoo, he'd have gotten his a long time ago."

Melanie rescued the hem of her long Indian cotton skirt from the floor. "According to Nev you know plenty about jungle voodoo."

"Not enough to get that bastard." She chuckled. "I got Tom, though, got him real good. I took his precious son away. Now Tommy, he understood life. We didn't need money to be happy, just a roof over our heads, a few clothes and some food." She sighed. "I never meant to get pregnant."

"Thanks a lot."

Her mother shrugged. "No offense, kid. I just never wanted babies. And that was the one time Tommy got stubborn. He wouldn't leave the States until after you were born."

"Yes, I know. I've always appreciated that."

"I'll bet you have." Cassandra drained her glass. "You're a brat, all right. Life became real easy when your daddy died and old Nev came down here to tell me he was taking you back. So who's stopping you, I said." She smiled. "I thought he was going to hit me."

Melanie hiked her skirt up a bit higher, propping her feet up on the cot. None of this really upset her anymore. Well, maybe a little, but it was too old to hurt like it had when she'd been a child.

"At least Nev understood that I didn't belong in a hut," she said. "You never did seem to get the message. So did Papa, he just never told you."

Cassandra shook her head. "I should have had Damien for a kid." Her hand shook slightly as she poured another glass of rum. "He might pilot planes for Romac, but he's still a jungle baby at heart."

"He's a full grown man, Mother. And his home's in Salvadore, Brazil. That's hardly the jungle."

"He went down the Amazon before college. Close enough." Amusement pulled at Cassandra's lips. "Bet old Nev had a fit over that. His grandson on the big river."

"Adopted grandson," Melanie reminded.

"It's all the same to Nev. What he couldn't have, he stole. You, Damien, Rolf, you all belong to him now. Everyone except the witch. How is she by the way?"

"If you mean Regan, she's fine."

"Too bad. She only married Rolf for Nev's money."

Melanie held back a sigh. Rolf was Nev's other grandson. Like Damien, Rolf had been adopted by Nev's son, his only child actually. One was a blue-eyed, blond-haired German, the other a dark-eyed, dark-haired Brazilian. But how Rolf's wife, Regan, had gotten into this conversation Melanie had no idea.

Pushing her long dark hair over one shoulder, she changed the subject. Or rather she moved it back to where she wanted it. "Mother, I don't care about Regan's motives. You drink too much, and that I do care about."

"You're lying."

"I am not."

"That's two lies. Go away."

Melanie held her temper, but she knew right then that she'd made a mistake coming down here. Let Cassandra drink herself to death if it was what she wanted to do. They never had been close the way a mother and daughter should. She should give up right now and go home.

A monkey screeched close by. Immediately after that something landed on the roof then scrambled across on its claws. As long as it wasn't a snake, Melanie could handle it. She'd learned the hard way how to cope in the rain forest. But coping wasn't loving. Although Cassandra had been born in Santo Domingo in the Dominican Republic, this was her home now. It had never been Melanie's.

"Tommy, listen to me," Cassandra had argued when Melanie was four with her ear pressed to their bedroom door. "We've lived in Caracas for three and a half years. You own a nightclub. But wouldn't you rather take pictures? Why don't we pack ourselves up and go to one of those remote villages in the rain forest?"

"Live in the jungle?"

Melanie's father had sounded appalled, but that didn't mean much. Anything Melanie's mother wanted she got.

"What would I photograph in a Venezuelan village?" he'd finally asked.

"Animals," Cassandra said in that velvet voice she often used on him.

Melanie bent her head. They were going to the rain forest.

"What about Melanie?" her father had asked. "She's four years old. She needs an education."

"Of course she does, darling. But you could teach her. And just think, she'll learn how to survive under the most primitive conditions."

"Well . . . maybe," her father conceded.

It was enough. They'd come almost straight to this collection of huts on the river. To Melanie's surprise three American families already lived there. Cassandra knew one of the men, which didn't surprise Melanie. Even by age four, she'd figured out that Cassandra knew a lot of men. Not the rich ones. She didn't care about money or power. She just liked men and liquor and living in squalor.

Cassandra called this last thing being free, but as far as Melanie could see, Papa didn't enjoy being free anywhere near as much as her mother did. He spent a lot of time in the cooler caves not far away.

"They're a world all their own, my caves," he would say to Melanie. Poor Papa, his mind was going. And it was Cassandra's fault.

By the time she was seven, Melanie had learned to resent her mother deeply. Her father was fading slowly away and not talking a lot anymore.

She was twelve years old the day Papa didn't wake up.

"He's dead," was all Cassandra said to her. "Nev wants his body and possessions shipped back to San Francisco." And off she'd gone to pack up his journals, clothes and camera. Melanie hated her.

"Your hearing gone, Melanie?" her mother asked now, cutting short the unpleasant memory. "The supply boat's here. One of the men is calling you. Maybe you've got an admirer."

"And maybe I'll move back here someday," Melanie said with an uncharacteristic blend of sarcasm and sadness. Cassandra didn't care, so why did she continue to put herself through these yearly visits?

"Señorita Melanie?" A skinny man with a beard and grimy pants appeared at the door. "There is a telegram for you, from America."

Her mother poured another drink, not stirring from the cot. "Maybe Romac's gone bankrupt," she suggested with a coarse chuckle. "There would go your cushy job, and your six-figure income."

Melanie sighed. "You're all heart, Mother." She took the smeared paper and unfolded it.

"Bankrupt?" Cassandra asked in a hopeful tone. But suddenly Melanie couldn't talk, couldn't do anything but stare in shock. She felt as if someone had kicked all the air from her lungs. The words blurred before her eyes. This wasn't possible. The message couldn't be true.

"Well, what is it?" her mother demanded. "If not bankrupt, then what?"

"Neville's—dead," was all Melanie could get out and she almost choked on that. "He died early this morning in the hospital."

"Did he really." Cassandra took a slow sip of her drink. "So he got his just deserts at last, did he? That should make the Circle boys happy." Then she tipped back her head and laughed.

"NEVILLE'S DEAD. Stay put. Damien will come." Cassandra tossed the telegram aside while Melanie shoved jeans and socks and boots into her knapsack. "Seems clear enough to me. Why are you packing?"

Melanie ignored the question. How could Nev be dead?

Cassandra yawned. "So the old guy's gone, what's the big deal? He was in his eighties, and trust me, he didn't deserve to live that long. Ask his former partners, if you can dig any of them up—in the non-literal sense, that is."

Shut up, Melanie begged silently, fighting her tears.

"He was a snake, baby, that cold and that mean. The only person he didn't swindle was your Grandpa Tom."

Melanie pulled on a pair of high-topped suede hiking boots and began lacing them up. "That's right, he never did swindle old Tom. When does the supply boat leave?"

"Not till tomorrow." Cassandra propped herself up on her elbow, then put a hand to her head and squeezed her eyes closed. "But you're supposed to wait for Damien, remember? He'll get you out of here faster than any boat."

Pushing her skirt down, Melanie stood and reached for her knapsack. Desperation clawed at her. She needed to be away from here quickly. "I don't suppose you want to come back for the funeral," she tried one last time.

Her mother fell back against the pillow. "Send pictures. Did you hear what I just said?"

"Send pictures," Melanie repeated. Burying her disappointment, she checked her watch. Four hours of light left, tops. Maybe the telegram was wrong. She shuddered. "If I hurry I can probably make it to Uguarta before dark."

Cassandra grunted. "Can't you read? The telegram says Damien will come for you."

"Well, he's not here now, Mother, so I'm leaving without him." Melanie was amazed at her calm tone. It didn't feel right. "Rolf sent the telegram, not Damien. For all I know my ride could be navigating the Rio Negro with a bunch of his Varig Airline pilot friends. Nev might not matter to you, but he matters to me. I want to be at the—" she hesitated, then forced the word "—funeral." She looked back sharply as Cassandra opened her mouth to speak. "Don't say it," she warned. "Mention the will just once, and before I leave here, I swear I'll dump every bottle of rum you have in the river."

"In that case, *hasta mañana*, kid. Have a nice hike."

Melanie couldn't think of another thing to say. Her brain felt totally numb. But for some reason she went back and kissed her mother's cheek. "Bye," she whispered, then she grabbed her knapsack and left the hut.

The skinny messenger was down by the dock, if you could call the little piece of rotting wood a dock. "Where's Captain Juarez?" she asked.

The man smiled. "He goes to find the women. You know—" he winked at her "—the ones who like pretty gifts."

"Figures." Melanie dropped her bag, pushing irritably at her hair. Nev couldn't be dead, he just couldn't. "Do you know—" she began, then broke off when a hand tapped her shoulder from behind.

She knew without looking who stood there. It could only be Damien. And suddenly Melanie wanted very much to sit down on the dock and cry.

She blanked her expression and turned to face him. "You came," she said. "I didn't think you would."

"Yes, you did. You just wish I hadn't because I remind you of Nev, and you'd rather not cry in front of me."

Bastard, she thought, wishing he would disappear. But that was a wish born of frustration and hurt—and the fact that he was exactly right. You could fight tears with anger, however, and Melanie usually found it easy to get angry after a few rounds with her mother.

Damien lived Cassandra's life, in a modified way, of course. Melanie figured Cassandra put it best when she said that Damien had the look of a devil with the expression of an angel. His hair was dark and wavy, somewhere between brown and black. Right now it was also very long, curling past the collar of his shirt. His features were slender if not especially fine; his eyes were a deep shade of gray, so much like charcoal they often looked black. He also appeared taller than six feet, which seemed odd to Melanie since at five foot nine she could hardly be considered short.

He wore khaki pants and a shirt, sturdy hiking boots and no hat. But then he never wore a hat, unless he couldn't fly cargo and was forced to wear one as part of his Romac uniform.

Melanie regarded him now at close range, feeling vaguely dizzy as the heat of the jungle pressed in on her. "It's true, isn't it? He's dead."

Damien nodded. Was he pale beneath his tan? His eyes scanned the river. "It was a heart attack," he said quietly. "Very sudden, according to Rolf. I don't know the details."

What could she say? Taking a deep breath, Melanie swung her knapsack over one shoulder. "How do we get out?"

"I have a jeep two miles from here. We can drive to Uguarta. There'll be a boat waiting to take us to Caracas. We can fly to San Francisco from there."

Melanie felt her lower lip beginning to tremble. "I loved him," she whispered, a confession she seldom made. "I really did."

Damien's dark eyes told her nothing of his feelings. "I know," he said. "Come on, we'd better go."

THE OLD MAN'S HAND shook as he reached for the buzzer beside his bed. He had a thought in his head. He must not lose it.

His blue-veined hand found the buzzer. *Come, Sonia,* he begged his granddaughter. Or Jessie, his housekeeper.

He saw something in his mind, the shadow of a memory.

Oh, it had been so cold that morning, wintertime in Chicago. Snowflakes were falling from the sky, "Jingle Bells" was playing on the radio. He'd had the steam heater going on full and a glass of eggnog in his hand. But the phone had been ringing and it was a very loud jarring sound. He hadn't wanted to answer it, hadn't wanted to know what he would hear when he picked up the receiver. He was old now, and sometimes he forgot what the voice on the wire said to him. Something about the Circle of Five, yes, that was it. And he was a part of it, wasn't he? One of five men in partnership.

But it didn't matter. It was the other thing he mustn't forget, that more recent moment when he'd seen the man's face.

Where are you, Sonia? he begged. *I have to make you understand. A man came and told me a story, a horrible story.*

"Grandfather, what is it?"

A woman's pretty, round face appeared over his bed. Sonia. He tried to smile.

She patted his shriveled hand. "Just relax, Grandfather, I'm here. Don't try to talk. You know what the doctors said."

No, Sonia, no. It's not what the doctors said, it's what he *said, the man who came here. Did you see him?*

But his lips barely moved. Only a tiny gurgle came from his throat.

"Shh." Again she patted his hand. "I have something to tell you, but I won't do it unless you lie still."

He stopped struggling and stared at her through half-closed eyes.

"That's better." She rubbed his frail arm. "It's about Neville McCall, Grandfather. You remember him. He got you into the Circle of Five. Well, he's dead. He had a heart attack last night at his home and died this morning in the hospital."

The old man's eyes fell closed. So it was true. Neville was gone. And Tom many years before him. Both their sons were dead, too. Now, there were only grandchildren left. That should be enough revenge for anyone. It should end with this death.

It should, the old man thought tiredly, but it wouldn't.

Chapter Two

The boat Damien hired had a canopy on it, but no mosquito netting. Melanie slathered insect repellent on her arms, draped a piece of long cotton gauze over her head and shoulders and told herself she was having a nightmare. She wasn't floating along the Orinoco and Neville wasn't dead.

"He's not dead," she heard herself whisper with force. "He can't be."

Damien handed her a cup of coffee from a thermos. "Accept it, Melanie," he said quietly. Didn't he ever show his feelings?

"I can't," she told him in a small voice. "He came and got me from here after my father died. He didn't send someone, Damien, he came himself and took me out."

Damien brushed tendrils of damp hair from his cheeks. "I know he did. I was angry because he wouldn't let me come with him."

She set her cup down, bracing her palms on the seat. "Look, I realize we don't know each other all that well, and this might seem like a rude question, but did you and Nev get along? I mean, you spend a lot of time in Brazil. I know Romac has flight crews based all over the world but you fly mostly out of São Paulo and Miami, never out of San Francisco. Why?"

His dark eyes regarded hers across the bench. "I don't like San Francisco. It's damp and foggy and I always catch cold when I go there." He shrugged and glanced at the trailing branches near the shore. "I was born in Brazil. I like the country of my birth. I'm happiest when I'm there."

Melanie heard a pop, like a cap gun shot off close by. Probably someone shooting at fish. "I understand why you like Salvadore," she said. "But you also loved Nev, right? And your adoptive parents?"

A tiny smile pulled on his lips. His eyes returned to her face. "Rolf told me you were curious. I didn't realize how much." Then the smile vanished, and there was nothing in his beautiful features. Maybe a trace of sadness deep in his eyes but if the emotion did exist, his lashes shielded it from her sight.

For some reason, Melanie couldn't accept that. She leaned forward. "Damien," she began, "don't you think—" She stopped suddenly and narrowed her eyes. "Why are my feet wet?"

Damien looked sharply down, then muttered something in Portuguese that was close enough to Spanish for Melanie to understand. Not that talk was necessary. The river water was already seeping through the laces of her boots, and getting higher by the second.

They were sinking! She twisted her head around. The boatman at Uguarta, a man Melanie knew and trusted, had assured them that his new assistant had checked the boat personally. It was in fine shape.

"Right," Melanie repeated, bailing with her hands while Damien struggled forward to dig out the pumps. "I'm going to get all covered with leeches, I just know it."

Damien tossed her a pump. "Here, use this."

"Damien, I don't think these things are going to be very helpful—what's this?"

With her left hand Melanie broke from the handle a small object wrapped in plastic. It looked like a castle battlement. A chess piece, maybe?

"Forget it, Melanie." Damien stood and tossed his hand pump aside. The water was up to his ankles. "It's no good. We'll have to swim to shore."

Swim? Gritting her teeth, Melanie climbed to her feet. She clutched the miniature castle tower tightly in her fist—for luck, she told herself. "I really hate the jungle," she said under her breath. Then slinging her backpack over one shoulder, she hoisted herself over the side and into the water.

The undertow was deceptively strong in this part of the river, but Damien had kept the boat close enough to shore that the distance was manageable. That didn't mean it wasn't difficult. Her clothing hampered her, especially her skirt, which of course she should have stripped off. Twice, the current dragged her under, but each time she surfaced and struggled on. It seemed like hours later that her fingers finally latched onto a fern that was strong enough to support her weight.

With a boost from Damien, she crawled out under a tree, waited to make sure he was safe, then tossed her bag and talisman to one side and began checking her arms and legs for whatever slimy creatures might have decided to attach themselves to her body.

"This place is worse than hell," she grumbled.

Damien collapsed on the bank beside her. "More jungle spite?" he asked, but he sounded distracted, vaguely suspicious. "That shouldn't have happened."

"Tell it to the boat." Melanie did a double take, shoving wet strands of hair from her eyes. "Where is the boat? It didn't sink already, did it?"

Damien nodded, his troubled eyes still on the river. He glanced sideways at her. "Did you hear a noise right before you noticed water in the boat?"

"You mean like a BB gun? Yes."

"How long before?"

"About a minute." Satisfied that nothing clung to her, Melanie picked up the plastic packet and unwrapped it. She'd guessed right. It was a chess piece. A rook. A bright red marble rook. "How odd," she murmured. She set it down and lifted her eyes to Damien's face. "Do you think the sound we heard is important?"

"Maybe." He indicated the chess piece. "What's that?"

"A rook. It was attached to the pump you gave me. Maybe it's a lucky charm. I've seen stranger things down here. Anyway, it doesn't matter. Tell me more about the sound, the gun or whatever it was. I thought it might be someone shooting fish. There was a man in our village who used to do that."

Damien's long fingers took the chess piece from her. "You must have had an interesting life."

"I didn't think so. I was very glad when—" Nev's name got stuck in her throat, so she substituted "—when I could leave."

Damien looked at her but said nothing. Then he frowned and nodded at her wet skirt. "Where did that come from?"

Melanie looked down into her lap, at the piece of folded paper that sat there. "I don't know." She picked it up. "It isn't wet. Maybe it came with the rook."

"A lucky charm with instructions," Damien murmured with a faint grin. "Anything written on it?"

Melanie unfolded the paper and her eyes scanned the words printed in red ink. It was written in English.

"Interesting," she answered, holding the note. "If this is meant for us, I think we might be in trouble."

"What kind of trouble?" Damien asked.

"'Rook threatens pawns,'" she read out loud. She could almost feel the venom of each word flowing into her bloodstream. "'This game we begin to play is under my control. I will have my revenge on the false king's heirs.'"

"MY GOD, WHAT HAPPENED to you?"

That was the first question out of Rolf's mouth when Damien dragged himself through the door of his brother's elegant Telegraph Hill home in San Francisco.

Damien located the nearest chair, an ugly blue plaid thing in the study, and all but fell into it. "We had some trouble," he said, wincing as he closed his eyes. Even his lashes felt scratched. "Our boat sank in the middle of nowhere. We had to hack through the jungle with our hands because

I lost my knife in the river. We finally conned a ride from a British archaeologist. Expert in the field, he claimed—right before he got us lost. We spent one night in a decaying hut, another in a cave, got bitten by every insect and stabbed by every thorn in sight."

"Sounds like your kind of fun." Regan strolled in wearing a red silk minidress. "The jet leaves for Chicago in an hour. That means we leave for the airport now. Melanie's coming with us. Are you?"

Damien ignored her. All the way to Chicago for a funeral. It probably made sense, though he hadn't thought about it until now. Nev had been born in Chicago. Tom and Isabelle and Nev's wife, Emily, were buried there. That meant he would be, too.

For a moment Damien considered telling his brother about the note Melanie had found on the boat, but that thought died the moment Regan appeared. She was a shrew, a tiny fine-boned London-born termagant with shorn-off auburn hair and a mean, snappish attitude.

Without opening his eyes, Damien answered quietly, "No," to the question of joining them. He ignored the face Regan made at him, then watched as she hauled Rolf out the door.

"Don't get the furniture dirty," she called over her shoulder. "The funeral's at four o'clock tomorrow afternoon Chicago time, if you feel the urge."

The only urge Damien felt was to snarl at her. He resisted, but it was difficult. What in God's name had Rolf ever seen in her?

Shuddering, he forced himself up and out of the study, determined not to dwell on any of this. Oh, but Nev's death did hurt. He thought about it all through the cold, foggy night.

HE WAS STILL THINKING about it the next afternoon as he approached the north end of the Chicago estate, which had for forty years been Nev's private lakeside retreat.

The Porsche Rolf had insisted on leaving for him at the airport handled easily despite the driving wind that had brought a mass of black storm clouds racing inland from Lake Michigan. Damien didn't appreciate the gloomy weather, but it seemed a fitting atmosphere for Nev's funeral.

Something very chilling had ridden in the air at the cemetery. More than the ground fog that clung to the gravestones late into the gray fall afternoon, he'd sensed a feeling of doom about the proceedings. Even the minister's words had had an eerie ring to them.

"Like a requiem knell," he'd heard Melanie murmur, not to him specifically, though he'd been the person closest to her and the only one who could have caught the remark. She'd known it, too. Eyes bright with unshed tears, she'd looked right at him and shrugged.

Was her comment connected to the note and the red rook? he wondered, then he blocked the thought. In fact he blocked the whole exhausting affair in Venezuela. Today was for Nev, not for mysteries, not even ones that involved Melanie Rossi.

A distant hint of amusement pulled at Damien's lips. They were two of a kind, he and Melanie, alike in many ways, yet complete opposites in others. He wondered sometimes why he'd never gotten to know her better.

In his mind he pictured her. She'd inherited all the best features from her Caribbean mother and her Italian-American father. Her hair, a rich shade of brown, was long and exquisitely thick, anywhere from wavy to curly, he'd discovered in Venezuela. She was tall and while he'd never realized it before he found he liked that. She had a slender frame, sleek but nicely curved. Damien had always preferred curves.

The leaves were just now beginning to change color, the inevitable flow into a new season. It was springtime in Brazil, autumn here. For a brief moment, he closed his eyes and wished he could be back in the country he loved so much.

"Well now, that's ingratitude for you." Regan's sharp tones echoed in his head, a memory that would hurt if he let it. "Lionel and Hilary take you, a South American street brat, into their beautiful San Francisco home, and all you want to do is go back to the dirt."

Damien shut the words out as he invariably did. Regan didn't know him. With friends in his native Brazil he would lower his guard, and only then to a certain extent. He had loved once, loved his real parents with all his heart. Then they'd died and he'd been made a seven-year-old orphan with no one except an old aunt left to take him in. Just another mouth to feed as far as she'd been concerned.

Damien shied away from all the memories, a difficult thing to do with Nev's mansion rising up before him.

It stood on a wooded section of land close enough to the lake that you could hear the waves crashing against the shore. Today the house looked precisely like the brooding manor Nev had intended it to be, a gloomy, sullen edifice, its Gothic windows and high peaked roof obscured by a wall of red maples and backed by the swollen mass of black clouds.

Damien eased the powerful Porsche through the iron gate, then along a sycamore-lined roadway wide enough to accommodate only one car at a time. It was like driving into a 1940s whodunit. His perception went from color to black and white. God knew he would rather sell his soul than face what came next. The reading of Neville McCall's will.

Damien peered through the deepening twilight. He could see Rolf, evidently waiting for him under the porte cochere. No sign of Regan, Melanie or Morgan Voss, Nev's personal assistant of twenty years.

"Straggler," Rolf accused mildly from the wall where he leaned. While Damien was dark and slender, Rolf was blond and rangy. Feline/canine was the comparison most often drawn between them. It was more flattering than a few others Damien had heard.

"There's a storm blowing in," his brother continued. "A big one by the look of it. I figure that, together with the outdated wiring, should make for a pleasant night."

"Probably," Damien eyed the gathering clouds. "Something feels wrong," he said softly. He regarded his brother's face, so unlike his own. "Have you noticed it?"

Rolf's blond brows came together in a frown. "What do you mean?"

Damien sighed. "I'm not sure. Forget it. I'm probably inventing ghosts."

"That's not like you," Rolf said with a small grin. "Oh, well, never mind. We better go in. Jorgensen, Nev's lawyer, wants to get started as soon as possible. But before he does that, Morgan insists he has to talk to us."

The clouds crept nearer. It was pouring out over the water. "Which of us?" Damien asked, zipping up his jacket against the chill. He'd worn a suit to the funeral out of respect to Nev, then stopped at a gas station on the way from Chicago to the house and changed into his usual jeans and cotton shirt.

"You and me, Melanie and Regan."

"Why?"

"I don't know, but he sounded peculiar, even for Morgan."

"He mentioned something about a note," a familiar voice put in.

Damien couldn't resist looking at the woman who joined them. It was Melanie, gorgeous as always in a black knit dress and black suede pumps. She had a tiny scratch on her cheek, the result of a low branch she hadn't seen as they'd slogged through the rain forest.

It took a moment but the significance of her remark finally sank in. "What kind of a note?" he asked warily. With his fingers he felt the chess piece and paper he'd tucked into his jacket pocket. Was the new note tied to this? he wondered. And yet for all its implications he still didn't quite see how the rook could have been meant for him and Melanie.

The time factor, the distance—it was too fine a line, wasn't it? "What exactly did Morgan say, Melanie?"

"I'm a woman, Damien," she reminded him. "Morgan doesn't talk to women, remember? Have you showed our note to Rolf yet?"

Rolf's brows went up. "*Your* note?"

Damien shrugged. "I'll explain as we go."

It was one of those explanations that took forever to get out and in the end made very little sense. "I don't know," was about the best response he could give to most of Rolf's questions.

They walked down a long hallway, then up a set of thickly carpeted stairs to the library. The room had a dusty old-book smell about it and three equally dusty men poking through the crammed shelves. They were relatives of Nev's deceased wife, Emily, if Damien wasn't mistaken.

"But you heard something just before the boat sank, you're sure of that?" Rolf pressed.

They passed through the library en route to Nev's private study. The sight of the familiar room was a knife blade in Damien's stomach. Damn, but he'd loved that old man.

"Positive," Melanie confirmed. She tugged on Damien's jacket to hold him back. "Are you all right?"

His lips curved slightly. "Don't I look all right?"

"No."

"Then I'll have to fake it." He nudged his brother's arm. "Don't mention this to anyone," he said. "The note might not even have been meant for us."

"What do you mean, might not?" Melanie demanded. "I thought we figured, time and distance and all that, it probably wasn't."

Damien cut her off with a quiet, "Shh," in her ear. "I told you in Caracas I had mixed feelings. Let's hear what Morgan has to say, okay?"

She regarded him in suspicion. "Why?"

"*Candomblé,*" he said, looking into her lovely gray-green eyes.

"Candomblé..." she repeated, frowning. "Wait a minute, isn't that some kind of African voodoo they do in Salvadore?"

"Not exactly. It has more to do with conjuring spirits. Let's say it can affect your instincts."

"Has it affected yours?"

"Maybe. I have a feeling."

"A bad one?"

He nodded. "Very bad."

Chapter Three

"It's disgusting," Rolf declared. "Everyone's eyeing the furniture and the paintings. One of Emily's cousins is actually on her hands and knees inspecting the rugs."

Damien located the bar and a can of soda. "Nev was loaded and uncommonly solvent," he said. "It was the same at Emily's funeral. Everyone hoped Nev would wither up and die without her."

"It feels like yesterday," Melanie murmured. She leaned against one of the carved rosewood walls, her eyes on the wind-tossed lake beyond the windows. "I can still remember it and I was only six when Emily died."

It was also the one and only time Melanie had gotten out of the jungle village, until Nev had taken her out forever.

Regan tapped a small impatient foot on the floor. "All right, can we cut the fond memories and get down to facts? Where's Morgan?"

"Why don't you go and look for him?" Damien suggested, lifting the can of soda to his lips.

Why didn't she go jump in the lake, Melanie thought with distant dislike. She watched as the clouds huddled closer together. They looked angry, bruised, the way she felt inside. *Hurry up, Morgan,* she pleaded silently of Nev's stuffy assistant. *This is going to be a horrible night. The power's bound to go out.*

"Ah, Rolf, Damien, you're both here. Good."

A tall man materialized in the doorway, a ghoul to Melanie's mind. There was really nothing in his physical appearance to suggest such a thing, but she always pictured a stitched-together monster whose scars had been magically erased. With his straight brown hair, his pale brown eyes and squared-off features, Morgan's was not a look to inspire trust, or any other pleasant emotion.

He didn't acknowledge either Melanie or Regan. He merely crossed to Nev's desk with his characteristic stride that seemed at once smooth and laborious.

"We might have a problem," he began, but Regan interrupted rudely.

"Yes, a note, we heard." She lit a cigarette, drumming her nails on the bar. "So why don't you produce the thing and be done with it?"

Her cap of super-short hair shone like copper in the soft study light. Pretty, petite and piranha. Melanie never would understand why Rolf had married her. But then why had her father married Cassandra? It must be some sort of selective blindness.

Morgan's long white fingers unlocked the desk drawer. "You won't like this, I'm afraid."

Melanie already didn't like it. A mysterious noise and a sunk boat, two notes, a red chess piece. What could be worse than that?

"The message is a bit disturbing.'

"You're a bit disturbing, Morgan," Regan muttered.

Melanie slid her gaze to Damien, a silent spectator behind the bar. It seemed he studied this scene from a distance. She wondered what he saw, what he felt. She'd spent two days in the jungle with him and she still knew virtually nothing about him. Well, nothing except that he was one of the most introspective people she'd ever met.

She forced her eyes away, recalling the time at Emily's funeral when she'd first met Damien and Rolf. Of course Damien had been meeting most everyone for the first time. He'd been nine and just off the plane from Brazil, a slender dark-eyed child who reminded her of wary animals she'd seen in the forest. He didn't trust anyone, hadn't spoken a single word that she remembered. In fact he'd closed his expression right down. Even as a young child, Melanie found that fascinating.

"Everyone's paying attention, I trust?" Morgan remarked, as he took a folded piece of paper from the desk and deliberately held it out to Rolf.

"Well?" Regan demanded. "What does it say?"

Rolf read the words out loud. "'Revenge is sweet, old man. Bittersweet.'"

"That's it?" Regan made a incredulous gesture. "That's the big mystery?"

"Shut up, Regan." Melanie pushed away from the wall, taking the paper from Rolf whose face looked puzzled. "Where did this come from?" she asked Morgan.

His shoulders stiffened. He hated women, no one knew why. Unfortunately, he was an extremely efficient man. No other person alive knew Romac as well as Morgan Voss.

"It was found in Mr. Neville's penthouse," he told them.

"By whom?" Damien asked softly.

"By me."

"Naturally." Regan's fingernails continued to tap. She glared at Melanie, then drew on her cigarette. "Well, if that's the lot, I suggest we go downstairs."

"But what is it? A warning of some sort?" Rolf still appeared mystified.

"Sounds more like a threat to me," Melanie said.

Damien left the bar. He came to stand beside her. Taking the note from her, he gave her a quick shake of his head.

Melanie wasn't quite sure what Damien meant. Don't mention the other note? Don't worry?

"When did Nev receive this?" he asked.

Morgan moved a shoulder. "I don't know exactly. I believe it might have been the morning he had his heart attack."

"Right, a little threat sent him into coronary arrest." Regan rolled her dark brown eyes. "Somebody give me a break. We're talking about a man who stole, sorry, bought an airline during the Depression and made a go of it. He played golf at his club the day before he died, and then he came to the office and yelled at me because some idiot in reservations overbooked three flights in one day. And you think a few words on paper could give him the screaming oopazootics?"

"We get the idea, Regan," Damien interrupted. Then to Melanie he said, "This note's typed. The one we got was written."

Melanie nodded as Morgan cleared his throat.

"There is more," he told them. This time his spidery fingers reached into the drawer and brought out a telephone answering machine. His eyes gleamed in the diminishing light from the lake. Then he pressed the Play button and stood back, an ominous sentry around which the sound from the tape at once began to flow.

A peal of laughter came first, more unsettling than the thunder from the lake that underscored it. Melanie shivered in spite of herself. She couldn't help remembering the river current that had tugged at her skirt, and the words of the other note. "I will have my revenge on the false king's heirs . . ."

Silence filled the study as the laughter faded away. Then slowly a voice took over, a mechanical sound, like a ventriloquist's doll controlled by a computer.

"Your time is up, old man," the voice predicted. "You can't stop Death and you can't stop me. But you can know this. All the king's horses and all the king's men won't put your heirs back together again."

There was a pause after that, a long drawn-out moment when no one moved. Melanie's skin crawled. Beyond the mansion's walls the thunder rolled on, a foreboding preface to the rest of the message.

"Rook takes king, old man," the taped voice warned. "The legacy you leave is death—to all those you love."

"CROWN ME," ninety-three-year-old Herschel Barnum ordered with a dry cackle. When his checker-playing partner didn't comply he swatted the man's arm with his cane. "No napping, you old buzzard. Crown me before Nurse Fuzz gets here."

"Nurse Fuzik, and I'm not napping." Rupert Skillings, ninety-one, plopped a red checker in the appropriate square then peered at his partner along the hooked beak of his nose.

He was shorter than Herschel, a little rounder, a little more arthritic and a lot more patient. He also had more hair, which was completely irrelevant, but he liked to point it out whenever Herschel got ornery and started waving his cane around like he was now.

Of course Herschel wasn't exactly being ornery tonight, but then why should he be? He'd just won his third game of checkers in a row. And there was that other matter, too. Now, what was it? Rupert searched his mind. A lot of dust in there these days. Something to do with someone dying, wasn't it?

Well now, that didn't help. Their old friends were dropping like flies, all those souls heading to that big retirement home in the sky. Hope Nurse Fuzik never came there.

"Retirement home, my foot," Herschel snorted in disgust, and Rupert realized he must have spoken out loud. He did that a lot these days. "That old clip artist's going straight to hell or my name isn't Herschel Barton."

"Barnum," Rupert corrected, but Herschel dismissed the mistake with a flick of his cane.

"Slip of the tongue. Means nothing. Let's get down to business before Nurse Fuzz gets here. Neville's funeral was today." He cackled again and smacked the tip of his cane on the carpet. "I tell you, Rupe, I'd give my eyeteeth to have been a fly on the wall at that little party."

Rupert was tempted to point out that neither of them had any eyeteeth left to give, but he stopped when his mind flashed a remarkably clear picture of Neville McCall. Tom Rossi's face was a little dimmer, but then he'd died a long time ago, almost thirty years back, wasn't it?

Rupert thought of the two men. Clip artists, cheats, swindlers, there weren't any words strong enough to describe Nev and Tom and what they'd done to the Circle of Five. Rupert saw red, then he saw Herschel's thin, lined face. That face looked downright nasty at the moment.

"They're both gone now." Herschel's smile was grinchlike; his cane beat a triumphant tattoo on the floor. "The old Circle of Five has come down to the Circle of Three. We're the survivors now. And by cracky we're going to get what's coming to us."

Rupert couldn't help it. He let a vicious little smile spread across his lips. "Is it all set up?" he whispered, just in case Nurse Fuzik snuck up behind him on those rubber-soled shoes of hers. "Is our Rook in place?"

"In place and already at work."

"Alone?"

"Hell no, he's got help on the inside."

"He does?" This was news to Rupert. Unless he'd been told and just forgotten. It happened these days. "What kind of help?"

"Don't know, don't care," Herschel stated flatly. "And neither do you." A bony finger stabbed the air over the checkerboard. "Don't you forget, they deserve this. They're kin to our sworn enemies. It's Nev and Tom who sealed those kids' fates, not us. You know old Sam would agree with me if he were here instead of stuck in that bed of his. Hell, him and me, we used to play chess by the hour back before we started nodding off in the middle of our games. He's gonna love that we hired someone who calls himself Rook to do our dirty work for us."

"Rook, pawns, two dead kings." Rupert shook his head. "It doesn't sound like this game will take very long to play."

For once, Herschel said nothing. But his smile was the picture of vengeance. And his cane tapping against the leg of the table sounded remarkably like a 1930s-style machine gun....

"IT'S LIKE Agatha Christie comes to Universal Studios," Rolf said immediately following the reading of Neville's will.

"Universal did a lot of horror movies in the thirties and forties," Melanie explained to Damien who appeared not to understand the allusion.

Rolf moved on toward the living room, where many of the disgruntled beneficiaries huddled in groups. It was all shadows in the house and had been since halfway through the reading when the wind knocked the power out. Unperturbed, Mr. Jorgensen had lit a candle and carried on.

Soon enough they'd all had candles and with only a few exceptions, resentful gleams in their eyes. Almost everything had gone to Rolf, Damien and Melanie, no surprise in that.

Truthfully, Melanie didn't care that she and Nev's two grandsons now each owned seventeen percent of all Romac shares, controlling interest. Added to the shares they'd already possessed, they really did have firm control. And if one of them should die, the others would split that person's inheritance. Very legal and proper. But nothing felt any different to Melanie. Nev was still gone, and that was really all that mattered.

She doubted that she would have given the will or its conditions a second thought if Regan hadn't sent her that long speculative look when the contingency clause was announced, and if she hadn't kept hearing that horrible mechanical voice in her head. What did the voice mean, "Death to all those you love?"

"So how does it feel to be filthy rich? Quite a change from the gutters of Brazil, don't you think?"

Tucker Smith, one of the few non-legatees here tonight came up behind Melanie and Damien as they made their way by candlelight into the downstairs study.

Sweet man, Melanie thought with sarcasm. Tucker was an accountant at Cable Car Foods, another of Nev's holdings. She didn't know how Damien kept from punching him for his mocking tone.

"So, how does it feel?"

"Not bad at all," Damien returned calmly. He added something in Portuguese that Tucker wouldn't understand, but Melanie did, then he walked off.

She halted, smiling a little. "Is there something you want, Tucker?"

"Of course not." He narrowed his eyes as Damien headed for the bar. "Did he just insult me?"

"Thoroughly. Why are you drooling on my shoulder? I didn't inherit any part of Cable Car."

"Ah, but you got the airline, and that's the accounting department I want into."

"Talk to Rolf. He's higher up at Romac than I am. I'm Elite Class, remember? I do the charters."

By candlelight, Tucker's rather square features appeared to harden. He was close to forty but wouldn't admit it. He wore his brown hair long, down to his shoulders, rather like an ancient Roman might have done. His eyes were flat brown, his lips thin, his nose usually flared—his imitation of an aristocrat. Abrasive was the word Melanie used to describe him, but of course he'd come to Romac through Morgan Voss, so what could you expect? No doubt that's the only reason he was here tonight, because of his connection to Morgan. He hadn't inherited a thing. But then why should he?

Morgan had told Nev that Tucker was an up-and-coming pilot who was also a wizard accountant. Well, he wasn't the latter, Melanie knew. Jonny Morelli at Romac was the wizard. Tucker was a mere apprentice. That's why he worked at Cable Car Foods and not with the big boys at the airline.

Melanie could hear the rain pelting the side of the mansion. A tiny draft in the study made her candle flutter. The velvet draperies had been drawn back, making the lightning over the lake visible. It flashed in great crooked forks, bringing a shiver to her skin.

"Why don't you go play the Ouija board with Addie?" Damien suggested to Tucker. He'd returned with a soda for Melanie. "Maybe it'll tell you what fate has in store for you."

Tucker frowned. "Who's Addie?"

"Addison Brown," Melanie told him. She sipped her drink. "He flew Rolf and Regan and me to Chicago. He's one of Romac's best pilots. Nev stole him from a rival airline."

"Correction, Mel, I defected." Addison's voice drifted over from the coffee table. "Nev just made it worth my while."

Another bolt of lightning turned the study a ghostly shade of blue, and made Melanie's heart lurch. Her nerves were stretched to the limit, past it in fact. She didn't need banter. And she definitely didn't need Damien beside her, looking as gorgeous and sexy now as he had in the jungle. But she had him anyway, didn't she? She also had other important things to consider, threats from an anonymous individual looking for revenge on Neville's principal heirs.

"Revenge for what?" she wondered out loud when Tucker was gone. "I know Nev wasn't a saint, Damien, but if you want revenge on a person, isn't it generally more gratifying to take it on that particular person?"

"Not if that person can't be touched." Damien ran his fingers through his dark hair, which was starting to curl from the rain. His mouth looked full and sensual in the candlelight. "I should have found out more about that boat before we left South America."

Melanie didn't want to go into that. "I don't suppose there's any chance that these notes could all be part of some elaborate practical joke?" She caught the grim light in Damien's eyes and sighed. "No, I didn't think so. Well, all right then, what do we do?"

Damien regarded the electric night sky. "For a start, we could go to the police, but I doubt there's much they can offer."

"Until one of us dies, then they'll step in."

"You're a cynic, Melanie." There was a note of humor in his tone. "If you were the police and I brought this information to you, what would you do?"

She hesitated. "Not a lot, I guess. Okay, what do you suggest?"

"We wait."

"That's not much of a suggestion."

"Best I can manage." He leaned against the table, studying his own glass. "What do you know about Nev's tactics, Mel?"

"In business?" She sighed. "Well, I know he could be ruthless. The word swindle came up a lot at parties, but mostly I'd hear it from older people—you know, rivals and former associates that he'd had dealings with for twenty years or more."

"What about Tom?"

"Same thing. At one Christmas party I went to, I heard a lot of Scrooge and Marley comparisons. But I don't think it came from the outside. I got the impression it was more something Tom used to say about the two of them."

Faint amusement curved Damien's lips. He had, Melanie realized suddenly, the most exquisitely beautiful mouth.

"Will you tell me something?" she asked him, and was a little unsettled when his eyes came to rest on her face. Those eyes were really quite remarkable. She liked their changeable aspect. They looked black in the next flash of lightning. Shaking the strange effect away, she went on, her head tipped to one side.

"You remember at Emily's funeral, when all those people were seeing you for the first time? Could you speak English?"

A tiny pull of humor at the corners of his lips pretty much answered her question. "Not really."

"But you understood it."

He shrugged. "My family was poor, Melanie, not stupid. My father drove buses for American tourists. He picked up a lot."

Melanie started to say that she understood since her mother had insisted she pick up Spanish, but a crash and an unexpected blast of wind through the study stopped her. Her candle blew out before she could cup the flame. So did every other candle in the room.

Someone next to the hearth uttered a short scream. "What happened? Oh my God, is it Nev?"

"That would be his entrance if it were," Tucker remarked from the direction of the Ouija board.

"The window's blown open," Damien said to Melanie.

His shoulder brushed hers. She felt the warmth of him and the sleek muscles of his arm even through all the layers of clothing. And that disturbed her, because she shouldn't have been able to feel anything at all. A shiver ran through her.

"Oh, Lord, what if it is Nev's spirit," the woman by the hearth moaned, then she let out another scream.

"I'll get the window," Damien said. He set his hands on Melanie's arms and turned her toward the fireplace. "You calm the screamer down. I'm no good at that sort of thing."

Neither am I, Melanie thought, grimacing as she bumped into a chair. But someone had to talk to the woman, and Addie and Tucker weren't making any offers.

Above the wind and the rain and the rattle of papers tossed about by the wet gusts, Addie managed to light a cigarette. He used the glowing tip to study the Ouija board.

"Will I get the woman of my dreams?" he asked it.

Tucker merely snorted with disdain.

"Don't help," Melanie muttered to them in passing.

Without lifting his tousled brown head Addie said, "Mel, bang the table or something, will you? This thing's not working."

"Neither's your brain," Melanie replied under her breath. Nevertheless she gave the table a kick.

To her left she heard the window click shut, felt the wind on her cheeks stop. She found the woman a moment later.

"It's okay," she said, taking a pair of plump shoulders in her hands. "Nev's not here, it's only the wind... Hey, watch it!"

Someone rushed past, banging rudely against Melanie's back and almost knocking her into the fireplace. Again the woman emitted a low scream. "It is Nev," she moaned. "He's come back."

Melanie caught her balance before she could pitch into the ashes. "Idiot!" she swore. "All right, who's the—"

A bright glare of light in her eyes cut her off. Then the light jiggled wildly and Regan's angry voice demanded, "Hey, what's going on here? Who's the Sunday driver? Damien, are you here?"

"By the window."

"Melanie?"

"In the fireplace."

With an impatient motion, Regan swung her flashlight to Melanie. "What are you doing in there? And who's screaming?"

Someone was tending to the frightened woman now, so Melanie abandoned her mission. She dusted off and started for the light. Rather, she would have if she hadn't suddenly realized that one of her hands was no longer empty. She was brushing her dress with an envelop.

Regan called out. "Damien! I want to go home, tonight. Can you fly?"

"No."

"Why the hell not?"

Damien's voice was closer to Melanie now. "I haven't slept for three days."

"I'll fly you back," Addie said. "Point that thing over here, will you, Regan? I want to see if Melanie's kick worked."

The light shifted just as Melanie was turning the envelope over in her hands. There was something on the back, but with the beam gone she couldn't read it.

"Where are you, Mel?" Damien asked.

"Right beside you." Her groping fingers found a candle on the mantel. "Do you have a match?"

He didn't answer, but then an orange light flared in the darkness next to her. A lighter. Melanie reached for his wrist.

"Look," she said, pulling the flame down. "Someone slipped this envelope to me when the candles went out."

He bent his head close to hers. "Another note?"

"I hope not."

Her breath caught sharply as she tipped the envelope into the little pool of light. Her name was scrawled there in black crayon, a chilling sight for all its childish aspects.

But that was nothing compared to the figures drawn with absolute precision at the bottom.

There were three of them, three chess pieces, set on paper by an artist's expert hand.

The symbolism made Melanie's blood run cold, her fingers go numb. She stared at the figures as Damien did, except that she knew her shock showed. She couldn't help it. She was looking at two kings laid out in long black coffins, and between them, a blood-red rook. A rook that was exact in every detail to the one she'd found right before their boat sank in the Orinoco River.

Chapter Four

From the diary of Neville McCall
December 15, 1933

You wouldn't believe what's out there on the streets of
Chicago, Diary. Death, despair, hunger—and more
broken dreams than even Tom remembers seeing as a
boy in Italy. They're everywhere, these lost souls, all
battered, destroyed by circumstances beyond their
control.

Beyond theirs, not mine. I refuse to see this. What's
more, I refuse to live in poverty, and I know Tom
agrees with me in spite of what his conscience says.

We're two of the lucky ones, he keeps saying. We still
have our shirts. But I tell him we won't have them for
long if we don't get rid of the outdated values we were
taught as children. Sorry Father, Mother, but honesty
isn't worth a plug nickel when the whole damned
country's falling apart. Compassion's a death knell,
and neither Tom nor I are ready for the grave just yet.
Suckers, that's what we need. And reluctantly Tom dug
one up today, a big strapping kid who's had his lights
punched out a few too many times. Says he wants to be
a boxer. He had the look. We'll set up a fight, give him
the usual one and a half percent, then pack him off to
Dublin. He'll thank us in the end, but even if he doesn't
it'll all be the same. We'll be on our way, Tom and me.

(Confidentially, Diary, I've been doing a little scouting of my own. I already have my eye on several naive business bunnies. A couple of strategically placed carrots, a little street savvy and nothing, not even the damned economy, will be able to stop us).
Who says Santa Claus is dead . . . ?

> For now,
> Nev

Damien read the diary pages from the envelope slipped to Melanie, what was it, two hours ago now? It felt like days.

They were aboard Nev's private jet heading back to San Francisco, a large group of West Coast legatees whose faces had paled when Mr. Jorgensen had loudly announced the possibility of a tornado passing through the Great Lakes area. Not to worry, he'd assured, but by then the exodus had begun, a swarm of rats scurrying for their rental cars.

"Stay or go?" Damien had asked Rolf and Melanie.

Rolf looked at the mansion's shadowy walls. "Maybe we should leave. Mel?"

She'd nodded, but it was the unopened envelope that held her attention, and Damien's, too. He didn't like the symbolism suggested by the chess pieces on the back. God knew what they'd find inside.

Well, they knew now, the four of them, sitting here at the rear of the plane while Morgan glared at them from his forward seat. He resented his exclusion from the group. Addie was flying and Tucker was talking to Jonny Morelli from Romac's accounting department. The other passengers were scattered, but none approached the solemn group gathered around the cherry-wood table.

Not that Regan was particularly solemn.

"You're jumping at shadows, all of you," she accused, shaking out a linen napkin as the steward served them each a steaming chicken dinner. "Someone wants us to know all the nasty things Nev and Tom did, that's all. Maybe it's the boxer they shipped off to Dublin on the cheap."

No, Damien's instincts said. It was closer than that, possibly a distant relative who felt cheated.

"Anyway," Regan continued, "Nev was a rat no matter how you look at it. Tom, too. Ireland was no fount of prosperity in the thirties. I know. I have cousins there. And as for their other dealings..."

Damien shut her out. He had deliberately seated himself next to Melanie, though that proved to be a mistake, if the heat in his blood was any indication. He'd already entertained too many times the prospect of having those luscious legs wrapped around his hips, her mouth on his, her hands...

He shuddered. All fine fantasies, but what came after them? She loved San Francisco. He hated it, hated the fog that rolled in from the Bay and the chill that hung in the air winter and summer.

She nudged him now in the ribs, diverting his thoughts. "What did Nev mean, 'business bunnies?'"

"Entrepreneurial fledglings?" Rolf suggested.

"More like marks," Damien said. "Nev and Tom were con men."

"In plain English, they were crooks," Regan translated. The idea seemed to please her. "Bloodsuckers." She speared a cherry tomato and popped it in her mouth. "Leeches."

"Survivors," Melanie shot back. "The Depression was a bad time."

Regan pushed her plate away and stood. "Always an excuse for Nev, but never a feeling for anyone else. Why should I defend him? He didn't leave me a bloody thing."

Rolf looked uncomfortable; Damien was tempted to lock her in the cargo hold.

He watched Regan stalk off, then saw Addison Brown emerge from the cockpit. Addie was a tall man with a lean build, dark brown eyes and a mop of brown hair. A handsome Ichabod, the female flight attendants at Romac called him. The office staff, too, but they preferred Jonny Morelli for looks, or so Regan claimed. And Regan would know.

She ran the Romac gossip pool, the way Tucker ran it at Cable Car.

Damien found the whole thing boring. How could Melanie, who had lived with nature in the jungle, possibly like such a dreary routine?

"What are you doing here, Addison?" Tucker demanded in a fury. He trailed Addie to their table. "Who's flying the plane?"

"Oh, put a cork in it, Tucker," Regan muttered, pushing past.

"We're on autopilot," Addie replied, shaking loose the fingers that clutched his sleeve. His brown eyes looked amused. "Do you mind, I have to use the john."

"But there's turbulence," Tucker objected.

"There's also a copilot," Rolf reminded him.

Melanie eyed the man doubtfully. "I thought Morgan said you flew jets."

Tucker stopped. "I did. I mean I do. I—well, I sort of had a bad experience last year. But I don't want to talk about it." He pointed at the table. "What's that?"

Smoothly, Melanie slipped both envelope and diary pages onto her lap. "It's personal," she said.

"A love letter?" Addie teased, emerging from the washroom.

"Not exactly."

"More likely a complaint from one of her Elite Class clients." Regan returned with a cigarette between her fingers. "Do you have a light, Addie?"

"No. If you're going to screw up your lungs, Regan, do it by yourself."

Grinning, he tossed her his lighter and started back up the aisle.

A rift in the air currents rattled the plane's hull. "We're flying into a storm," Damien said to Melanie, but storms didn't appear to worry her.

"'Rook takes king, old man,'" she quoted from the telephone message. She set the envelope up in front of his water glass. "Now, look at this drawing."

He shrugged. "Two dead kings."

"Right." She waited, then said, "Well, don't you see? In this picture, it looks like the rook has killed the kings."

"Or the rook has remained alive after the kings are dead."

The plane lurched again. "Maybe," she agreed. "But either way it's a progression, isn't it? The kings are gone, the rook's alive—and what are we?"

The word, "Pawns," was quite literally torn from Damien's mouth with a suddenness that surprised him. It wasn't turbulence that rocked the plane this time, it was a hole in the air, like only one other he'd experienced before.

This time the screams of fear were understandable.

The bottom had quite literally dropped out of the current they'd been riding. Like a vertical roller coaster the jet plunged downward. Toward what?

Damien struggled to pinpoint their position by time and flight plan. They should be over Nevada by now, he judged.

They leveled off in a few seconds that passed like hours even to an experienced pilot.

"Hell of an air pocket," Addie called back, righting himself and guiding a frightened man toward an empty chair.

"Seat belt," Damien said to Melanie. He started to stand, but felt her pulling on his jacket.

"Wait a minute, where are you going?"

"Up front."

Her grip tightened. He saw the anxiousness she tried to hide. "Why?"

He pried her fingers loose, then, acting on impulse, something he never did unless he was flying solo, he brought her hand to his lips. "Because," he answered, which was no answer at all, only the best he could do right then.

His mind clicked over swiftly. The plane was settled, more or less. The turbulence continued, no problem there. But something didn't feel right to him.

Giving the strap of Melanie's seat belt a tug, he glanced at Rolf and startled Regan. "Stay put," he told them all, then he fought his way up to Addie who was trying to shake loose three pairs of hands clutching his uniform.

"It's like fending off an octopus," the pilot murmured. The plane heaved unexpectedly, knocking him into Damien's chest. "Sorry." He got his balance while Damien got his breath. "What is it, do you figure?"

"Don't know." Damien rubbed his sore chest.

Jonny Morelli rescued Addie from the last frantic pair of hands. "Who's in the right seat?" he shouted.

"Brogan. Twenty-seven years of experience."

Addie started forward again, but this time it was Jonny who grabbed his arm. He grabbed Damien's too. His black eyes were locked on the window, glazed over with something stronger than fear.

"My God," he whispered. "Look out there."

Out there was night and the darkness of a storm in motion, black clouds tinged with an unnatural glow. Damien's eyes closed. Pretty... And deadly.

Ahead of them, Morgan's mouth dropped open. "Why, it's as if we were flying into another dimension."

"We should be so lucky," Addie muttered. "Sit down, and buckle up."

"We're in trouble, right?" a teenager yelled to Damien. Who'd brought a kid on board? "Maybe we're going to crash?"

A screech of metal shot through the air. Damien felt the spiral that pulled at the outer shell, saw with clarity now the blue glow that came from under the wing. He'd been through this before. He knew the sounds of fatigue and everything that went with it.

It was impossible to walk a straight line, harder still to listen and to know. Did anyone besides him smell the smoke?

"Brogan's lost it," Addie yelled above what sounded like the pounding of a thousand angry drums. He'd reached the cockpit door.

Damien lost his balance when he looked back. Where was Melanie? And Rolf? A chill of horror crawled down his spine. He couldn't see them, couldn't see anything except a smoke-filled cabin and Tucker's frantic look.

"Go fly the plane, Damien," one of Emily's cousins beside him begged. She beat her frail fists against his arm. "You're supposed to be flying the plane."

"No, I'm not." Damien shook the punches off, sat her down and at the same time shoved his feelings away. They didn't need him up front, but he was going anyway. Better to be up there where he could see the controls.

"The plane," Morgan gasped. "It's on fire, isn't it?"

Every terrified eye was on Damien's face when he nodded. And he knew it didn't make any of them feel better when he said, "The plane and one of the engines."

"MINA..."

The name slid through Melanie's head, a great foggy blanket of sound, confused, distorted, faintly preternatural. In her mind, she had visions of giant bat wings closing about a skull moon. The world was all shapes and vague shadows, darkness shot with streaks of pink and red, like a sunset over the ocean, filling her thoughts with color.

What a strange dream this was. There was a sense of falling through space, of catching a vine and swinging through the trees. Except the trees were all on fire!

Smoke billowed around her. It seared her lungs, like the talons of a hawk tearing at her chest. She couldn't breathe. Where was the air?

Hands touched her body, her throat, her face. Strong, deft hands. How did she know they were Damien's?

"Where are we?"

The question drifted out of the smoke. The voice was Regan's. She sounded frightened more than cross.

"We're in Mina." Someone else spoke now, a man. Was it Damien? "It's a small city in Nevada. Relax, Regan. We're all out and safe."

Fingers brushed Melanie's cheek, stroked the hair from her forehead. Then a stream of air came into her lungs. Her eyes flew open in shock. Damien's mouth was on hers! He was breathing life back into her limp body.

More doors opened in her mind. The whole ugly scene replayed itself in slow motion. They hadn't crashed, not exactly. So why did everything seem hazy to her, out of focus?

"Lie still, Melanie."

Damien spoke to her. How dispassionate he sounded. Never a hint of panic. How did he do that?

"What happened?" Was that her talking now? She hardly recognized the croak that came from her throat.

Damien's hands continued to touch her. He hadn't touched her like this in the jungle, not in the hut or the cave or even on the river. The river...

"We made an emergency landing," he told her. His face was very close to hers. What a perfectly beautiful man he was. "We landed at an airport just outside Mina, Nevada."

Melanie tried to move, to flex her aching muscles, but Damien held her fast, and belatedly she felt the soft bed of grass and earth beneath her. Though the pain remained, the fog in her head began to clear. "Is everyone all right?"

"Lie still. Everyone's fine. Tucker twisted his ankle and you and Rolf and Morgan banged your heads. But other than that no one was seriously hurt."

Figures dressed in white took shape around her, ghostly specters outlined with flashes of red and blue neon.

The smell of electrical smoke was strong in the night air. Fire! She struggled to concentrate. They'd made an emergency landing. These were medical people hovering about.

Cool fingers stroked her hair, then pressed against her skin just enough to make her sore muscles relax.

If she stopped breathing would Damien put his mouth on hers again?

A light glared suddenly in her eyes. Voices murmured in the background. She picked out a word, but confined it to the shadows of her mind. She didn't want to hear it. Make the red and black chess pieces push it away. Except that the black kings were dead, weren't they? Only the red rook lived.

What did it all mean?

The diary pages, the notes, the taped message, were they threats or mere pinpricks designed to wake the sleeping conscience? And what about that horrible word she held in limbo in the back of her mind?

"She has a slight concussion. She'll be fine," a doctor said.

Less fearsome ideas crept in. Damien still stroked her hair. Had he really kissed her earlier? Maybe not. Her thoughts were fuzzy, cloaked in the most bizarre mist, like blue smoke.

"Sabotage..."

The trapped word shot through her head. Had someone said it out loud? She listened hard to Rolf's whisper.

"It was sabotage, Damien, it had to be."

Damien didn't answer. He didn't have to. The horror crashed through anyway.

Rolf went on. "This wasn't a coincidence. You'll see, Damien. Someone wants us dead!"

THEY COULDN'T PROVE a thing.

That much Rook knew for a fact, and the knowledge brought a smile to his lips. A full day had passed since the airborne incident. The police couldn't help them; no one could. Sabotage was so easily arranged. Not perfectly so in this case—the plane's electrical system wasn't supposed to catch fire—but he'd made his point in any event. Of course, he hadn't really wanted to be on the plane....

Darkness closed in around him, cool and moist. He smelled the inevitable dampness that was San Francisco, tasted it, felt it clinging to his warm skin. He liked the Bay area, especially Hyde Street Pier, with its wicked name.

Jekyll and Hyde, that was him all right. But then Rook was a more appropriate name. He'd watched the kings die, now he would destroy the pawns. What a birthday present he gave himself.

He stood by the seawall, his eyes traveling over the Golden Gate Bridge as he considered his options. He'd arrived in San Francisco late that afternoon. So had the others. His lovely, confused pawns.

He must do something to shake them up again. He did not want them to regain their emotional balance.

Ah, but there was little chance of that, he thought with a chuckle. He had a plan, a way to make them see what they might otherwise deny. They would know the truth, and suffer for it.

The wind lifted strands of his hair. The tang of salt and diesel fuel permeated the night air, a rejuvenation in many ways. He should go to talk to Herschel and Rupert, but they'd be tucked in their beds by now. And then there was old Samuel, the invalid. He was always in his bed. Three swindled old souls, no longer a part of the Circle of Five thanks to Neville and Tom.

A snarl fell from Rook's lips. Three men destroyed by two vipers. But he would make things right. Time was on his side. Time and inside help.

It was going to happen finally, the plan of a lifetime. And no one would ever figure it out, or even know who he was. Some secrets should never be told.

Chapter Five

A high-placed banking executive wanted to charter one of Romac's Elite Class jumbos for a Halloween party.

Normally Melanie would have enjoyed making the arrangements. Three days after the will reading and subsequent forced landing in Mina, Nevada, however, she could scarcely pay attention to the details.

"San Francisco to Boston on the twenty-seventh." Melanie massaged her pounding temples. "Okay, we can do that." She cracked an eye at her new assistant. "Can't we?"

"Yes, ma'am."

He was too polite, too perfect. She didn't trust people who looked and acted like department store mannequins.

She sat up straighter at her desk in the eighty-three-story office building that looked out on Coit Tower, and of course her beloved Bay.

Nev named it the Romac Building, although he could have used only his name. Tom had been dead by the time the plans were conceived. He'd died of a perforated ulcer one year before Melanie was born. One measly little year between gravestone and grandchild. It wasn't fair.

"Can I get you an aspirin, ma'am?"

Melanie continued to make circles on her temples. "No, and don't call me ma'am."

"Yes, Ms. Rossi. Shall I contact our decorators about Mr. Hiroshi's Halloween flight?"

"What motif does he want, dragons or vampires?"

"Something innovative, he told us. I'm not sure what that means."

"Where I come from it means put a witch's hat on the dragon's head." Romac's number one accountant, Jonny Morelli, poked his head in after a quick knock. "Sorry, Mel, but your secretary's at lunch and I can't find Rolf."

"No problem." She eased her eyes open. Why did the sun have to be out today? Even through a wall of smoked glass the glare hurt. But was it the sun that had created the pain in her head or all those horrible questions that kept chasing themselves through it?

"You can go, Sidney. Call our decorators. Tell them to send me three or four design sheets." She stared at her cold coffee. "Okay, Jonny, what's the problem?"

"I need the afternoon off." He grimaced as he poured her a fresh cup of coffee. "Apparently my basement's flooded. The plumber can come either today or two weeks from today, nothing in between."

Melanie leaned back in her oversize chair. Across the room and with the light shining in his face she could almost talk herself into believing that Jonny was Damien, that's how much alike the two men looked. Jonny was a little heavier, his dark hair a little shorter, his black eyes soft and unchangeable in aspect, but it was a close resemblance. Not that she should care.

"As far as I'm concerned you can go," she said. "Where's Rolf, do you know?"

He nodded, leaning back against the door. "Thanks, and I have no idea. Maybe with Regan, but I doubt it. She left this morning, hasn't been back since. How's your head?"

"It hurts."

His smile was faint. "It's your own fault. You weren't supposed to come to work so soon after the, uh—well, you know."

"The near-crash. You can say it, Jonny. God knows the police and the FAA and half a dozen other lettered agencies keep bringing it up." She looked at her watch. "What time is it?"

"One-thirty." He started out the door, then paused. "Oh, and Damien called the switchboard while you and Rolf were in that board meeting this morning. He's on his way back from wherever."

"Anchorage."

"Really? You know where he went?" Jonny's voice contained a note of sadness. "You never know where I am."

"I know where you'll be," she said with a somewhat uncomfortable twinge. Jonny liked her, and she liked him, just not the same way.

"Right, I'll be wet and grumpy in my basement." He tugged on the large carved wood door. "Anyway, Damien phoned to say that he's not coming in. There's probably a message somewhere on your desk, but I gather he's going to be buried under six feet of blankets. I don't think the Alaskan climate agrees with his Brazilian blood."

It wouldn't, Melanie thought. But then crash landings, threats and sinking boats didn't agree with hers. Neither did the idea of sabotage, especially when no evidence could be found to support the theory.

"It was deliberate, Damien," Rolf had insisted well into the day after the crash, long after they'd left Nevada. "You say you feel things, well, I feel this, and I don't like it."

Neither did Damien, Melanie had seen that, not so much in his face, but in his body language. He'd looked restless, caged, unable to sit still. She'd also decided that he was avoiding her, but it might have been her imagination. No one had talked much to anyone on the milk-run commercial flight from Mina to San Francisco.

Once Jonny was gone, Melanie set her mind on her work. The Gonzales's wedding flight to Mexico City departed tomorrow. Were all the details in order? She went methodically down the list. But other thoughts kept creeping in to distract her.

Why chess pieces for symbols? What did the diary pages mean? Who were the business bunnies Nev referred to? Had Damien actually kissed her, or was that just wishful thinking?

Stop it, she ordered herself, tossing her pen down in exasperation and pushing once again on her temples. *Forget that man!*

Her intercom gave a soft purr, followed by her secretary's voice. "Melanie? There's a young woman from accounting to see you. Lucy Farmer."

Should she know that name? Melanie checked her watch. Three o'clock already? "Okay, send her in. And tell Sidney to check with Cable Car about the food for the Gonzales flight."

A slight woman with brown hair and huge round glasses ventured through the door. "Ms. Rossi?"

Lucy Farmer sounded tentative. She must be new.

Melanie nodded. "Come in, Lucy. Is there a problem?"

"Not exactly. I mean sort of, but they say you're very nice, and there's no one else around."

"I beg your pardon?"

She scuttled over to Melanie's desk. "Well, you see, Mr. McCall, Rolf McCall that is, has left for the day. And I can't talk to Mr. Voss about this."

Melanie felt a smile tugging at her lips. Poor Rolf, he'd inherited Morgan Voss by default, and he was too nice to fire him. On the other hand, Morgan was very good at his job.

"I guess you know that Mr. Morelli went home, as well," Lucy went on. "So that meant I could either come to you or go to Mrs. Drexell, the supervisor. But Mrs. Drexell's hard to talk to and they told me in the rest room that it would be better to talk to you anyway." She let out a nervous sigh. "Am I making any sense?"

Melanie smiled. "I think I get the idea. Go on."

Lucy relaxed visibly. "Well, anyway, I'm new here, but I sort of noticed that my desk was messed up this morning. And I think maybe somebody's been using my computer without clearing it with me. I figured maybe someone in charge should know about it."

"Is that all?" Melanie asked.

"Not quite." Lucy fidgeted with her fingers. "The thing is, I saw Mr. Voss leaving the office where I work really early this morning. I couldn't figure out why he would have been there, and it was right afterward that I noticed my desk was wrong."

Melanie frowned. "I see." She didn't, but it was an interesting story even so, significant perhaps in that Morgan Voss knew nothing of accounting, or so he claimed.

"Is it okay, then?" Lucy wanted to know. "I mean I don't want to get anyone in trouble, not even Mr. Voss, but I thought I should say something."

It was a telling remark. "You won't," Melanie promised. She stood, swayed slightly and crossed to the door. "It was good that you came to me, Lucy," *Except my head feels like it's going to explode, and I really need to get some work done.* "I'll mention this problem to Mr. McCall."

Lucy's smile widened. "Thanks," she said with obvious relief. "Everyone said you'd understand, but Mrs. McCall—well, you know."

No, but she could imagine. She'd also have to make a point of going into the staff washrooms more often.

Lucy smiled again, then scuttled back through the outer office.

"Sidney," Melanie said to her assistant from the doorway. "Do you know where Mr. McCall and Mr. Voss are?"

"Yes, ma'am, I mean, no—uh, Ms. Rossi."

A stammer from the ever polite and perfect one? She walked over and leaned her palms on his desk. "Spill it, Sidney," she ordered. "Where are they?"

He looked away, a flush staining his cheeks bright pink. "It's just gossip," he mumbled. "I'm not sure how true it is."

Melanie sighed, too tired to argue. "What, Sidney?"

He hesitated, then sent her a conspiratorial look. "Well actually, they say his wife's, uh, having an affair. Of course," he added quickly, "like I said, it could be just a rumor."

Melanie considered the idea. "An affair with whom, did 'they' say?"

Her assistant shook his head. "No." His eyes darted back and forth, then his voice dropped to a confidential level. "But if you ask me, I think it's old Mr. Voss."

Melanie almost laughed, then she thought of Rolf and was tempted to go for Regan's throat. But suddenly a very different idea occurred to her. What if it wasn't true?

A cold chill slid down Melanie's spine. It was a monstrous thought, but what if Regan was up to something else, something darker? Neville hadn't left her a thing. She'd pointed that out angrily enough on the plane. And there was that reversion clause in the will.

Melanie tried to erase her unworthy suspicions. They persisted even so. Cassandra said that Regan had married Rolf for his money. But maybe Rolf didn't have enough money for her. Maybe Regan wanted it all.

THE *EMILY-MAC* WAS MOORED at Neville's private pier in Sausalito. The pier led to an even more secluded home, but Damien wasn't prepared to deal with those memories just yet. Besides, Regan might show up there. She wouldn't come within a hundred yards of the *Emily-Mac,* or any other boat.

Damien parked the hunter green Jaguar, which Nev had specifically willed to him, at the end of the pier. He shivered and climbed out. It was almost as cold by the Bay as it had been in Anchorage. Early afternoon sun had turned to cloud and finally to fog, thick and ghostly white, a depressing mass of damp air that would slither silently around the decks behind him. Too bad about the tailwind that had blown them into San Francisco ahead of schedule.

He squinted at the outline of the large craft as it bobbed silently in its moorings. For this yacht Nev had had a particular soft spot.

Emily had loved boating; she'd practically lived for it, or so the story went. Nev had bought the beautiful cruiser for her three months before her death. They'd sail around the world, he'd promised, but they never had.

There must be a history of tragedy in the McCall family, Damien decided as he retrieved his flight bag from the trunk. Lionel had died before Rolf's twenty-first birthday, and Damien's nineteenth. That meant he'd been dead for fourteen years now, and Hilary, their mother, a mere eight months less than that.

So now he'd lost two sets of parents, the ones he'd loved in Salvadore and the ones he'd tried very hard to love in San Francisco. He'd been alone, except for Nev who'd somehow understood that he'd never been happy away from Brazil.

Rolf didn't miss his native Munich at all. He didn't understand. But then Rolf had Regan, and that had to be like living in hell.

"I think she might be seeing someone," Rolf had confided to him only yesterday morning while Damien was getting ready to leave for the airport. "I'd talk to her about it, you know, but I think she'd probably lie if it was true. I know she'd get furious with me one way or the other."

A picture of Melanie's face formed slowly in Damien's mind. God, he'd spent two days fighting her image and suddenly all he could do was visualize her on the deck of the *Emily-Mac*, waiting for him, wearing nothing except a long piece of cotton gauze on her head with the ends draped over her shoulders so they flowed down her back.

He sighed and mounted the gangplank, wishing distantly that his Quallofil jacket was warmer, or that Melanie really would be waiting for him.

"I'll probably fall in love with her," he muttered, shaking damp tendrils of hair from his face as he boarded the boat. Fall in love and maybe even agree to endure this climate just to make her happy. Then he'd be miserable and it would all fall apart, anyway. No matter how he looked at it he'd be better off back in Brazil.

Ah, but there was that other problem. Someone wanted something from Neville's heirs. Revenge, he suspected, and that could get very ugly.

Unwilling to lock himself in the well-equipped living area below deck, Damien wandered to the far rail. Seawater slapped the hull, but it wasn't especially rough today. Still, he would have preferred at least another twenty degrees of heat. How did Melanie survive in this damp weather?

A shiver gripped his entire body, one not entirely born of the temperature. He was thinking of Melanie again, thinking that she could get rid of the cold in his bones and the one starting up in his chest. She could probably do a lot of things. . . .

Shaking his head to clear his thoughts, Damien pushed off from the rail. He was about to head for the stairs when a shadow darted swiftly through his peripheral vision.

His first thought was Melanie, then Rolf, but neither of them would duck away from him. There'd been stealth in the movement, a furtive air that suggested an intruder.

He waited by the rail, motionless, his eyes roaming the foggy upper deck. Nothing stirred. He kept watch on the gangplank. He could see it, but just barely and only in those rare moments when the fog thinned a little.

Water continued to slap the hull; a foghorn moaned up ahead, but these were constant sounds, things he could separate and set aside.

He heard it maybe thirty seconds later, the shuffle that sounded odd, rubber soles on the wooden deck. He caught the shadow again, someone wearing a black trenchcoat, collar up, with no face visible. It appeared for an instant, then melted back into the fog.

The intruder wasn't going for the gangplank. Why? Damien wondered, still not moving. Hadn't the person seen him?

But he must have, his instincts said.

Without warning the figure bolted. It made straight for the gangplank, and now Damien moved. He could cut the stalker off, he realized in mild surprise. He was faster and more mobile.

Damien cursed the fog when it swallowed the intruder yet again. A skidding sound warned him of a sharp direction change, but the figure wasn't fluid enough, it didn't quite make the turn at the bow, and Damien was able to grab his coat.

He got a better hold and started to jerk the wearer around. But then a blow like nothing he'd ever been hit with in his life caught him directly between the ribs.

The breath was driven from his lungs, every scrap of strength torn from his muscles. His body went limp, numb. Those things he knew even though his mind was gone, too dizzy and disoriented to understand anything except that he was no longer standing on the deck of the *Emily-Mac.*

He was being laid over a strip of hard, smooth wood. It dug into the sorest part of his ribs and brought a moan of pain to his throat.

He swallowed it, but he still couldn't fight. He couldn't do anything except wait for what he somehow knew would come: the chill water of San Francisco Bay rushing over his limbs.

No face registered in his mind, only the impression of male strength. The figure made no sound, did nothing to give itself away. It merely heaved Damien's body over the rail as if he were a broken doll.

The ocean came up to meet him, an icy, gray mass pulling at his clothes and hair. He forced his eyes open. He'd swallowed too much of the salt water in the first ducking; it was choking him. But the ladder was there, only a few feet away, his lifeline if he could manage to catch it.

Less than half-conscious, he tried for the bottom rung. To his amazement his fingers found it. He hauled himself toward the boat, the short swim sapping every last bit of his strength. Releasing a shuddery breath Damien wrapped his arms around the ladder, rested his head against its cold steel frame and let the blackness of unnatural sleep close slowly in around him.

Chapter Six

Damien had no idea where he was. He knew only that he was cold and soaking wet, and he was climbing a ladder. Or was someone pushing him?

"Take my hand, Damien."

A voice reached out to him, Melanie's, soft and low and sounding faintly urgent.

His cheek slammed hard into a metal rod. Pain sliced through his face.

"Rolf, be careful, he's hurt."

Damien felt his brother's hands pushing at him from underneath. The wet denim of his jeans clung to his legs, making movement difficult. Nothing made sense to him, least of all how Melanie and Rolf had gotten here.

His mind tumbled in endless circles until slowly it became a giant buzz of non-sound. Great blotches of darkness hovered in the corners. He thought they must be creeping in because as hard as he struggled he could not concentrate. One thing did get through, however. Melanie's fingers had caught hold of his wrist, and there was surprising strength in her grip.

"Come on," she shouted down to him. "Climb. Don't pass out, not now."

He fought the blackness and the shaking in his limbs and the sickness that rushed into his throat. There was an ache deep inside his chest as if he'd been struck by a hammer fifty times normal size. Breathing was next to impossible. He listened to what Melanie and his body's automatic reflexes wanted and obeyed their instructions.

Gradually he became aware of Rolf behind him, pinning him to the ladder, but it was Melanie he actually saw, her face that left the imprint on his mind. Her beautiful gray-green eyes were wide with fear, her cheeks pale, her hair loose and wonderfully messy. It occurred to him that she was wearing a dress, moss green cashmere that would be hugging all the curves his eyes couldn't quite bring into focus.

The ladder went on forever. Each movement was an agony, a fight not to topple back into the water and just let the blackness consume him.

"One more rung," Melanie panted, still tugging. "Just a little farther."

He knew it must be her fingers that touched the bruise on his cheek. Behind him Rolf gave a final boost and the climb was done. He stumbled through the rail, managed a few steps, then collapsed facedown on the deck.

"WHAT HAPPENED?"

Damien came to so swiftly that Melanie jumped. She'd been sitting beside him on the sofa below deck for close to an hour, holding his hand and running her fingers through his hair, willing him to wake up. Somehow, though, she hadn't expected him to go from unconscious to conscious in a split second.

She recovered quickly, pinning his shoulders to the cushions when he would have sat up. "Don't move," she said. "And I don't know, you tell me."

He rubbed the side of his head, his eyes scrunched shut, probably in pain. He'd whacked his cheek a few times before she and Rolf had gotten him down here.

"Someone hit me," he said at last. "There was someone on board when I got back from the airport. I thought I had him, then the next thing I knew something slammed me in the chest and I was being dumped into the Bay." He opened his eyes. "Where's Rolf?"

"Gone up to the house for supplies. He thought you needed brandy and better food than what's in the fridge." She fingered the tender skin on his right cheek. "How do you feel?"

"Lousy." His eyes looked confused when they stared at her. "What brought you and Rolf to Sausalito?"

"I live in Tiburon, remember? But that's not why I came. I got a message from my secretary as I was leaving the office. She said you wanted me to meet you on the *Emily-Mac*. I don't know about Rolf. He was on board when I got here—what are you doing?"

"Sitting up." He ignored her restraining hands and propped himself up on one elbow. In Portuguese he murmured the equivalent of "feeling like hell," then he glanced down at his naked chest and the blanket that covered the rest of him.

"You or Rolf?" he asked.

"Me. Rolf's not good at playing doctor. He told me he fainted when you were both kids and your cat had kittens."

"He did." Damien sat up straighter, coughed hard and winced. "Son of a bitch that hurts."

"I'll bet. But I still don't think you should move. You swallowed a lot of water."

"I'd rather not hear the details." His eyes lit briefly on her face then shifted to the left. "What's that?"

She regarded the unopened envelope on the coffee table. "You won't want to hear about that, either. I know I don't."

He was reaching for it. "Another note?"

She smacked his hand. "Or more diary pages. I found it in your bathroom when we brought you down here. I didn't show it to Rolf and I haven't been able to bring myself to open it. Presumably it's the reason for your intruder being here. You must have come back sooner than expected and caught him."

"Yes, it was a him," Damien told her, biting his lip as he reached again for the envelope.

"Here." Melanie retrieved it, then gave his shoulders a gentle but firm shove. His skin was smooth and tanned—

and, thank heaven, finally warming up. He'd been like a block of ice when she'd pulled his wet clothes off, so cold that she'd been tempted to shed her dress and crawl under the blanket with him. But then she was tempted to do that right now in spite of the fact that he seemed to be recovering nicely.

"Look, I'll open it," she said, her hands still on his arms. "But you have to promise me you'll lie there and rest. You were half drowned when we found you, Damien. The least you could do is act like it."

He managed a faint smile, dropping back against the pillows with no further protest.

His eyes were black and beautifully shaped, and watching her closely, she realized. It made concentrating on the envelope difficult, but Melanie did it. There was a red rook drawn on the back this time and nothing else.

She shook the pages out, telling herself it was better to know. You couldn't do battle with an unknown enemy.

"It's more diary pages," she said, her eyes skimming the writing. "Do you want me to read them out loud?"

He nodded. He was still watching her, but thinking what, she couldn't imagine. Taking a breath, she began to read.

From the diary of Neville McCall
August 23, 1933

What a horror this decade has become. You toughen up or you die. Tom and I both know this now and we're acting accordingly. It's time to make deals, I told him last month. No, we won't mess with the big boys on the South Side, we'll do it quietly, keep things more or less legit.

We started the ball rolling two weeks ago. We settled on three other Chicago businessmen, perfectly suited to our plan. Smart men but not brilliant and maybe just a little too honest. "Yes, these ones will do just fine, Mr. Marley," I said to Tom, but I don't think he appreciated the humor.

He will. In time he'll come to agree with me that this is

the best and only way. No, we are not crooks, Diary,
not even con men. We're forming an alliance here,
Tom's named it already: The Circle of Five. And we're
exactly what we appear to be. Survivors of a doomed
era. We are five and we are for the moment strong.
What happens from this point on no one can know.
But I promise you one thing, Diary, whatever it takes,
Tom and I will not go under!

Melanie knit her brow as she finished reading. "That
sounds ominous."

"It would," Damien said, sitting back up with an effort.
"To anyone except your grandfather."

She stuck the pages back in the envelope. "I wonder who
the other men in the Circle of Five were?" She paused and
frowned. "The Circle... You know, that sounds familiar to
me."

Damien wasn't sure what hurt worse, his head, his torso
or his stomach. He glanced at his watch while continuing to
ease himself up. Eight-something. His vision was blurry, but
it wasn't as late as he'd thought.

Melanie's hands found his shoulders again. "What do
you think you're doing?" she demanded.

"Getting up. Did you leave any clothes on me?" He
checked under the blanket. Not a stitch, not even his un-
derwear.

"Of course not. You were soaking wet." Was she blushing? "Anyway, it doesn't matter." She pushed harder. "You
couldn't possibly walk yet."

A burst of pain in his cheek momentarily made him dizzy.
"I plan to do a whole lot more than walk, Mel."

"Like what?"

He looked her in the eyes. "Take a drive."

"You're crazy." She hesitated, then asked in a suspicious
tone, "Drive where?"

He fought for patience, a next to impossible thing with all
that was going on in his body. Not only did every single part
of him hurt, he was also starting to react to Melanie. An-

other two minutes and he'd give in to her restraining hands. He'd fall obediently back on the sofa cushions and try to think of some clever ploy to get her to join him.

"Where, Damien?" she repeated when he didn't answer.

He shook the thoughts away. "Some pier in the city. Nev had a warehouse there. Rolf and I both have keys. If I can get in maybe I can find out more about this Circle of Five. I have a feeling it's important."

"Well, so do I, but couldn't a warehouse search wait until tomorrow?"

He pulled both her hands from his body, raising her fingers to his mouth and kissing them. "No."

She wasn't about to be politely seduced. She gave him an exasperated look. "For God's sake, Damien, why not? It's entirely possible, even probable, that someone tried to kill you today. You were hardly breathing when we pulled you from the water. And now, not an hour and a half later, you want to go rushing off to a pier to learn the identity of three businessmen, none of whom could possibly have dumped you into the Bay."

"That's right. Now would you mind getting off the blanket?"

She didn't budge. "Why tonight?"

Despite tremendous resistance from his muscles, he set her firmly aside. "Because as bad as I feel tonight, tomorrow I'm going to feel ten times worse, and it wouldn't be fair to put this off on Rolf."

She ducked her head. "No, I guess it wouldn't. Did you know—" she began, then stopped. "Never mind."

Damien probed his bruised cheek. It felt on fire. "If it's about Regan, I heard."

"Rolf talked to you?"

"Yesterday. How did you find out?"

She darted a guilty look at his face. "My assistant told me. I, uh, gather it's all over the Romac grapevine."

Damien swore at Regan under his breath. "Bitch."

Melanie placed a forestalling palm on his chest, right on the spot where he'd been hit. He caught back a sharp breath of reaction. "Not there," he said through his teeth.

"Sorry," she murmured, then raised the same fingers to his good cheek. "You're hot. I don't think you should go anywhere."

"Melanie . . ."

"No, wait." She held him back. "I wanted to say something about Regan. I had a idea, and I think you know her better than I do."

"No, I don't."

"Well, you know Rolf better anyway, and you must have some opinion of your brother's wife."

Damien managed a wan smile. "I have several. What's your point?"

"Do you think she could be involved in any of what's been going on?"

That was blunt. "Honestly?" he said, trapping her hand for the last time. "No."

"Why not?"

"Because she's mercenary, not malicious. I doubt if she really wished Nev dead, just nicely retired and planted on an island in Greece so she could get more money out of Rolf." His gaze moved to the cabin door. "Where is Rolf by the way? How long's he been gone?"

"At the house, I told you, and not long. Maybe twenty minutes."

It would take that long to reach the place on foot, half that time by car.

Damien combed his fingers through his sticky, tangled hair. He should take a shower, but there was no time for that. He needed to get up, for more than one reason now, and get out of here before Rolf returned and felt obliged to come along.

"Uh, Melanie," he said, shifting uncomfortably, "I'd like to get to the bathroom."

"And you want me to look away?" Yes, she was blushing, but only a very little. She was also smiling. "Remember who undressed you, Damien. And don't forget, either, that I lived in a more primitive part of South America than you did. The natives around our village didn't always bother with clothes."

He shoved the blanket aside anyway and slid from the sofa with a silent groan. Damn her, she didn't look away, but then she didn't really look down, either. For a moment he considered his plan. Search a warehouse on a wet, foggy pier or stay here on the *Emily-Mac* with Melanie?

There was no contest of course, but he had to go with the search. He'd never be able to do it tomorrow.

"You're really going through with this, aren't you?" she asked in a slightly strangled voice that made him stop and re-reconsider.

He glanced back, forcing her eyes to his. "I really am."

"In that case," she said, "I'm coming with you."

His bumps and bruises made dizziness a constant state. "Fine," he said, steadying himself on the wall.

"You mean you're not going to fight me?"

She was right behind him now. He stared straight ahead at the bathroom door. "No."

He couldn't believe that she actually slid her fingers through the ends of his hair. He felt them move slowly down his back. "You're a masochist," she told him softly.

A very small ironic smile cross his lips. "I know."

ROOK SAT IN HIS CAR on Neville McCall's private pier. It was dark now and the fog was thick, but he'd be able to see if Damien left the boat. Knowing Damien, he would. This was not a man who'd take kindly to being deposited in the cold waters of the Bay. He also would have read the diary pages by now, or Melanie would have read them to him, because he surely had to be seeing double after the shot he'd taken in the chest.

Damien was a curious person, and he didn't like being threatened. Neither did Melanie, although at least her grandfather had cared. But Tom had also "rooked" his Circle partners, and for that she must pay.

Nev had a warehouse on Pier 16. He kept just about everything there, even his old diaries. Those Rook had found buried deep in dust and cobwebs. He kept information on the Circle of Five there, too, but only a bare minimum. Rook knew the truth of the situation because of who he was, not because of any written documents he'd dug up. No, there was very little, if any, of that to be had. And of course Neville's son, Lionel, and Tom's son, Tommy, were both dead. Whatever knowledge they might have possessed would not be passed on to their offspring.

The thought brought a smile to Rook's lips. He had only to wait. If Damien planned to go to the warehouse, he'd do it tonight, regardless of his physical condition. And anyone who knew Melanie had to know that she wouldn't let him go alone. No, she was a curious little cat as well. How unfortunate that she must die.

That was the price for revenge. Rook takes pawns. It had to be that way.

Pulling his coat tighter, he hunched down in his seat. In his mind he began counting down to his birthday, which was coming soon. This was the very best present he could ever get.

Chapter Seven

This was a stupid thing to do. Fog and darkness and danger were only three of the elements hanging in the air. Damien was a mess, Rolf would be frantic when he got back to the boat and found their message, and Melanie was convinced that someone had followed them from Sausalito.

"We should have gone to the police," she said when they finally found the right pier.

"Quiet. Try the keys."

She shoved the first of seven in the appropriate lock. "You look like a ghost," she hissed at him. "And don't tell me to shut up because there's no one here except us, and quite likely the person who attacked you this afternoon."

He leaned against the corrugated metal, his eyes closed, his dark hair framing features that were far too pale. "Maybe you're right," he agreed. "But if you are, I want to know about it. I want to know who we're dealing with. And if he's one step ahead of us tonight, then I want to know that, too."

She finished with the locks, shoving the keys in the pocket of the jeans Damien had lent her. They were baggy and the legs were too long, but tucking them into her boots eliminated that problem, and a narrow belt readily handled the waistband.

"You still haven't told me why we can't just go to the police," she reminded him.

"Because police investigations are time-consuming. I don't have that kind of patience. I'd also prefer not to be dropped into the Bay again, and I can't imagine you or Rolf want something like that happening to you. Besides, if we *were* followed, that means the person who's behind all this expected us to do something tonight, probably to come here. I'd like to know why."

"If," Melanie repeated with meaning.

She had to lean her full weight on the door to open it, but better she do it than Damien. He was in no fit state even to be here, let alone wrestle with a rusted door.

"I feel like a prowler," she said, giving the metal a kick. "Okay, let's say your attacker did figure we'd come. Aren't we sort of playing into his hands by doing this?"

"I'm afraid so."

Reaching around her Damien gave the door a shove. It opened with a creak that echoed around the deserted dock. Well, semideserted. Melanie had seen a few bundled creatures scurrying around near the water.

The building was small compared to many in the area, eerily silent except for the foghorns out on the water, and it smelled musty.

"Nev didn't come here much, did he?" she said. There were boxes everywhere and stacks of crates, both metal and wood. "Is there an order to any of this, do you know?"

"There was an order to everything Nev did." Damien shone a flashlight across the wall nearest the door, located the electrical panel and pulled a narrow black switch. Odd rows of fluorescent lights flickered overhead, enough to see by.

What Melanie saw first was Damien's face, pale as she'd suspected despite his tan.

She remembered watching him on the boat, recalled the warm flush that had washed over her skin when he'd gotten up from the sofa. He was so beautiful. She didn't know how she'd resisted touching him. And she hadn't really, come to think of it. But when he'd gone into the bedroom to change she should have followed him there too, gone and made him get into bed instead of waiting politely in the hall for him to dress.

"The oldest records will be in the back," Damien said now, switching off the flashlight and closing the door. He locked it as well, she noticed. "We'll start at 1933, the date on the first set of diary pages, and go from there."

"Okay." But she hung back, pulling on his sleeve as a thought that had been plaguing her for some time came into her mind again. "Damien, I assume you didn't leave a message with my secretary for me to meet you on the boat, right?"

He nodded, his eyes scanning the stacks.

"Then who did? The man who attacked you?"

"I imagine so."

"So then he didn't necessarily intend for you to die."

He glanced sideways at her. "How do you figure that? I could have drowned long before you and Rolf showed up."

"Yes, but you didn't. You were clinging to the ladder when we found you. Maybe he wanted you to live so you could read the diary pages and come here."

"Why?"

"To find out more about the Circle of Five?" She gave the loose sleeve of his jacket a frustrated swat. "Damn, I wish I could figure out why that sounds so familiar to me. Damien!" She caught his waist in alarm when he swayed slightly. "Are you all right?"

"Fine. Just dizzy." He waved her off. "It'll pass." He took her hand. "Come on, let's get this over with. I'm beginning to think this wasn't a very good idea."

He'd given her a green flannel shirt to wear, and a lined leather jacket that was wonderfully battle scarred. She felt like a burglar, looked like a hood and wanted badly to go home.

But that kind of thinking would accomplish nothing, she told herself with a forcefulness that was habit with her. Damien needed to go home far more than she did, so that meant she had to dig in, find whatever information she could and try to make sense of it.

It was a simple idea in theory, but a grueling exercise in fact. Even locating the Depression-era crates was tedious work. Yes, there was an order to the seeming chaos. Unfortunately the old files they sought were at the bottom of the stacks and shoved way back into corners thick with spiderwebs.

At one point she accidentally touched a big dead spider and her reaction sent her flying straight back into Damien's lap.

"Sorry," she apologized with a sigh. "I really hate those things."

Did his arms tighten about her for a second? She knew for sure that he pressed his forehead into the back of her shoulder.

"It's no problem. Have you found anything?"

"No." She wanted to twist around and hug him, but that was probably a bad idea, all things considered. "There's a lot of early Romac stuff, several bank balance sheets and ledger books and even memos he sent to Tom, but I can't find so much as a mention of any Circle of Five."

"Neither can I." Damien stopped suddenly, lifting his head. "Did you hear something?"

She listened but heard only the clang of a ship. "Like what?"

"The door!" Damien set her swiftly from his lap. "Stay behind me," he cautioned.

Melanie kept one pace behind and slightly to the left, her eyes combing the shadows as they moved through the towering stacks. When one of the shadows in the corner stirred, she clutched at his arm. "Over there," she whispered. "I saw someone."

"Where?"

"By those metal boxes... What's this?"

She'd set her hand on a piece of paper taped to the side of a large filing cabinet. No, not a paper, a picture, a very old-looking black and white photograph.

For a moment she forgot about the intruder. The picture showed five men, five faces to be precise, set around a black center, so it was really a collage rather than a single photograph. But it was also a circle and Neville and Tom were both there. Nev and Tom and three other men. The Circle of Five, circa 1935, it had to be.

Melanie passed her fingertips over Neville's young face. "Damien."

"Shh."

"But there's a—"

"He's going for the door. Wait here."

Damien took off so fast he was gone from sight before Melanie could react. She paused just long enough to grab the photo and check the shadows, then she ran after him.

She was very good at running in stealth. She'd done it many times in Venezuela to escape from Cassandra. This was really nothing, except that the person she chased was undoubtedly responsible for knocking Damien out earlier. Who knew what tricks he might have up his sleeve tonight?

She spied Damien several yards ahead of her. He was motionless, watching something. Melanie stopped and waited, her breath held, feeling more like an animal hunted than the hunter. What did Damien see?

She got her answer when a figure dressed in a bulky black raincoat sprang suddenly from the shadows. He wore a black ski mask and gloves, and he was heading toward the door.

Damien followed, was closing on the man, when the figure unexpectedly paused and pulled an object from his coat. In one uninterrupted motion he launched the thing straight at Damien's chest. Damien caught it neatly, but in the moment it took, the figure was gone, racing through the now-open door and vanishing like a ghost into the foggy night.

Melanie shoved the picture into the waistband of her jeans and ran to the door where Damien stood listening.

"Where did he go?" she whispered.

"I don't know. I can't hear anything."

Melanie was about to suggest that they split up and search, when her ears caught the sound of approaching footsteps. They were quiet rubbery steps, sneakers on wet pavement. Had the intruder been wearing sneakers? She hadn't really gotten a clear look at his feet.

She squinted into the fog but couldn't make out a thing. Then slowly an outline began to form.

"It's Rolf." Damien sounded exhausted. He tipped his head back, letting his eyes fall closed. "What are you doing here?" he asked with infinite weariness.

"What you'd expect." Rolf drew closer, frowning at both of them but speaking strictly to Melanie. "He didn't look this bad when we fished him out of the Bay. What have you two been doing down here?"

"Chasing phantoms," Melanie said. "You didn't see anyone run past in a big hurry, did you?"

Rolf's confusion deepened. "Not a soul. Why?"

"It wouldn't be hard to hide," Damien remarked.

His dull tone was starting to worry Melanie.

"Okay, that's it," she said, placing her hands on his waist. "You've had enough, I've had plenty and I'm sure Rolf doesn't want any part of it."

Rolf slid his gaze to Damien's face. "Well, I would sort of like to know what's going on."

"Who wouldn't?" Damien murmured. "Don't push me, Mel. We can't leave yet."

"Why not? Rolf can lock up."

He held the object the figure had tossed to him over his shoulder so she could see it. It looked like a remote control.

Suspicion gave Melanie's voice an edge. "What's that?"

"A detonation device," Damien told her with remarkable self-possession. "Our disappearing rook planted a bomb in the warehouse."

THE NEXT THIRTY-SIX HOURS were a complete blur to Damien. Even the events on the pier got jumbled up in his head.

He remembered Rolf saying, "Well, that's it then. If this guy's setting bombs we have to call the police. You two could have been killed."

"No police," Damien managed to argue. "Melanie, tell him." Not that she should have had to. After twenty-five years together Rolf should know all about his distrust for authorities. Police, social workers, he didn't like any of those people messing around in his life.

"Hire a private detective if you want to," he told his brother. "But leave the police out of it for now."

Melanie tapped his arm. "Damien, you're forgetting the planes."

"What about them?"

"If our flight from Chicago *was* sabotaged, couldn't the same thing be done to the commercial flights?"

Dizziness pressed in on him. He nodded, closing his eyes and fighting it. "You're right," he said tiredly. "Okay, Rolf, call the cops. Just leave me out of it."

If Rolf answered, Damien didn't hear the words. From that point on, only snatches of things registered in his brain, bits of conversation he heard but didn't have the strength to respond to.

The first thing he remembered was a vague sense of motion and Melanie saying, "Can you handle this, Rolf?" Presumably she meant the incomplete bomb Damien had discovered in the warehouse. Rolf must have answered because he felt himself being pushed forward. "Okay, I'll take him home then and get him into bed."

"How much should I tell the police?"

"Whatever you think." There was a brief silence, then, "Where's Regan?"

Another silence, this one on Rolf's side. "I wish I knew," he said.

Melanie sighed. "I'm sorry, Rolf."

"So am I."

Something very pleasant and warm drifted into Damien's mind after that. First there was the movement again, then a door opened and he was suddenly back in the jungle. There were plants everywhere and dark polished walls and a stone fireplace. Throw rugs adorned hardwood floors, so this wasn't the jungle, but the abundance of greenery certainly suggested as much.

"Come on, be good and sit down," Melanie said.

Damien's head felt so heavy.

"Don't fall over until I get your shirt off."

"No."

"You want me to leave your shirt on?"

He heard his fly unzip. "Um, you can fall over now."

That memory ended when he landed on the bed, and few others after that possessed such clarity. He knew he must have said things because Melanie talked to him, but he couldn't always get past the pain to sort out the words. Whatever had slammed into his chest had done one effective job on him.

Time slid by without meaning. He slept uneasily, moving constantly about the bed, often getting tangled up in the sheets. But whenever he did that, Melanie was there to untangle him.

She touched him, too, in ways that even his aching body couldn't ignore. She put something on his breastbone right where it hurt the most. It felt hot and cold at the same time and smelled very strong, something antiseptic and faintly fruity.

She ran her hands along his naked sides, bringing a shiver to his skin. "Lie still," she told him. "You're going to make it worse."

"Maybe you should call a doctor," Damien heard Rolf say. When had he come in?

"Don't call," Damien murmured.

Rolf's voice came closer. "Are you awake?"

"Not really," Melanie answered for him. "We've had a few conversations like this. I doubt he'll remember many of them. He keeps saying he doesn't know what hit him on the boat, but whatever it was made a huge bruise."

"Maybe it was a club or a bat."

"I don't think so. He insists he didn't expect it. You'd see a bat coming." Her palm pressed lightly against Damien's ribs, below the hurt. "Anyway, I think he'll be all right, and he keeps telling me, no doctor, so I'll let it go for now."

"I give up," Rolf muttered.

"Good." A heavy paper rustled. "What do you make of this?"

"It looks like an old photograph."

"It is. Five faces in a circle and two of them belong to Nev and Tom. It was taped up in the warehouse. I assume our bomb-happy rook wanted us to have it."

"Why?"

"I don't know, but he seems to be trying to make a point of some sort. Apparently he wants us to know all about the Circle of Five. You read the diary pages we left for you, I assume."

"Several times. Did you find anything useful in the warehouse?"

"Just the picture."

"And a bomb," Rolf added. "But the police say there wasn't much explosive material involved. A sufficient amount to blow up a few crates, but nothing more than that."

Now that was interesting, Damien thought.

He drifted off then, coming back only briefly whenever he sensed Melanie doing something to him.

"You need a bath," she said finally with a sigh. It must have been the next day because there was muted light falling across the bed and his face. "I bet I could do it without disturbing you."

He bet she couldn't, but he wasn't about to fight her.

Her hands on him were exquisitely gentle, the warm soapy cloth felt good where it slid across his limbs and stomach. She even washed his hair and that was another delicious experience.

"God, you're beautiful," he heard her murmur. She brushed at his damp hair. "I want to do your back."

Damien obeyed, relaxing against her. Everywhere she touched him his body reacted. It was unfortunate that he couldn't be just a little more aware.

He was alert enough when Rolf came to see him again because this time he brought Regan with him.

"Detroit," he remembered waking up to mumble. "I have a flight today. What time is it?"

"Well, you're right on top of things, aren't you?" Regan remarked in her usual caustic fashion. "A full third of our flight crews are out with the flu and you go and fall into the Bay."

"Addison can do the flight to Detroit," Rolf began, but Regan cut him off sharply.

"No, he can't. He's been out sick for the past two days. It's been hell in reservations. And now we have to do another shuffle."

"We have lots of pilots, Regan." Damien caught the irritation in Melanie's tone.

He saw Rolf pulling his wife away, heard him murmuring a quiet, "I'll call you later, Mel. Come on, Regan, I think maybe we should go."

Please do, Damien thought tiredly. *I want another bath....*

More hours slid by. The next time he woke up it was Morgan's voice he heard. But the words seemed to come from a great distance, as if they floated up from a point directly below him.

"This is completely improper, Melanie," Rolf's assistant was declaring indignantly.

"This is none of your business, Morgan," Melanie shot back. "What do you want?"

"I heard Damien had an accident. I came to see how he's feeling."

"Rotten," Damien mumbled with a sigh. "Go away."

Morgan couldn't hear him. He was downstairs by the front door, far away and busy warning Melanie that nothing had better happen to Neville's grandson, or there would be lawyers swarming all over her.

"Remember the reversion clause in the will, my dear."

"Go to hell, Morgan."

"In time," the man said with a chuckle that set Damien's groggy nerves on edge. "All in good time."

It was dark when Damien came around again. He felt Melanie's hair on his cheek as she leaned over him for something. She had beautiful hair; it smelled like tropical flowers.

"Lucy Farmer," she was saying into the telephone. "Oh, I don't know, Rolf. She seemed sincere. She works in accounting. She said her desk was messed up Thursday morning, but right before she noticed that, she saw Morgan coming out of the office where she works. So you tell me, what would Morgan Voss be doing in the Romac accounting department?"

Twinges of increasing awareness made Damien uncomfortable. Too many little things were happening. Regan's suspected affair, Morgan's threats to Melanie, bombs not powerful enough to kill, the reference to the Circle of Five, and now an old photograph.

When he really woke up, it was still dark, extremely late by all appearances. He looked over and saw Rolf sitting in an antique rocking chair beside his bed. Except that this wasn't his bed, it was Melanie's. Redwood beams that climbed to a high peak overhead indicated an A-frame, and he knew Melanie had just such a house in Tiburon. Well, at least he knew where he was. It was an improvement.

"Welcome back," his brother said. He looked rumpled and unhappy. "I thought I'd come over and give Mel a break."

Damien's whole body hurt, but it was a fading ache, the kind you knew would soon be gone. He moved a tentative shoulder.

"Did you have a fight with Regan?"

Rolf's smile was uncharacteristically cynical. He drained the glass of brandy in his hand. "I confronted her earlier tonight. She threw a figurine at me."

"Did she admit anything?"

"No, she just yelled and called me a bastard. How do you feel?"

"Better. Where's Melanie?"

Rolf nodded at the bed. "Right there. She figured you wouldn't care."

Damien made it up onto one elbow, pushing the hair from his face as he looked at Melanie asleep on her stomach beside him. She was fully clothed, if you considered cream leggings and a long navy sweatshirt clothes. On her, he considered them highly seductive, about the same level as a black bra and garter belt.

He dragged his eyes away. He didn't dare touch, especially not with Rolf here.

"What are you going to do about Regan?"

"I don't know. And we've got bigger problems now anyway."

"Such as?"

"That flight to Detroit you were supposed to take."

A knot of resistance formed in Damien's stomach. "What about it?"

"The pilot had to make an emergency landing in Denver. We're lucky it was cargo and not commercial. The hydraulics were a mess."

Damien fell back onto the pillows, rubbing one eye. "What do the inspectors say?"

"Nothing definite. Whoever's doing this is good."

"Or has good help."

Rolf nodded. "One way or the other, it seems that someone's doing his damnedest to bring Nev's little empire down."

Chapter Eight

Someone was watching her.

Melanie could feel two eyes staring in the darkness. But her limbs were floaty, unresponsive, and the fear inside her had more to do with a homicidal rook than the eyes that studied her every move. Was she dreaming?

With a start she woke up, her own eyes flying open to Damien's face. But no, that wasn't right, she couldn't see him. He was too close for that. And suddenly she felt his mouth on hers, a quick kiss that was over before she was even fully aware of it.

"Stay awake," he said against her shocked lips. He gave her a trace of a smile that was almost as disturbing as his kiss, and pressed his thumb to her lower lip. "I want to talk."

She pushed her hair from her face. "I have news for you, Damien, that's all you've been doing since Wednesday night."

"Did I say anything interesting?" He seemed fascinated by her mouth. It occurred to her that he might still have a fever.

She collected her resistance and rolled onto her back. "You kept trying to get me into bed with you. Does that count as interesting?"

"It depends."

"On what?"

His eyes glittered in the faint light that didn't quite belong to the dawn. "You're here, aren't you?"

"Fully dressed," she reminded him, then sat up swiftly and checked, just in case. It was almost a disappointment to discover her sweatshirt and leggings still intact.

His smile widened a bit, disarming her totally. "You weren't sure, were you?" he asked.

"No, but then I've heard stories about you."

"No, you haven't. I'm not around here enough for stories to start."

Now it was her turn to unsettle him. Rolling over, she placed her palms on either side of his body and kissed him full on the mouth. "That's what you think, jungle boy."

She didn't expect him to react, but he did and with a thoroughness that threw her completely off balance. He pulled her on top of him, not even flinching when she landed on his bruised torso. He was kissing her before she realized what was happening—and by the time she did she no longer cared.

Except that she should, because he wasn't going to be around San Francisco for very much longer.

"I thought you wanted to talk," she said with great self-restraint against his mouth. "I can't do two things at once."

She felt him smile. "I can."

"I don't doubt it." She pulled away, refusing to acknowledge his eyes or his smile or the fact that he was fully aroused beneath the sheets and her own highly responsive body.

A curious mixture of relief and regret slid through her when he let her go. She escaped to the far side of the bed where she felt relatively safe, if not at all satisfied.

"Talk," she said, sitting cross-legged and shoving back her hair.

If he'd been vaguely amused, it vanished in the next second. He came up on one elbow to stare at her. "I spoke to Rolf during the night. He told me about the Detroit flight."

Melanie shuddered. "It was horrible, not so much in the air as on the ground. The pilot didn't know if he'd have brakes."

"Rolf said he had just enough."

She nodded. "It was meant to happen to you, you know."

"Was it?" Damien didn't seem convinced. "Knowing Romac, there wasn't a person who wouldn't have realized that I couldn't fly yesterday. It feels more like we're being manipulated. Or maybe deliberately confused is a better way of putting it."

Melanie pulled a pillow onto her lap and hugged it. "All right, let's say that's true. What can we do about it? Did you and Rolf come up with anything?"

"Not much. Rolf's talked to the police."

He made a face at that, like a child eating asparagus, and Melanie laughed. But there was nothing funny in this situation.

"He's also hired a private investigator."

"To look into the mysterious Circle of Five." She nodded. "He mentioned that." She leaned over and took the picture from the oak nightstand. "Rolf was asking around all day yesterday. Do you know that so far he can't find anyone who's ever heard of the Circle of Five, even people Nev's been associated with for thirty or more years?"

Damien shrugged. "Nev and Tom formed the Circle during the Depression, Mel. That's almost sixty years ago. Anyone who might have known or been involved is probably dead, or at least well retired." He tested his sore cheek with his fingers. "Besides, if there was a swindle involved, the whole thing was likely hushed up on both sides. No one likes to be labeled a sucker."

Melanie only half heard the last thing. "The Circle boys," she said. She rocked back and forth, holding the pillow with the end tucked under her chin. "Ask his former partners—if you can dig them up. That's it!"

"What's it?" Reaching out, Damien tugged gently on the pillow. "Hey, are you here?"

"Yes!" She practically flew across the bed. He caught her but the momentum threw him onto his back, with her on top of him, straddling him. "You don't understand. Cassandra said that to me."

"Said what?"

Melanie contained her enthusiasm, but didn't move. "The Circle boys. She mentioned the word circle, and then later she said that Nev didn't deserve the life he had and if I didn't believe her I should ask his former partners, if any of them were still alive. She knows, Damien, about the Circle of Five, anyway. Maybe she can give us the names we want." Melanie hesitated, then added a distracted, "She drinks a lot, though. She might not remember." She looked down at Damien's face, a picture of wonder and distant amusement.

"It's worth a try," he said patiently, not stirring beneath her. "Get off me, Mel."

"What?" Her distraction faded as she realized where she was, and exactly how he was reacting to her. "Oh, sorry."

"Don't be," he said as she slid off. "I'd love to fall in love with you, but I can't live your life."

With the deepest regret she'd ever known, Melanie removed herself completely from the bed. "I wouldn't ask you to." Turning, she started for the loft staircase. Over her shoulder she said firmly, "I'm going to send a telegram to Cassandra."

THE OLD MAN DIDN'T WANT his granddaughter to leave.

Not yet, Sonia, he begged her silently, but of course she couldn't hear him.

She bent with difficulty to kiss his cheek. "I'll come back later," she promised. "I have to see my doctor this afternoon."

He stared at her. She was very pregnant, she shouldn't even have come here today, but she was a good girl, so patient with him. He loved her very much. If only he could explain his suspicions to her. Something was happening, something connected to the old Circle of Five. But would she believe him even if he could make the words come?

She left with a kiss blown from the bedroom door. His housekeeper, a woman devoted to routine, was downstairs vacuuming the living-room carpet. She wouldn't come up to check on him for another twenty minutes. What would he do to fill the time until his next injection?

He didn't want to think about old Neville anymore or the Circle of Five. Those things always led to other thoughts, ones that distressed him and made his blood pressure soar.

"You must stay calm," Sonia told him repeatedly. "I know you want to say something, but it's impossible, you have to understand that."

If only he could force his shaking hands to write, but that was as far beyond him as speech. It was torture to know all that he did, to suspect even more and then be unable to communicate either of those things.

"Samuel?"

A man's voice seemed to emanate from the woodwork. The old man recognized this voice. He wanted to withdraw from it, to hear anything but what it would say to him. What had been vague in his mind last week was now abundantly clear. Oh, how he wished it would all go and leave him in peace.

"I saw your granddaughter leave," the man said. He emerged from the shadows in the hallway, approaching the bed with slow, measured strides.

Samuel would have flinched if his muscles would have responded. Why did this person come here? Why didn't Jessie, his housekeeper, ever finish her vacuuming early, come up here and catch him? Did he torment old Rupert and Herschel this way, or were they happy to see him and to hear his twisted plan?

The old man's heart gave a lurch as a thought came to him. Maybe Herschel and Rupert wanted this man who called himself Rook to succeed, a fitting payment for Neville and Tom's misdeeds—for none of what they'd done could really be considered a crime.

"You stare at me as though we were strangers," Rook said now. He looked down at Samuel's unblinking eyes. "Don't you remember what I told you the first time I came here? We're related, you and I." He made a gloved fist. "We're bound by blood."

No! Samuel denied this fiercely, though he knew with an unerring sense of doom that it was true.

"I went to see Herschel and Rupert today," Rook continued. "They were pleased to see me."

But do they know what you're really doing? Samuel wondered. *Who you really are?* He felt frantic inside, helpless. A sound of disgust gurgled in his throat. How could his blood have produced something so evil?

Rook's gloved fingers touched Samuel's fine white hair. "Maybe you don't understand," he said sadly. "I want you to know that I'm doing this for the three of you as well as for myself. They deserve to be punished, to suffer for what their grandfathers did."

A smile that brought Samuel out in a cold sweat crossed the man's lips. The expression in his eyes made it clear that his thoughts were far away.

"Did you know I set a bomb in Neville's warehouse?" he asked softly. "I wanted to scare them. But it didn't work. They spotted me, or rather Damien did." His eyes hardened, and his tone, but the eerie amusement remained. "I didn't appreciate that of course, but as long as they know what could have been."

Don't kill them, Samuel pleaded. On the bedsheet, his hand became a feeble claw. *Let it go. Go on with your life.*

But no words came out, and Rook misread the agitation, as one so consumed by thoughts of vengeance was bound to do.

He squatted down until his face was level with Samuel's. Was there a family resemblance? Maybe a little around the eyes, but who would ever notice it?

"Don't worry, old man," Rook said, patting Samuel's papery hand. "They'll never find out about me. They can't. I'm safe and so are you and your two old friends."

Samuel closed his eyes, too weary now to fight this creature. When he forced them open again, the man was gone.

What a dreadful mess this was, he thought with a moan. Nothing Samuel could do would stop it. No one could hear him. He had only one prayer left: that he was old and senile, and that no part of this nightmare was real.

THERE WERE CERTAIN benefits to owning the airline you flew for, Damien realized days after the incident on the *Emily-Mac*. You could rearrange flight rosters and no one could object. He booked himself on the first cargo flight to Miami, checked the 767 over personally and, satisfied, took off early Sunday morning.

"You can't be leaving!" Rolf had exclaimed in disbelief, catching him at the airport right before he left. "Not for good, I mean."

Damien didn't blame him for having doubts. "I'm not," he said. "There's something I want to do in South America. I'll be back as soon as I can." He paused, then added, "If you see Mel, you might tell her that."

Rolf's brows went up. "Why didn't you tell her?"

"Because."

"That's not a reason, Damien."

"It's the best I can do." He gave a thumbs-up to his co-pilot across the hangar. "I have to go. How is it between you and Regan?"

Rolf dipped his head. "It isn't. She left to visit her cousin in Nassau this morning."

"I didn't know she had relatives in the Bahamas."

"I don't think she does." Damien wasn't sure what to say, but Rolf saved him the trouble by shrugging and clapping him on the shoulder. "Don't worry about it. Like I said before, we've got bigger problems. Our private eye's come up empty so far. It's as though the Circle of Five never existed. Even the picture hasn't helped."

"Something'll turn up," Damien told him. "Talk to Mel for me, huh? Tell her I'll call her when I get back."

"Whatever you say. And no fiesta breaks, okay?"

Damien smiled. "No fiestas going on that I'm aware of. See you in a few days."

He'd left with mixed emotions. He should have talked to Melanie himself, and in a politely removed way he supposed he had. She knew he had a flight today, he'd told her that much; she just didn't know where he planned to go from there.

She thought her mother might know all about the Circle of Five. Unfortunately, telegrams to remote jungle villages took forever to convey. Something told him they didn't have a great deal of time, so he'd decided to go to Venezuela and talk to Cassandra personally.

He wished that made him feel better, but it didn't. He'd been polite with Melanie yesterday. Polite! He couldn't believe it. He'd gotten out of bed, dressed and thanked her very nicely for taking care of him. Then he'd cursed himself all the way back to the boat.

He was a fool and he knew it. He'd hurt her. One thing about Melanie, she got tough when she had to. She hadn't let him see a thing. She'd been every bit as polite and distant as he had.

Damien was still swearing at his stupidity when he set the plane down in Miami, and thoroughly distracted as he went to check in with Romac Operations. He was so lost in thought that he didn't immediately recognize the man he all but walked into in the approach corridor.

"What are you doing in Miami?" Addison asked him in surprise.

Damien came back to the present with a small frown. "I changed the roster. Why are you here? I thought you were doing Honolulu today."

Addison grinned. "I like Miami better."

Did he? For some reason Damien found himself doubting that. He leaned against the sterile beige wall characteristic of all airports, his hands in his jacket pockets, his eyes on Addison's narrow face. "I don't think so," he said. "You're not the Miami type. What's the real reason?"

Something Damien couldn't read glittered in the pilot's eyes. Guilt maybe? It was gone before it really formed. "Is it important?" Addie asked, his smile fading slightly.

"Maybe."

"What do you mean, maybe?" Mild annoyance showed on his features now. "What's with you and Rolf? Is it the planes? Is that what's bothering you?"

"Isn't it bothering you?"

Addison made a rapid motion with his hand. "Look, Damien, we've known each other for close to two years now, so cut the crap, huh? Rolf was all over me yesterday because I should have been the one to fill in for you on the Detroit flight. He wanted to know if I was really sick. Now, I'm not stupid. He might not have come right out and said it, but he was really asking did I book off sick because I knew the hydraulics were going to pack up. Okay, that's fair. The word sabotage has been quietly creeping along the Romac grapevine, but don't forget, I booked off before you did. How was I supposed to know you weren't going to take the flight?"

Damien didn't bother with the obvious answer. He also didn't entirely trust Addison's defensive attitude.

"We're all kind of edgy," he said, pushing off from the wall. "It sounds personal, Addie, but it isn't intended to be. Rolf's been questioning everyone, even Morgan."

Addison's dark brows went up. "You mean he doesn't even trust his own assistant?"

Damien felt his muscles relax. A tiny smile played on the corners of his mouth. "Would you want Morgan around you every day?"

Addie snorted. "Not a chance. Why doesn't Rolf fire the guy? No, never mind. Rolf wouldn't fire his worst enemy."

"Rolf doesn't have any enemies."

"No, but Nev did." Addie's expression sobered. "I guess I shouldn't be snapping at you guys. I mean, if we're dealing with sabotage, that's serious stuff."

"If," Damien agreed. "It might just be bad luck."

"I hope so. I'm coming up on a big run of jumbos this month." He nodded toward the runways. "Are you going back today?"

"No. You?"

Addison tugged on the bill of his uniform hat. "Big date," he replied with a grin. "Which is the real reason I didn't want Hawaii."

Now that, Damien could believe. He gave Addie's uniform a look rich in meaning then started off. "Have fun," he said over his shoulder.

"I always do."

"WHAT MAKES YOU THINK I know who the Circle boys are?" Cassandra demanded. She waved at Melanie's telegram on the cot beside her. "First my kid wants information, now you show up asking for the same thing."

She was half-drunk, a constant state according to Melanie. She was also a beautiful woman. She'd given many of her exquisitely shaped features to her daughter. Looks aside, however, the two women couldn't have been less alike.

With mild regret, Damien watched her pour a glass of rum. "We need to know who they are, Cassandra," he said.

She lifted her head in a challenge. "Why?"

"Because it looks like someone's trying to destroy Romac."

She brought the glass to her lips, chuckling. "Good."

"And us with it."

"Ah, I see. And you think that one or more of those feeble old men must be behind this plot." She arched her delicate brows at the rum she was about to toss back. "Hope I'm that alert when I'm ninety-something."

Damien walked around the hut, looking absently at the crude furniture. The place was a dump, decaying and dirty and crawling with bugs. He couldn't believe she lived like this.

"Oh, you don't like my house either, do you?" she said with theatrical disappointment. "I'm hurt, Damien. I thought you of all people would appreciate it."

"I appreciate the idea, not the reality. You'd be as well off in a cave."

She closed one eye, regarding him shrewdly. "My husband spent most of his time down here in caves." She laughed. "I think he told me once that the caves were actually cleaner than our hut."

Damien said nothing, merely watched her from across the room. There was something in her, some feeling still lurking inside her for her husband and daughter. If only he could tap it.

"I'll bet Melanie keeps a clean house," she said, half closing her eyes and lifting one hand. "I picture a whitewashed plaster mansion. Tell me I'm right."

"You're not. It's a plant-filled redwood A-frame." Damien hoisted himself up onto the windowsill. "Names, Cassandra."

"I don't remember names, and I don't give a damn if Romac falls." She stretched both her long arms up, then gestured at his bruised cheek. "Just out of curiosity, gorgeous, what happened to you?"

"Melanie punched me."

Cassandra's laugh was rough and delighted. "And Nev said I didn't teach her anything." She pressed the glass to her lower lip. "But you know, you really are a beauty, a jungle cat. I knew you would be. I could tell even when you were nine and resentful as hell. I saw you years after that, too. Did you know I came to Rolf's wedding? Melanie didn't. I would have told her except I was drunk and I couldn't stand watching the witch in her moment of virginal triumph. I went to a bar instead with a man I met in the back row of the church. I would've invited Melanie but she says I drink too much. I don't think I drink too much, do you?" she asked her glass. Then she pointed at the window. "Who's that?"

Damien looked behind him at the tangle of trees and vines. "It's a macaw."

"Really?" She fell back on the cot. "Maybe I do drink too much at that. You didn't answer my question before."

"Which one?"

"About the Circle boys. Do you think they're plotting against you?"

"Depends how sharp they are," he said. "It wasn't any ninety-year-old who tossed me into the Bay or set a bomb in Nev's warehouse, but people can be bought to do things like that." He glanced again out the window. "Did you know the boat Mel and I rented at Uguarta sank?"

"Actually, yes." Cassandra confronted Damien's gaze, then looked away. "The boatman came to see me early this morning. He said—well, never mind what he said. What it boils down to is that he had the boat dredged up and what do you think he found when all the gunk had been cleared away?"

Damien eased the damp cotton T-shirt away from the middle of his back. "Sabotage?"

She saluted him with her tumbler. "Beautiful and bright."

"Does he know who did it?"

"His assistant. I gather the little squirt lit out right after you two left, but not before he told a pretty female conquest all about his hot deal. No names, though, if you're interested."

"Rook must have paid him off."

"Who?"

Damien waved it away. "Just someone's calling card."

"Your hired toppler of empires?"

"Probably." He slid from the sill and the sun that was making him hot. "Who are the Circle boys, Cassandra?"

She tipped her head to one side. "You really are gorgeous, you know that?"

Damien raked his fingers through his hair, holding it off his warm forehead. "Tell me, Cassandra."

"Did someone really push you into the Bay?"

"Yes."

Her tone sharpened, only by a fraction but Damien noticed it. "What about my kid?"

"She's fine so far."

"What does that mean?"

"It means that all of Nev's heirs are targets. Melanie's an heir."

"The witch, too?"

Damien sighed. "I don't know. Probably not. Anyway, she's Rolf's problem. It's Melanie I'm worried about."

"Oh really?"

He just kept looking at her, and finally she released a heavy breath.

"Oh, all right, I'll tell you what I can. But just so you know, I'm doing this for Melanie, you and Rolf. I wouldn't lift a finger to save anything that Neville McCall or Tom Rossi built. You got that?"

"I got it."

"Okay." She settled back and gave an eloquent shrug. "First of all there was Nev and Tom, and according to Tommy, a lot of seedy little scams that saw them pretty nicely through the start of the Depression. Now, I don't know exactly what it was but I do know the Circle thing was a planned scam from day one. And if you think old Tom was any less of a bastard than Nev, you're wrong."

"How do you know that?"

"Tommy told me. And I have no idea how he found out. He just knew, the same way he knew it was really old Tom's idea to call it the Circle of Five. So you see, Mel's grandpa was nothing but a martyr. He sacrificed his conscience for money. And what a cause!"

"And the Circle itself? What did it entail?"

"Exactly what I said. Money." She wiggled her fingers. "Details I don't have, Damien. I only know there were three other men involved. Businessmen actually. They went into some deal with Nev and Tom, and then got screwed. And I think you can guess that when the dust finally settled it was Nev and Tom who emerged victorious."

Damien frowned. "Emerged from what? Don't you have any idea what the deal was?"

"Nope. Only that it must have been dirty. Tommy'd know, but then he's long gone and probably better off for it."

Damien arched a dark brow. "That's a pretty callous attitude."

Giving a short, sharp laugh Cassandra drained her glass. "Yeah, well, I'm a pretty callous person." Her eyes flicked to his. "I'm also a realist. You think I'm to blame for Tommy's death, don't you?"

"I didn't say that."

She shrugged. "You didn't have to. I may be a lush, but I'm not stupid. Old Tom hated me and I hated him. Why is that, you ask? Because while we were totally dissimilar in almost every way, we were both uncommonly perceptive. We each understood what the other was. We pulled poor Tommy in two different directions. For whatever reasons, I won. Tommy turned away from his old man, existed for a while and finally turned away from life. So you tell me, whose fault was that?"

Damien thought for a moment, then asked, "Why did you drag him down here?"

"Because he didn't want to be up there." Her hand trembled as she groped for her rum bottle. "Trust me, I couldn't have dragged Tommy anywhere if he hadn't wanted to be dragged. Melanie never believed that, but it's the truth. Tommy got turned off Romac and he ran to me for escape. And I'll tell you something else, he only once talked to me about the Circle boys. Then he clammed up about everything."

Damien was startled. "You've never told Melanie any of this?"

"No point. Melanie sees things her way, I see things mine. That's life." Yawning, Cassandra settled back on her cot. "So, is there anything else you want to know?" She sent him a wry look. "About the Circle boys, I mean."

For a long time Damien studied her, then he made an accepting gesture. "Their names, for one thing."

"I'll write them down." She stared at her fingers. "If I can remember how to write, that is. Anything else?"

"No—yes." Damien started to turn away, then stopped. His head was spinning from this conversation. "Are these Circle partners still alive?"

"Who knows? But if they aren't, you might want to check out their kids, or their kids' kids. You know, poor heir bent on sticking it to rich heir." She hesitated, her hand shaking badly as she went to refill her glass. "Just do me one favor, okay?" she said in a subdued voice that wasn't like her at all. Her eyes came up to meet his. "Don't let whoever's doing this hurt my kid, huh?"

Chapter Nine

"Ah, Mel, just the lady magnate I've been looking for." Tucker Smith's moist hands clamped themselves around Melanie's arms from behind. "You make the descent into the Cable Car caverns at last."

She kept walking. "I'll break your hands if they aren't off me in three seconds."

"Oh, come on, Mel."

"One, two..."

"Okay, they're off." He backed away, arms raised.

She stopped in the long carpeted corridor. Like the airline, Cable Car Foods had its business offices in the Romac Building. Normally that wasn't a problem. Today it seemed it would be.

"What do you want, Tucker?" she asked with forced patience. "I'm very busy."

"I want you to talk to Jonny for me."

"No."

"About a job in Romac Accounting," he went on. Then he stared at her. "What do you mean, no?" His eyes showed incredulity.

"I mean, no, I won't talk to Jonny."

"Why the—why not?"

"Because you're doing just fine here."

His expression got ugly for a second, a Roman centurion denied his deepest desire. "You're not being fair, Mel."

"Don't whine."

He'd just love to hit her, Melanie could see it in his muddy eyes. But Tucker was too afraid of being hit back to ever try anything. Besides, he wanted in at Romac. He'd never get there if he blew her vote.

"Look, Melanie," he said, placing an arm around her shoulders, "I'm already—"

"Get your arm off me."

His smile came dangerously close to a leer. "Do I disturb you?"

"Three seconds, Tucker."

"God, I give up." He removed his arm and glared. "Look, Melanie, as I was saying, I already work upstairs one morning a week."

"Why?"

The glare became a look of superiority. "The companies are interconnected, you know," he said as if speaking to a child.

"Don't be obnoxious. I mean, why you?"

Now he seemed offended. "Why not me?"

"Because at least three people I know of at Cable Car have seniority over you. How did you get the crossover job, Tucker?"

"I asked for it."

"In other words Morgan got it for you."

"Yes—no!" He swore under his breath. "You're really making this difficult, you know."

"I'm not making it anything. I told you in Chicago, I do the Elite charters. For whatever reason, Morgan seems to be your champion. Get him to talk to Jonny."

She was sure she didn't imagine Tucker's reaction to that remark, because it surprised her. There was a definite glitch in his expression and in his voice. "Uh, no, I don't think so. Not this time. Look, Mel, Morgan got me this job, I admit it, but he's not my champion. He's just an old friend of the family doing a favor. I can't expect him to keep pushing me up the corporate ladder. Some things you have to do for yourself."

Melanie studied Tucker's eyes carefully, and his body language. "This is a new attitude for you."

He wouldn't look at her for a minute. When he finally did, his expression was calm. Only his fingers rubbing on his pant legs betrayed his nervousness. But was he nervous for himself or for Morgan?

"I change as I have to, Mel," he said with a smile. "Isn't change the first law of the jungle?"

She'd lost the moment and her chance. "No," she answered with a smile of her own. "The first law is survival."

"HE WANTS IN AT Romac awfully badly," Melanie told Rolf after work.

It was a balmy evening for the latter part of October. There was still light in the sky at five-thirty. Rolf had invited her out to Nev's house in Sausalito for a talk, because he said he didn't want to be in his own place in the city, at least not until Regan got back from Nassau and they could iron things out.

Not much chance of that, Melanie thought, but it didn't matter to her where they went, just as long as she didn't have to be alone. Time to herself meant thinking of Damien and what good would that do? The lines were drawn between them. He liked his life as it was and she liked hers. To carry a misplaced attraction beyond the very dangerous point it seemed to have reached would be nothing short of idiotic. It had to end. That meant she must keep him out of her mind.

She lounged barefoot in a rattan chair in the big kitchen, eating grapes while Rolf fixed himself some concoction in the blender.

"For my ulcer," he said in a resigned tone. "Why do you think it's so odd that Tucker should want to work upstairs?"

Melanie shrugged. She wished she knew where Damien was. "I don't, really. It's his insistent attitude that's bothering me, and something else."

"What?"

"It's hard to explain." She propped her feet up. "He looked strange when I asked him how he got the crossover accounting job between Romac and Cable Car."

Rolf flicked the blender on. "Morgan got it for him, that's not news."

"I know. But when I said that to him, he looked away, as if he was uncomfortable with the idea."

"And since when does Morgan's or anyone else's help make Tucker uncomfortable?" Rolf drew the remark out. "I see your point. Anything else?"

"Well, then I wondered if maybe it was Morgan's name that made him uncomfortable."

"Sorry, you'll have to explain that."

Melanie leaned forward on her elbows. "Morgan's been hanging around the Romac accounting department lately. That woman, Lucy Farmer, the one I told you about the other day, well, she's seen him twice now coming out of the accounting offices early in the morning."

"Suspicious I'll grant you, but what's she doing there early in the morning?"

"Ah, well, now that's another thing. I didn't know this but she's Jonny's junior assistant. And Jonny's been leaving early these past few weeks. Sometimes he asks, but evidently other times he just sort of fades out of sight. She's been coming in to cover for him."

"Did Lucy Farmer tell you this?" Rolf sounded distracted as he looked around the colonial kitchen.

Melanie sat back with a handful of grapes. "Lucy and a few others I talked to. That's why I was down on the Cable Car level today." She waited until he'd turned off the blender and poured the thick white ulcer cure into a glass, then she said, "You're thinking about Regan, aren't you?"

He didn't deny it. "I can't believe she'd have an affair."

Neither could she, Melanie thought. Her eyes traveled to the *Emily-Mac,* gleaming silver-white in the distance, from here a mere speck on the water in the early evening sun. "Maybe it's not true."

"No, it's true, I'm sure of that. I just can't figure out who she's seeing or why she's doing it." Rolf raised his head to look at her, his face momentarily tinged with guilt. "I did remember to tell you about Damien, didn't I?"

Melanie stiffened inside. "That he was going to South America. Yes."

Rolf sighed. "He's crazy."

"No." She mirrored his sigh. "He's homesick."

"He's back."

"What?" Melanie's head snapped up. Rolf wasn't teasing. Damien was back and heading up the path to the house, his pale blue denim shirt open at the throat, his jacket and backpack a bulky weight over one shoulder.

She closed her eyes briefly. How in two short days could she possibly have forgotten how gorgeous he was? She should get out of here.

She didn't move and the moment for a quick escape vanished.

His features were unusually somber as he let himself in the screen door. His dark eyes skimmed their faces, coming to rest on Melanie's.

"You two are hard to find," he remarked finally, wincing a little as he eased the burden from his shoulder. He looked scratched. He couldn't have been in Salvadore.

She kept her eyes on his. "How long have you been back?"

"About an hour." He collapsed into a chair beside her, pulling a piece of paper from his shirt pocket and sliding it to her across the table. "From your mother."

"You went to see Cassandra?" She stared at him. "That's where you've been?"

"Don't yell at me, Mel. I've been bitten by every bug on the Orinoco."

"Serves you right," she muttered, setting her teeth. She wanted to check the bruise on his torso, to smooth the hair from his face with her fingers. "You should have told me you were going."

He glanced at Rolf, then away. "I know."

Rolf jumped in quickly. "Uh, Melanie said she sent a telegram to Cassandra about the Circle of Five. Did her guess pan out?"

"Uh-huh." Damien was watching her; Melanie could feel his eyes on her face and breasts. Her skin burned beneath the dusty pink cotton of her T-shirt. "Read it, Mel," he said softly.

The paper was under her fingers. She forced herself to unfold it and look. Three names were written there, in her mother's hand.

"Herschel Barnum, Rupert Skillings and Samuel Taggart," Damien said to his brother. "She doesn't know where they live or if they're even alive, but your private investigator should be able to find that out."

Rolf stood. "I'll call him right away." Melanie's head was bent down. He pulled on a strand of her hair. "Can I have the note?"

She read the words one last time, surprised and oddly upset by Cassandra's shaky postscript. "Love ya, kid," her mother had scribbled in the corner. And for the first time since she'd been very young, Melanie wanted to cry for all the things the two of them had missed.

Nodding mutely, she pushed the paper toward Rolf's fingers, waited until he was gone, then looked sideways through her hair at Damien's impassive face.

"Why didn't you tell me you were going?"

"I knew you'd want to come."

"I could have done it alone, Damien. I don't like it down there, but that doesn't mean I can't cope."

She recognized the faintly regretful light in his eyes. "It was easier to go by myself than to argue about it. I don't want to fall in love with you, Mel."

It took everything she had to look tough, or at least unmoved. "Then don't," she said, and prayed she didn't sound like a sulky child. She forced herself to sit up. "Look Damien, I don't want to fall in love with you, either, but I don't like polite relationships, especially with men. I go through that at work every day. I don't need it in my off time, too." She bit her lip and offered a tentative, "Couldn't we just try to be friends?"

A smile laced with irony crossed his mouth. "We could *try*," he agreed. He studied her for a minute—she couldn't imagine what he was thinking—then he relented and said, "I'll tell you what. While Rolf's P.I. does his homework, why don't we go to a concert in the park?"

She didn't want to be too hasty about this. "What kind of a concert?"

"A sixties revival. I heard about it at the airport."

She regarded her torn jeans and baggy T-shirt. "Can I go like this?"

"To Hippie Hill?" His smile widened. "You'll probably be overdressed." Pushing back his chair, he held out his hand to her. "Come on," he said. "Rolf won't care. And anyway, there's something I want to tell you."

Her muscles tightened as his fingers curled around hers. "More *candomblé?*" she asked, telling herself firmly that the shiver sweeping through her did not come from two sources.

"Cold, hard fact," he said with a shake of his head. He pulled her up. "The boatman's assistant was paid to sink us."

"HEY, YOU TWO," Jonny greeted as Melanie and Damien made their way through Golden Gate Park.

A cool breeze blew off the Bay, ruffling his dark hair. He looked dead tired and very much like Damien, though not a fraction as sexy. But she'd promised herself she wouldn't think about that.

Jonny appealed to them with a grimace. "Look, I hate to ask this, but would it be okay if I took a couple of days off?"

Damien sent him a questioning look. "You tracked us to the park to ask that?"

"No, I saw you and thought I'd save myself a phone call later."

Melanie sensed caution in his tone. "Is there a problem?" she asked.

His eyes flicked to her face, then to a grove of shadowed trees. "No. I just need a couple days to myself."

Damien shrugged. "Take them," was all he said.

"Thanks." Jonny jerked his head toward the gathering crowd, milling ex-flower children, many now upward of forty. "You here for the music?" At their silent nods, he said, "Well, enjoy it. I wish I could hang around, but I have to clear out my attic. I think I've got mice."

Melanie pulled her jacket a little closer. "How's your basement?"

"It's fine. No mice down there."

"I mean the water."

"What water?"

"I thought you said your basement flooded."

He didn't miss a beat, didn't falter or give any sign of unease. "Oh that." He chuckled, a slightly forced sound, hooking his thumbs in his belt loops. "All fixed." With a grin and a pleasant, "Thanks again," he moved off toward the bridge, which was not the direction he lived.

Melanie stared after him. "He lied to me," she said, not liking the idea one bit. "He told me his basement flooded last week."

"Sounds like he forgot about it," Damien remarked.

"Maybe because it never happened." A tremor that didn't come from the coastal chill ran across Melanie's skin. "Damien, this is awful. I'm starting not to trust anyone."

"THINK OF A WORD," Damien told her, "or a feeling. Anything except notes or diary pages or red rooks or people who lie."

Melanie's gaze landed on a pair of striped bell bottoms with frayed cuffs and a big pink daisy stitched to the back pocket.

"How about a flower?"

"That'll do."

They sat cross-legged on the grass, alone in the midst of many similar pairs. It reminded Melanie of a love-in. A woman with a gravelly voice and beaded vest sang songs on the makeshift stage.

"Okay, do you have a flower in your mind?"

"Uh—" she conjured up a purple orchid "—yes."

"Good, now close your eyes and concentrate on it."

She felt his fingers making small counterclockwise circles on her temples and sighed to herself. This meditation he wanted her to try didn't stand a chance of working. It had been doomed from the moment he touched her. Closing her eyes made it easier to endure, but Melanie could still feel Damien's fingers on her forehead, still inhale the scent of his skin and hair.

"You're not concentrating, Mel," he said in tempered amusement.

She couldn't do this. She opened her eyes. "I don't understand transcendental meditation."

"Neither do I, but Rolf swears by it."

"Rolf has an ulcer."

Damien smiled a little. "That's a point." With his thumbs he brushed her temples one last time, then let his hands fall away from her face. He took a quick look at the bandstand. "We could dance, I suppose."

"Do the pony?" She grinned, leaning back on her palms. "And here I thought you were more the samba, lambada type."

A humorous light invaded his eyes. "I know the lambada."

"I figured you might."

"Friends don't do it."

Friends? Well, she'd made the suggestion, hadn't she? It didn't have a prayer of succeeding, she realized now, but she couldn't tell him that. She had trouble even admitting it to herself.

The music changed to a slow beat. Bodies with braided hair and headbands swayed on the grass. It felt like the sixties, at least Melanie's perception of that time. They hadn't been singing songs for freedom in Venezuela.

She gathered her jacket more closely around her. She'd vowed fifteen minutes ago that she wouldn't shiver from the cold, although the temperature had dropped substantially in that time. Damien might put his arm around her, and that would be the end of her already shaky facade. So long as he didn't touch her, she could half believe she wouldn't fall in love with him. Any more contact between them would destroy the lie in a second.

"Dim sum," she heard Damien say when the set broke. "Or pizza." He sent her a speculative look. "Which do you like better?"

She rubbed her arms though the sleeves of her jacket. "Which is closer?"

"Chinatown, but Nev's Jaguar has a good heater."

She made a face. "Your Jaguar," she reminded him. "And is there anything you miss?"

"Too much, most of the time." He pulled her to her feet and then he did it. He put his arm over her shoulders, tucking her in close to his warm body. It was probably to her disadvantage that she knew what lay beneath his clothes. His smile was a bit too knowing. "It doesn't get this cold in Salvadore," he reminded her.

"You can't get yellow fever in San Francisco," she retorted.

"Stop comparing my home to a tropical village, Mel."

"I can't help it, it's what I know." She refused to relax against him. "Did we decide, pizza or Chinese?"

"Beer and pizza?" he asked with a hopeful arch of his brow.

"As long as we're inside. Damien?" He glanced down at her, a definite threat to her emotions in the shadows of the park. "Is Cassandra all right?"

"I think so." She felt him shrug. "She drinks too much."

"Well, I know that. But she couldn't have been herself. I mean, she gave you those names and that just isn't something she'd do normally. She always told me she'd love to see Nev and Tom's empire crumble.''

Damien scanned the skyline. "Maybe it deserves to crumble a little."

"Why, because of Nev and Tom's business ethics? You can't blame them for being a little unscrupulous back in the thirties."

"A little, no. But Cassandra seems to feel it was more than that."

Melanie hunched her shoulders. "Cassandra hated Tom. She'd call him a crook for jaywalking."

"Maybe." Damien slid her a sideways look. "She did it for you, you know."

Melanie's expression was mistrustful. "Did what?"

"Gave me those names."

"She gave..." Melanie stopped, staring at him with a blend of surprise and suspicion. "Why would she do that?" Her eyes darkened. "You're not lying, are you?"

"Your faith in me is staggering."

"Don't be sarcastic. What makes you think she did it for me?"

"Because she said so. She also wanted me to make sure nothing happened to you."

"Talk about faith." Melanie looked away, then added softly, "I wonder why she never says those things to me?"

"Ask her," Damien suggested.

"I beg your pardon?"

"Go back down there when this mess up here is over, and talk to her." His tone became faintly amused and he turned his face into her hair. "You might want to take a broom with you, though."

"You see, even you can't stand it."

She smiled and let herself lean against him, then suddenly it hit her, what he'd said: when this mess is over.

"*If* it's ever over," she said out loud. They began walking again. "Who could be behind all this, Damien? Surely not those three old Circle of Five men."

"Check out their kids and their kids' kids," Damien murmured obscurely. Melanie felt his lips press against her hair, but maybe he didn't realize what he was doing. His thoughts seemed far away from her. "There's a connection, Mel, there has to be. All we have to do is find it."

"It and him," she said, inching closer despite her misgivings. "He wants more than the airline destroyed, Damien. He said in that telephone message that Nev's legacy to us would be death. He meant it. I don't know how I know that, but I do. Whoever this Rook is, he wants us all dead."

Chapter Ten

The phone rang in Rook's darkened bedroom. He let it ring four times then picked up the receiver.

"Good, you're there," a voice on the other end said.

Rook had no time for small talk. "What do you want?" he asked his helper without inflection.

"Damien's back from South America."

"I know."

"Yes, but do you know where he was?"

"In Brazil, I imagine."

"Wrong. He was visiting Melanie's mother, who was married to old Tom Rossi's son. Does that suggest anything to you?"

"Get to the point," Rook said coldly.

A sigh came across the line. "Maybe she told Damien something you didn't want him to know."

Rook considered the idea. Much as he hated to admit it, there was merit in the suggestion.

"Where are you now?" he asked.

"I've been following them like you wanted me to. They're at Nuno's, eating pizza and talking."

Rook glanced at his watch. Eight-thirty. He'd had plans for this night, but he supposed they could be delayed, postponed if necessary, though he hoped it wouldn't come to that. Torment was so enjoyable.

"All right," he said, pushing himself out of the bed he'd just collapsed on. "Keep your eye on them until I get there."

"You think they're up to something?"

"I want to make sure one way or the other. I'm not finished with Damien and Melanie."

"You mean you don't want them dead?"

Rook smiled. "Not yet."

THE RESTAURANT WAS COZY and Damien found himself mesmerized by Melanie. He didn't need to be doing this to himself. She polished off her beer and leaned forward to study him across the table.

"Trying to make a point, Mel?" he asked, focusing on her with difficulty.

"No, I was just wondering about you."

"What about me?"

"You don't drink, you don't smoke—do you do anything wrong?"

He almost choked. "I don't drink because I like to be in control. I got drunk once when I was fifteen, took Rolf's car, drove it into a ditch and woke up the next morning in a town called Skull Valley, Arizona. There were four of us, me and three of my friends, and not one of us could remember how we got there."

Melanie's smile was delighted. "Where in Skull Valley did you wake up?"

"A motel."

"Like those places in Mexico?"

"No, like a dump where hookers go and you might wake up after a night in a bar. Except we never went to a bar and I never liked the idea of paying for sex, even with Rosa."

"Who's Rosa?"

"The waitress who hauled me up to my room. She threw a blanket over me when I passed out and missed the bed."

"Then what happened?"

He frowned. "I don't remember. I woke up the next morning on the floor, threw up, paid for the room and found my friends. Rosa gave us coffee and told us to come back and see her in a few years. Then we hitchhiked home.

It was the first and last time I ever drank. I was sick for two days after that.''

"So what did Hilary say?"

Damien shifted uncomfortably in his seat. "I never told her. I just pretended I had the flu and stayed in my room until I felt human again."

"But what about Rolf's car?"

"It was back in the garage when I came out. No questions asked, and I wasn't about to volunteer any information."

Melanie propped her chin up on her hands and gave a sad sigh. "He's a great brother. You're lucky. Cassandra didn't want even me, let alone any other children."

Damien was faintly shocked by the remark. Or was it panic he felt? What would he have done if Melanie had never been born?

"Papa was nice to me, though," she continued. "His mind came and went, but every once in a while he'd get me a toy to play with."

Damien found himself growing intrigued. "What about other kids?"

"There were two in the village," she said. "A boy and a girl. I played dolls with the girl and climbed trees with the boy. Until I found a spider in one of the branches and that was it for tree climbing." She fiddled with her last piece of pizza. "You don't think I'm very tough, do you?"

"I think you're very tough. Why?"

"I could take care of myself in the jungle before I could read, did you know that? Except for snakes and spiders, I always hated those things. And leeches. I can't stand leeches. But I could still take care of myself. I could survive. It doesn't sound like much, I know, but I think it was. I mean, Papa couldn't survive and he was a lot older and stronger than me."

"Not stronger, Mel."

"Oh yes, much stronger. It's just that he loved my mother, so he gave in to her and then he had to change his whole way of life to accommodate her."

"Are you sure that's how it was between them?"

"Why? Did Cassandra give you a different version?"

"Slightly different."

"Well, maybe the truth's halfway between. Anyway, Papa started with a burden of change. I didn't. All I knew was the rain forest, so what could I do but adapt? Papa had memories to fend off, of people and places he loved a lot more than Venezuela. That made it harder for him than for me. But that's not what I'm trying to say. I just want you to know that I really can take care of myself. I know how not to hurt, or at least how not to let it show. I also know how not to fall in love. At least I did until I met you again—and you don't need to look so shocked. I don't want anything from you, because I'm not my mother, and I wouldn't ever try to change another person."

Then why was she saying these things to him? Damien opened his mouth to speak, but she stopped him with a quick shake of her head.

"No, don't grope or try to be polite. I really wouldn't want the kind of relationship my parents had. I mean, you saw Cassandra when you went down to ask her about the Circle of Five. Did she seem happy to you?"

"No, but—"

"I know," Melanie interrupted, leaning back in her seat. "You're going to say she gave you the names of the Circle members because of me, so she can't be all bad."

Damien hid a grin. "Something like that. Anyway, I don't think your father would have married her if he hadn't wanted to get away from Romac."

Melanie narrowed her eyes. "What, you mean Tom drove him away? I don't believe that."

"Your father knew about the Circle of Five, at least Cassandra claims he did. Maybe he thought the deals Nev and Tom made were too sordid and he wanted to get out and find something for himself."

"He did like to take pictures," Melanie conceded, her voice and expression far away. "And he liked writing, too. Well, sort of. He always kept journals. Cassandra must have shipped fifty of them back to San Francisco after he died. Come to think of it, he wrote down every—'' She halted abruptly, her eyes coming up to his. ''Journals,'' she whispered. ''Damien, he kept journals, about everything. And you said he told Cassandra about the Circle of Five, that he knew what it was.''

Reaching across the table, she pounded her fist lightly on his hand. ''What are you saying?'' he asked.

''Nev has those journals,'' she revealed. ''Or he had them, anyway. He had all of my father's stuff. And Tom's. You remember, he stored it at the Sausalito house, up in the attic.'' Her fingers dug urgently into his wrist. ''Don't you see, Damien? The answers we are looking for might be in my father's journals.''

Now Damien did see. Taking her hand he stood and murmured, ''We've got to get to Sausalito.''

ROOK MANAGED TO STAY behind them despite the heavy bridge traffic. He didn't trust the look of purpose they'd had on their faces when they'd left the restaurant. And now they were driving through Sausalito.

Well, the house and the *Emily-Mac* were both here. Maybe he was overreacting. But no, his instincts were too good for that. And he didn't want things getting messed up now. Not that his plan was in any danger of falling apart at this point, but caution was better than carelessness. And a warning might not hurt, either.

A smile curved his lips at that thought. Yes, a warning would be a very good idea. Now the dilemma. Just how graphic should that warning be?

I met a woman today, a beautiful red-haired island queen. Old Tom calls her a voodoo queen, but what does he know about anything, especially human nature...?

In the cluttered attic of Nev's Sausalito house, Melanie sighed and stopped reading. ''That has a bitter sound to it,'' she said. "But I don't see anything in here about the Circle of Five. I don't see anything in any of these books, do you?"

Damien shook his head. "Only a page on bats torn out of an old *National Geographic*."

"Papa liked bats."

Melanie scanned the pile of books they'd unearthed from one of the trunks. It was cold and drafty up here and her head was starting to hurt from reading her father's spidery handwriting in the light of one forty-watt bulb. Rolf hadn't been here when they'd gotten back, though where he'd gone Melanie couldn't guess, unless of course Regan had come home.

"Maybe my father felt duty-bound not to write anything down about Grandpa Tom's dirty deals." She picked up another book. This one was dated several months before the one she'd just finished reading. She bent back the cover. "I wish we could figure out what Rook really wants."

"Revenge," Damien replied with a shrug. "In whatever form he can get it."

His eyes were so large and dark in this light. She could get lost in eyes like that. But she wouldn't, she resolved, giving herself a shake.

"Murder is pretty drastic revenge," she said. She removed a yellowed envelope from between the pages and continued flipping. "They must have done something pretty horrible."

Out of the corner of her eye, she saw Damien move closer. "What's that?" he asked, and she looked down at the envelope in her hand.

"A letter. Why?"

"That's old Tom's handwriting. I recognize it from some of the documents at Romac."

Melanie took another look and frowned. He was right. And her father's name was written on the outside.

"Open it, Mel," Damien said softly.

She hesitated, but complied. Quickly she skimmed the pages inside.

"Anything?" Damien asked.

"Everything," she said, biting her lip. "Or enough anyway. Do you want me to read it?"

He nodded and she took a deep breath.

"Dear Tommy,

I know you're upset about the things I told you last night, but I really did think you'd understand. We were all businessmen back then, small-time but stable. Well, as stable as you could be during the Depression. I thought it would be all right at first, I really did. But then the economy got more fouled up and even the stable businesses started to fail.

Now, I know you don't believe me about wanting the Circle of Five to work out, and I'll admit there was a big part of me that knew it didn't stand a chance in hell of succeeding, but choices were limited in those days. Just because a partner toppled, that didn't mean you had to fall with him. Nev and I understood that from the start.

As for your accusation that we'd counted on our partners falling into financial ruin from the start, what can I say? The possibility existed. And you can be sure Nev and I had no intention of sinking with anyone.

Inevitably it happened. Our partners' businesses began to falter. Naturally, we bought them up, 'made a killing' to use your words.

Now I'll agree, maybe our strength-in-numbers precept was a little underhanded, but who knew times could ever get that bad?

Oh, I can hear you, Tommy. You don't believe a word I'm telling you. You think we went into the partnership intending for this to happen. We had plenty of money, you're saying to yourself. Nev and I were looking beyond the Depression long before we ever formed the Circle. Vultures, I believe you called us, swooping in for the kill when disaster struck. We bought our partners' businesses, sat back and waited for the turnaround. Then, when it came, we cleaned up by selling off those same businesses.

Well, maybe there's something to that, but then you weren't alive during those years. You have no idea how difficult it was merely to survive...."

"That's enough, Mel," Damien said, rubbing a weary eye.

"Sort of removes any doubt about what the Circle of Five really was, doesn't it?" Slowly Melanie slid the letter back inside her father's journal. "And, I suppose it also supports some of what Cassandra told you...." She broke off and glanced over her shoulder at the window. "Did you hear something?"

"Like an engine?" Damien nodded and got up to look. "I don't see a car, or headlights for that matter." Then he paused and peered through the pane. "Wait a minute, there's someone down there."

"Doing what?" Melanie came to stand beside him. She didn't see anyone, only shadows and a light film of mist swirling in from the water.

"I'm not sure, but I don't like it. Wait here."

He was gone before she could object and for a moment Melanie simply stared at the vast grounds. Then suddenly it occurred to her that she was alone up here, and turning, she ran across the attic and down two very dark sets of stairs to the even darker kitchen.

"Damien?" she whispered, easing open the swinging door. "Are you here?"

There was no answer so she pushed through and crept over to the main door. The silence was too heavy, it made her skin crawl—but not half as much as the hand that came out of nowhere to clamp itself onto her wrist.

She started to scream and jerk away, then felt herself being hauled forward against a man's hard body.

"It's okay, Mel," Damien said in her ear. "It's me."

She relaxed against him, the tension sliding from her limbs. "God, you scared me," she said weakly. "What are you doing sneaking around in the dark?"

"Because someone else has been sneaking around." He pulled her over to the wall and flicked on a small table lamp. "Look at this. It was taped to the front door."

Melanie forced her eyes down to the large piece of white paper he held in his hand. On it she saw four chess pieces, the leering outline of a personified rook and three toppled pawns.

No, not toppled, she realized with a start. Dead. The pawns were all covered in blood.

THE SOUND OF THE telephone ringing in his ear the next morning dragged Damien out of a sleep filled with vicious rooks and bleeding pawns.

When he found the receiver, a thick, "What?" was the best he could manage to mumble.

"Did I wake you up?" Rolf asked.

"If it isn't after nine, you can go to hell," Damien growled, forcing his eyes open a crack. Still pitch black beyond the portholes. He was going to strangle Rolf.

"It's six-fifteen. What time did you get in?"

"Five-thirty."

"You're joking."

Damien crooked an arm over his bloodshot eyes. "I had a lousy night, Rolf. What do you want?"

"The private investigator has a location on our ex-Circle partners."

"At six-fifteen in the morning?"

"We're paying him a fortune. He can work nights." Rolf paused. "What were you doing out till five-thirty?"

Damien's bad mood was deteriorating rapidly. "Don't ask."

"Okay." His brother sighed, sounding exhausted now, and miserable. "Regan came home last night, a couple hours after you and Mel left. She called from the airport. We've been talking all night. She says her cousin in Nassau is fine, which should give you an indication of how the conversation's been going. She's still playing the wounded party."

Damien called her a name in Portuguese. He considered telling Rolf about the letter and the picture, then decided against it. "I suppose you want me to call these three Circle guys."

"I'd appreciate it. But forget the phone, you can go and talk to them personally. Two of them, Herschel Barnum and Rupert Skillings, are in a nursing home in Berkeley. Samuel Taggart has a place just outside Monterey."

Damien ordered his brain to work. Obviously none of these men was dead. "How old are they?" he asked.

"All in their nineties. I don't know about their mental faculties. You'll have to phone the nursing home about visiting hours. I have the address and Samuel Taggart's too. Hopkins, the P.I., is going to check on their descendants, because I guess we all know that these men aren't likely to be running around boat decks and warehouses at ninety-odd."

"Could be hired help," Damien reminded him, although deep down he didn't really believe that. This seemed too personal to have been bought.

"I'd do it myself, Damien," Rolf was apologizing, "but I've got to get this thing with Regan straightened out. You, uh, might want to ask Mel to go with you. Her assistant can cover for her today."

Damien flinched, but didn't let it come across. "I'll think about it," he agreed. "Give me the addresses and phone numbers."

Two minutes later, he was flopping back on the mattress. His eyes stung from salt air and smoke, his head was a buzz of San Francisco noise. With a groan and a shudder, he rolled over and buried his face in the pillow.

He kept seeing dead pawns in his mind, and the only thing that would block them out was a picture of Melanie. And that made him nervous enough that finally he kicked off the covers and got out of bed.

He looked at the clock. Six-thirty a.m. A shower, maybe breakfast and a quick trip to the airport to check on the outgoing planes, then he'd see about talking to Herschel, Rupert and Samuel.

What, if anything, did the ex-Circle of Five partners know about recent events? He might not learn the whole truth today, but if these men were lucid he should be able to get some sort of a feeling from them. He'd better, because people bent on revenge almost always became consumed, if not completely crazy.

"DO YOU HAVE ANY IDEA what time it is?" Melanie stared at Damien in disbelief. "What are you doing here?"

"It's 7:17 in the morning, and I need your help."

She brought her eyes into focus, giving the belt of her emerald velour robe a precautionary tug. Why did he have to look so somber and gorgeous?

She turned for the living room of her A-frame, leaving the door open for him to follow. "Help with what?" she asked, thinking "coffee" as she went. "More threatening drawings?"

"The Circle of Five partners." He kept his distance behind her. "They're old. I'm not good with old people."

She tossed him an exasperated look over her shoulder. "What makes you think I'm any better—and if you say because I'm a woman, I'll hit you."

"Sexism's not really my burden, Mel." She caught the small smile in his voice. "I only know I'm not good with this sort of thing, so I figured you'd have to be better."

He trailed her to the kitchen, a big room of wood and glass and copper. She didn't know what to say, so she headed for the counter and said nothing.

He commented on the silence, which struck her as odd since he tended, when he wasn't burning up with fever, to be uncommonly reserved. Today he leaned the other way.

He hoisted himself onto the center island while she found the coffee tin. "Okay," she said carefully. "So how do you figure I can help you with three old men?"

He kept his hands in his jacket pockets, shifting his eyes to the windows. His eyes looked black today, which made his hair seem darker and his skin lighter. All of which made him seem more vulnerable, and that was not a good thing to notice at 7:21 on a cold foggy morning with her bed only one flight of stairs away.

"Pretend they're Elite Charter clients," he said. "Fussy ones. How would you deal with that?"

"I'd grit my teeth, smile and get through it. Then I'd sic my new assistant on them for the details."

"Is that a punishment?"

"Not as much as if I handed them over to Morgan. Nev had him doing Elite with me when I first started, you know."

"Why?"

"I'm not sure." She took two mugs from the cupboard. "Probably because he wanted me to learn fast. You tend to do that when you work with Morgan. As soon as I knew what I was doing, he went back over to Nev's office and I got a string of up-and-comers for assistants. Sidney's the latest. I'd transfer him to reservations and let him 'Yes, ma'am,' Regan to death, but no one deserves that, so I'll have to think of some other place to relocate him."

Damien brought his eyes back to her face. He could manage so much serenity in his expression. Or was it innocence? In either case she wasn't prepared for his quiet, "Regan came back last night from her fling in the Bahamas."

Melanie wished she could pour hot coffee over Regan's shorn head. "She's crazy."

"So's Rolf."

"No, he's just sweet and misguided where she's concerned. Then again, at least Regan isn't dragging Rolf off to the back of beyond."

Damien took the steaming mug she handed him. "Not dragging, no, but she might still drive him there." He made a dismissing motion. "That's their business, though. Mine—ours—is a confrontation with the ex-Circle partners. I'll warn you now, Mel, I think someone followed me this morning."

A chill ran through her. She glanced out the kitchen window. "Do you think he's out there now?"

"I think it's possible. It would be a lot easier to tell without the fog."

"You're being sarcastic again."

"I know. I'm like that when I don't see the sun." Draining his coffee, he slid from the counter. The glimmer of amusement on his mouth was deadly. "Do you want me to help you dress?"

She held his gaze with difficulty. She kept wanting to look away, or better still, say yes. "You're forgetting, Damien, I'm not shy about my body." In this case, that was a big lie, but he didn't have to know it. "I'll dress myself. You watch the fog."

His eyes narrowed on the white bank beyond the window. "That's not a bad idea. Maybe I'll take a look around outside."

"I didn't mean—"

"I know you didn't," he interrupted, zipping his lined jacket. "But it's still a good idea. I don't think our rook wanted us to have those Circle members' names yet or he'd have supplied them."

"You mean he didn't know about Cassandra."

"Probably not."

"Then he's going to get mad."

Damien released a heavy breath. "I have a feeling, Mel, that he already is."

"THEY'RE COMING, Hersch." Rupert Skillings shuffled swiftly into the game room in his slippers. He still had his pajamas on and his white hair was sticking up all over his head. "They phoned the desk. Nurse Fuzik told me. Two of Neville's heirs are coming here this morning."

Herschel sat at the card table with three other men. Two of them were dozing, so he tossed his cards down and levered himself to his feet.

"I wonder why Rook didn't call," he said, looking more grouchy than upset. They shuffled out of the room and over to a bench in the hall near the base heater. "He said he'd call when he slipped them the news on us."

"Maybe he forgot."

Herschel's cane banged the floor. "Rook wouldn't forget."

Rook might not, but Rupert almost did. What were they talking about? A phone call? Yes. Now, what had Nurse Fuzik said?

"Maybe they found out about the money," Herschel continued.

"What money?" Rupert's confusion deepened. Why was he sitting in a drafty corridor in his pajamas?

Herschel's cane poked his foot. "The money he promised to get for us from the airline."

Money... Rupert thought hard. His mind worked better after his daily shot of Scotch. That wasn't permitted here, of course. "Rook is getting us money from the airline," he said at last. "That's right, I remember now."

"Coot," Herschel grumbled. "Oh now, don't look so damned offended, Rupe, I was talking about Nev. The gall of that old codger, sending his heirs out here."

"Sending!" Rupert frowned. "But Nev's dead, he couldn't have sent them."

"'Course he could. Ornery old cuss. He's probably got a line to them from hell. Rook should have called and warned us." He sucked on his lip for a moment, then snapped crossly, "Which ones are coming?"

"I think Nurse Fuzik said it was a woman on the telephone."

The cane hit the floor hard. "That'd be Tom's girl. Can't remember her name, but she was a bright little thing when old Neville rescued her from that native village in Africa."

"I don't think it was Africa, Hersch."

His friend glared. "You wanna argue countries or figure out how to handle these two?"

"But we don't even know what they want."

"They want to take up where old Nev left off, that's what they want. Maybe they found out about the money and they're going to say we're stealing it."

"But you said Rook had help on the inside." Rupert paused, a trifle uncertain. "Didn't you?"

"Did I—I mean, yes, I did." Herschel's wrinkled brow puckered. "Can't quite remember the name though."

"Rook never told us the name."

Now this, Rupert recalled clearly because he didn't like the way Rook came to them, sneaky, underhanded and hidden. They met like enemies did in spy movies, out in the garden, with Rook on one side of the hedge and them on the other. They'd never even seen his face.

"So the woman's coming and one of Nev's adopted spawn." Herschel's cane rattled on the floor, and on Rupert's nerves. He gave it a sudden eager thump. "You know something, Rupe, this could be fun. We're the geezers here. We can play 'em, just like old Nev and Tom played us. We'll fox them good. We won't tell 'em anything about anything, especially about Rook."

"We don't know anything about Rook."

Herschel waved a bony hand. "Doesn't matter. They won't know that. We'll just sit here and smile and listen. And remind ourselves that their money will pretty soon be ours."

Chapter Eleven

"You're not going to answer a single question I ask, are you?" Melanie said to the two very old men across from her in the sitting room of the Berkeley Parkside Lodge.

The thin one with the skeletal limbs and hawk nose beamed at both of them, although Damien had remained silent for most of this visit. He hadn't lied, he really wasn't good with elderly people, except Nev, who wouldn't have acted old on his deathbed.

"We don't know anything, miss," the other one said. His name was Rupert, and they might just get something out of him. His faded brown eyes had lit up when he'd seen Melanie. "You want to know did we do business with your grandfathers, and we've told you, yes. Did they cheat us, yes. Did we like them, no. Would we send someone after you with notes and pages from Neville's diary, no. What would be the point?"

Melanie sat back in her hard chair, regarding them closely. Damien slouched back in his, hands in his pockets, legs stretched out in front of him.

"Maybe you want us to know what Tom and Nev did to you," she replied softly. A nice touch. These men were no hard of hearing.

"And maybe we just don't know anything," Herschel put in with an impatient whack of his cane. "The old cheats are dead, and I say good riddance to them. Why should we send threats to either of you?"

Rupert, in a baggy sweater and wool trousers, reached out to tap Melanie's hand. "How did you find out about us, miss?"

"Melanie. And we talked to someone who knew about the Circle of Five."

Herschel stabbed his cane at her. "You watch your tongue, girl. We don't use that name around here." The tip dropped a bit to her legs. "Why are you wearing pants? I thought you were an executive."

"I'm not working today."

Herschel snorted. "The hell you're not, girl. You're working Rupert here like an old pro." The cane swatted Rupert's leg. "You remember that, Rupe, she's got her granddaddy's blood. We can't trust her an inch. This other one, I don't know. He doesn't say much."

Nao entendo, Damien was tempted to murmur, but instead he asked, "What would you like me to say?"

"Nothing. The girl's prettier, let her talk. I just wanted to make sure you had a tongue." Herschel dismissed him, turning back to Melanie. "Okay, girl, spit it out. Why did you come all the way out here to cross-examine us?"

"You don't believe me about the threatening notes and the phone message and the diary pages?"

"Nonsense. You're wasting my time. Get to the meat if there is any."

She studied them through narrowed eyes. She'd worn jeans today, a white silk top, an oversize black jacket and black boots. She looked about eighteen. If Herschel didn't appreciate the simplicity, Damien certainly did.

"Do you want all of it?" she asked them. "The whole truth?"

Rupert's head bobbed. Herschel merely stared back at her, his features hard.

She shrugged. "Okay. You're right. It is more than I'm telling you."

"I knew it!" Herschel's cane hit the floor in triumph.

"It's a bomb, a boat deliberately sunk in the Orinoco and sabotage on two of our planes and—"

"What?" Rupert stared at her in horror.

Her nod was entirely for him. "There's more, too."

"No more!" Herschel looked like a thundercloud. "Are you blaming us for these things?"

"Of course not," Melanie denied hastily. "I'm asking you if you know of anyone who might be willing to go that far for revenge."

"Absolutely not," Herschel said flatly. "And you shut your mouth, Rupe," he ordered when the other man began to protest.

"But what if he—"

"Who?" Melanie demanded, and now Damien leaned forward.

"Who is 'he,' Mr. Skillings?"

"No one," Herschel answered. Using his cane, he struggled to his feet. "I've heard enough. Both of you go away. You've got no business coming around here badgering us. My friend here forgets things sometimes."

"Now wait a minute, Herschel—"

"I told you to be quiet, Rupert. I'll handle this. And you!" His cane landed dangerously close to Damien's foot. "Get out. You're liars just like your grandfathers. Coming in here, trying to get us to admit to blowing you up—I bet there never even was a bomb."

"Yes, there was," Melanie insisted. She appealed to Rupert. "You believe me, don't you, Mr. Skillings?"

"Yes, certainly." He climbed to his feet and faced Herschel. "Now see here, you old goat—"

Herschel ignored him. "Go!" he roared.

A nurse in a pink cardigan hurried toward them.

Damien touched Melanie's arm. "We'd better leave," he said.

She resisted him. "In a minute. I think Rupert wants to tell me something."

"No, he doesn't." Herschel hobbled right up to her. "Go home and leave us be. Bombs can kill. We're not sticking our necks in any noose for you."

"But I—"

"Come on, Mel." Damien tugged on her hand.

"You should go," Rupert told her. "Herschel's right, we don't know about any bomb." He looked a little shaken. "Really, we wouldn't do anything like that. Not a bomb, not that." He hesitated, then shuffled closer while the nurse pleaded with Herschel to calm down. "He calls himself Rook, miss, but that's all we know about him. We never see him. For the most part he telephones us. I didn't think he'd get violent."

"So you didn't hire him," Damien said.

"No. He came to us."

"Why?" Melanie asked. "What did he want?"

Rupert opened his mouth, then closed it again firmly. His brown eyes toughened up. He wasn't going to tell them any more.

"There was no mention of a bomb, miss," he repeated, "or of sabotage. That's not what we wanted. He calls himself Rook. That's all I know. Now go."

"I COULD HAVE GOTTEN more out of him, Damien," Melanie declared as he pulled her through the front door of the lodge. "Why didn't you let me try?"

He kept a firm pressure on her resistant body. "Didn't you see that look on his face at the end?" he asked her. "He was through talking, Mel. He might not want us blown away, but he wants something. He came right out and admitted that much."

"Romac?"

"I doubt it. More likely the two of them want to bring us down."

"Which means Rook is someone at the airline, right? Or Cable Car."

Damien started to argue, then stopped. It was a logical assumption. "It would make things easier to be on the inside," he agreed. "Although he could have hired help in that area."

She twisted free of his grasp. "Don't worry," she said, sending him a displeased sideways look. "I'm not about to run back and start grilling Rupert again. But he knows more than he's admitting, and I still think we left too soon."

Vague amusement played on Damien's lips. "You say that, Mel, but I'm the one Herschel would have gone after with his cane." He pushed back his sleeve to look at his watch. "Almost eleven. Are you hungry?"

She grinned and gave him a little shove. "We can stop at a burger place on the way to Monterey. Did you call Samuel Taggart?"

Damien shivered in the chill air. He'd get pneumonia before he left this place. "The lines were down." He slid her an ironic look. "Probably the fog."

"Only if, like the movie, there's something evil in it. Anyway, you should be thankful it rolled in. It's grounding our flights today. That'll give the mechanics a chance to triple-check the planes."

"True." He squinted into the wet shroud that didn't agree with his lungs or his body temperature. "It's too still," he started to say, but the words never quite made it out. Something solid and extremely forceful glanced off his shoulder, almost knocking him to the ground. He stumbled but caught his balance, then reached automatically for Melanie.

"Down," he gasped at her, pain making his voice tight.

They dropped to their knees behind a bush.

"What happened? Are you all right?" Obviously bewildered, Melanie pushed at the collar of his jacket, but he caught her fingers in his.

"Later." His vision was blurred, possibly from the fire in his shoulder. He couldn't bring the parking lot into focus. It was the *Emily-Mac* all over again. "Do you see anything?" he asked, his mouth close to her ear.

"I never did to start with," she whispered back. "Why did you stumble?"

Pain sliced up and down his left arm. "Something hit me. Are you sure you don't see anything?"

She shook her head.

"Okay." He took her hand, nodding at the foggy lot. "The car's straight ahead. Let's get there and then get the hell out of here."

They climbed to their feet together, warily, listening for any break in the immediate silence. Traffic hummed in the distance, one or two cars rolled past on the street, but that was normal enough. Now if they could only make it to the Jag.

Damien stepped from the curb with a near ridiculous caution. It made no sense, but he couldn't seem to think clearly. What did Rook hit him with? A poison dart on the end of a sledgehammer?

He heard Melanie gasp and felt her fingers tighten suddenly on his sleeve. "My God, Damien. Look!"

But there was no time even for that small act. No time to look or think, almost no time to react.

Directly in front of them a powerful engine roared to life. Tires squealed on the wet pavement, and out of nowhere came a black monster of a car. It was on them before Damien could twist his head around.

It could have killed them, he knew that. They wouldn't have been able to elude it. He couldn't even have shoved Melanie away, that's how fast it appeared. But just as it reached them it stopped dead, as if it had run into an invisible wall.

The engine settled down to a low growl as the headlights snapped on. Then the door opened and a figure in black stepped out, an indistinct outline in the glare of the lights and the swirling fog.

His hand seemed to go to his face. "Leave them alone," a voice told them, that same grotesque synthesized voice they'd heard on Nev's answering machine, the one the police lab for all its technical advances could not break down. "You follow my plan or you follow nothing. This is my game, not yours. You'll learn what I choose when I choose. Do you understand?"

"Christ, he is crazy," Damien muttered.

"We understand," Melanie replied in a determinedly steady tone.

"Damien?" the figure demanded.

"What?"

"Answer me."

Go to hell, he thought. "I understand," he said through his teeth.

The voice made an irritated sound. "Be sure you do, both of you. Talk to him, Melanie," it warned, as if it knew Damien's muscles were slowly working themselves into knots of rage. "He can be a hothead, and that'll only make things worse for you. *Comprendo?*"

Damien swore quietly at the taunting figure. He could lunge for him, maybe knock him down with the car door.

"No!" Melanie whispered, clutching at his sleeve. She must have read the tension in him. "He's bound to have a gun."

"Answer me," the voice insisted.

Damien gave Melanie a quick head shake to silence her. *"O que deseja?"* he tried, curious to see if this Rook understood Portuguese or if he was just baiting him. It didn't work. The figure merely stiffened.

"I'm warning you, Damien," he snarled. "Don't play games with me."

"What do you want from us?" Damien repeated in English.

"You'll find out," the figure promised. Did he sound hostile beneath the layers of distortion? "Rook takes pawns, amigos. Leave the Circle of Five partners alone."

"And if we don't?" Melanie challenged.

The voice growled but didn't immediately answer. When it did, it simply said again, "Leave them alone."

His hand came slowly down, and with deliberate care the figure slid back behind the wheel. A second later the headlights flared to bright. Damien heard the engine being gunned and in the next instant saw the car roll backward. Rook reversed it into the fog, then killed the lights and turned out of the lot, an exit as understated as his entrance had been theatrical.

In silence Damien breathed the damp air into his lungs.

"He's going to kill us," Melanie said softly.

Damien pulled her close against him, pressing his face in her hair as his shoulder began to throb all over again. "No, he won't," he promised. "But he's going to try."

"THE WORD FOR YOU isn't hothead, it's stubborn." Melanie shoved the Jaguar up a gear as she cleared traffic on the route to Monterey. "Rook specifically told us not to do this. So what are we doing? We're going straight to Samuel Taggart's house."

Damien was slumped back in the bucket seat, in too much pain to fully explain his reasoning. "It'll throw him off," he murmured. "He won't expect us to go there today."

Melanie made a disbelieving sound in her throat, then rammed the car into a lower gear as they approached the city limits.

Watching her now as he had been all the way from Berkeley, Damien acknowledged that he found this act singularly arousing. She handled the Jag with a forcefulness he'd never seen in a woman, like a wild animal she wasn't afraid to tame. He only wished she'd pull the car over for a while so they could climb into the back seat and make love. Because he did love her. His problem was he didn't know what to do about it.

Closing his eyes, he hunched deeper into his seat. Love and misery. Somehow he'd always known those two words would be constant companions in his life.

"Woodland Road." Melanie read the sign, slowing the car to a crawl. "This is it. Right or left?"

Damien kept his eyes tightly closed. "Right."

He heard the stick shift jam and felt the heat between his legs soar. Whatever had hit his shoulder hadn't been quite strong enough. Thoughts of Melanie and the reaction they engendered reduced his other body pains to minor aches.

They bumped along an unpaved road for close to five minutes before she commented, "It's awfully remote. That housekeeper I spoke to must live in. She sounded funny on the phone, did I mention that?"

"Twice. Maybe the guy's a hermit and doesn't have many visitors."

"She mentioned the word invalid, not hermit."

Damien opened his eyes to a dotting of oak and spruce trees and behind them a two-story clapboard house with flaking white paint and dark green shutters.

"Is there anyone following us?" he asked, grunting as he struggled to sit up.

"Not a soul. *I've* been watching."

He caught the amusement in her tone and couldn't help smiling a bit. "Now who's being sarcastic?"

"Damien, wait." She put her hand over his before he could climb out. "I've been thinking."

"You want to ditch this whole mess and come back to Salvadore with me."

"I'm serious."

"So am I." He pushed damp tendrils of hair from his cheeks. "Is it hot in here?"

"No, and it's only fifty-one degrees outside."

"And raining," he noted. He flopped tiredly back in his seat. "Okay, tell me, what have you been thinking."

"About Rolf."

"He can handle, Regan, Mel."

"No, not that."

Twisting around, she hooked her leg beneath her. The movement brought her knee up against his thigh and a few choice words to his throat. He swallowed them and let her continue.

"Haven't you noticed how these awful things keep happening to us—well, actually mostly to you, but you know what I mean. Except for the flight home from Chicago, Rook doesn't seem to be going after Rolf."

"Going after Romac is the same as going after Rolf."

"No more than you or me."

Damien frowned at her. He had to be misunderstanding this. "Are you saying you think Rolf's involved in some way?"

She smacked his leg. "Of course not, don't be ridiculous."

"Then what? And don't touch me."

"What?" Now it was Melanie's turn to be confused. "Did I hurt you?"

His meaningful look brought a small, "Oh," to her lips.

"Go on," he told her.

She pulled her knee away. "I—uh—" She frowned. "What was I saying?"

Good. He'd thrown her. It was only fair. "About Rolf?" he prompted gently.

She recovered her composure quickly. "Oh, that's right. Well, don't you think it's odd?"

"Maybe," he conceded. "But I wouldn't wish any of this on him even so."

"Neither would I. But think about it, Damien. It only makes sense that Rook will eventually start in on Rolf, and maybe because he's been left out, so to speak, he'll be more susceptible than we are. I mean, I'm starting to jump at shadows. I'm even considering buying a big dog."

Damien had a better idea, but he kept it to himself. "So, what? Do you want me to move in with Rolf and Regan?"

"No!" She sounded revolted.

"Well, what then?"

She leaned a little closer, temptingly so. All Damien had to do was move his head and he could catch her mouth with his.

"Warn him," she said, enunciating each word. "Tell him to watch his back."

"Don't take the Cessna up alone?"

"Exactly."

Damien nodded. He tossed a distasteful glance at the house. "Not that I want to do this, but let's get it over with, huh?"

Melanie hesitated. She looked for a moment as though she wanted to touch him, to stroke his damp hair or something equally protective and tender. Damien wouldn't have minded. Any contact from her would have made it all better.

She pulled back instead, which disappointed him, but he understood that, too. He knew it was the best thing. Still, it made him grouchy to admit it.

"Come on," he said, kicking the door open with more force than was necessary. "Maybe Samuel Taggart can solve all our problems."

Melanie sighed, regarding him through the curtain of her dark hair. "Not all of them, Damien. Only the simple ones."

Chapter Twelve

"Sonia, is Mr. Sam awake?"

The housekeeper poked her head into an upstairs bedroom, then opened the door wider for Melanie and Damien. A woman with straight mahogany hair, obviously in her ninth month of pregnancy, maneuvered herself out of her chair and smiled at them.

"Hello," she said very softly, indicating the frail man in the bed with a cautionary lift of her finger. "Thank you, Jessie, you can go. We'll have our tea downstairs in a few minutes."

The housekeeper vanished, leaving them alone with the woman she'd called Sonia.

Melanie rubbed her palms together, feeling decidedly awkward. Damien seemed more contemplative if no less self-conscious.

"I, um, suppose we should introduce ourselves," she began. "I'm Mclanie Rossi, this is Damien McCall."

"Yes, I know. Jessie told me you called. My name is Sonia Benson. Grandfather?" Bending over with an effort, she spoke to a bedridden man whose eyes evinced the only sign of life in an otherwise wasted body. "These are Tom and Neville's grandchildren."

Melanie lifted her gaze to Damien, who seemed as surprised as she was by the casual introduction.

"Are you sure you want to tell him that?" he asked, but Sonia waved the concern away.

"Oh, Grandfather doesn't bear any grudges. And even if he did they certainly wouldn't extend to you." She patted the old man's hand. "He can't move much or talk, but he understands us, and he likes to have company. That's why Jessie didn't tell you about his condition. She said you were coming out here to see him, and being that so few of his old friends are alive these days, I thought it might be nice for him to see some new faces. At any rate, if you have questions, perhaps I could answer them. I've always been very close to my grandfather." She bent back over the bed. "You don't mind, do you, Grandfather?"

A tiny sound trickled from his throat.

Sonia sighed. "I really hate to see him like this, you know. It's so unfair. He had a stroke eight years ago and then another last November. It left him completely paralyzed."

Melanie wanted very badly to go home. Certainly, she didn't want to see this poor man lying in his bed any longer than she had to. But you couldn't ignore a tragic sight, or will it away simply because it horrified you.

Damien stood back from the bed, she noticed. He was no more comfortable with the situation than she was.

"Does what happened to your grandfather, this stroke, have anything to do with Neville and Tom?" Damien asked in a somewhat cautious tone.

"You mean with the dissolution of the Circle of Five?"

Mild shock passed through Melanie. "You know about that?"

"Of course. It's family history." Sonia gestured to a small brown and white photograph on the wall. "There they are in all their glory." She pointed to five men seated around a table in what appeared to be a crowded tavern. "If you're interested, that's a bordello, but of course it looks like a bar. Just a tidbit I thought you might like to know. They used to do all their business-after-business meetings at Kelly's Place, one block down from the train station." She smiled at the bed. "You were all a bunch of dirty old men, weren't you, Grandfather?"

Melanie inched closer to the picture. The faces in the foreground were the same as the ones in the photograph provided by Rook, except that here all the men were smiling.

"That's Grandfather," Sonia said, pointing out a man with blond hair and big dark eyes. "He was very handsome in those days, what people used to call a lady-killer. I—" She stopped speaking and looked down as the old man made another feeble sound.

"What is it?" she asked. Then she laid a hand on his shoulder. "Now you know what the doctor said. You're not to get excited. Is it the window? Do you want me to open the window? No? Water then? Are you thirsty?"

"Maybe it's us," Damien suggested from the door.

"I can't—" A puzzled frown invaded Sonia's face. "Well, maybe it is. But I don't know. He's been like this quite a lot lately. He never used to be. He wants to say something, I'm sure of that. I just can't imagine what it is."

"You're sure he doesn't resent us for our relationship to Tom and Nev?" Melanie questioned, feeling more guilty than ever, and more helpless.

Sonia pressed one hand to her swollen stomach, another to the small of her back, as if standing too long was a trial for her. "I'm sure, really I am. Now my mother was a different story. Shh, now, Grandfather, here's Jessie with your medicine. You take it and relax while I have tea with our guests." She put a finger to her lips. "We'll go to the kitchen," she said in a hushed tone. "I'll explain about my mother there."

Melanie nodded, glanced at Damien whose features were completely impassive, then offered a tentative, "Uh, it was very nice meeting you, Mr. Taggart," to the man in the bed.

Samuel gave no indication that he noticed her. His eyes were wide open and rolling back in his skull, and the most dreadful noises were issuing from his throat.

"Come on, Mel," Damien urged, and this time she didn't have to be dragged out. "We'll wait for you downstairs, Sonia."

Five minutes later, Samuel's granddaughter was lowering herself into a swivel chair in the Mexican-tiled kitchen.

"When are you due?" Melanie inquired politely.

"Any day now. My husband runs a shoe store in Monterey. He says I shouldn't come out here so close to my time, but I can't leave Grandfather with only Jessie to care for him."

Damien sat braced with one hand on the edge of the table. He didn't have a lot of color beneath his tan. Either seeing Samuel made him squeamish or his shoulder hurt more than he'd let on. Melanie suspected the latter.

"There's no one else in your family who could spend time with him?" he asked.

Sonia inhaled with deep regret. "Not really. You see, we aren't a big family. There's only me and my brother Randy and right now he's living in Hawaii. My mother's dead. She was Grandfather's youngest daughter."

"What about Samuel's other children?" Melanie prompted, and Sonia smiled.

"Are you sure you want the gory details?"

"I didn't have much of a family," Melanie told her. "I'd love to hear a few gory details."

Laughing, Sonia settled back in her chair. "Well, let's see. Uncle Bert, that's Grandfather's son, he teaches high school in Cleveland. His two kids are all wrapped up in their own lives. They haven't come to visit since they were children, so they couldn't take care of him. And then there's Aunt Rachel. She's our family question mark."

"In what way?" Damien asked.

Sonia sighed. "To start with, nobody's heard from her for more than forty years. She left for Hollywood a few years after World War II ended, and that's the last time anyone saw her. It's probably for the best, though. I mean if you want to talk about grudges, Rachel and my mother both had big ones. They figured by Grandfather losing his business in the Depression, they got cheated out of a lot of money."

"But you don't feel that way?" Damien said carefully.

Sonia spread her fingers. "Not a bit. That's how it goes in our family. You either resent what happened or you don't. There's no middle ground as far as I can tell. My Great-aunt Millie, for example. She's Grandfather's sister. She hated what happened. Even now she'll tell anyone who'll listen all about what she calls 'the big swindle.'" Sonia frowned slightly, sliding her eyes from Melanie to Damien and back again. "I heard Neville died recently. Is there a problem? Is that why you've come here?"

"It's a minor problem," Melanie lied.

"To do with the Circle of Five?"

"In a way."

"So that's why you're interested in our family. But I don't understand. That partnership was dissolved back in the thirties."

Damien regarded his teacup, then Sonia's face. "We think someone's trying to revive it."

"But why?"

"Have you ever heard of a man who calls himself Rook?" Damien asked.

She gave a disbelieving laugh. "No. What kind of a name is that?"

"Think of it as a nickname," he said, "like Snake or Slasher."

Sonia sobered. "Oh, I see. Is there anything I can do?"

"No more than you've already done," Melanie told her. "Really, we appreciate your talking to us. Herschel Barnum wasn't quite as receptive."

She smiled. "Ah, good old Herschel. Did he threaten you with his cane?"

"Once or twice," Damien murmured.

"Well, don't let him bother you. He's really a harmless old thing."

"Maybe Herschel's harmless," Melanie said in a somber tone, "but I have a feeling Rook's going to be deadly."

"No, I DON'T WANT to go to bed," Damien objected three hours later aboard the *Emily-Mac*. "Not unless you get in first. And stop pulling off my clothes."

Melanie shoved him gently into a chair. "I just want to see your shoulder, and don't joke with me. We're not going to bed together. You're hurt."

He stared up at her, his eyes black and disturbing as they invariably were at night. "I'm not that hurt."

Leaving his jacket on, she unbuttoned his shirt. "You've got a bruise the size of a baseball." She paused, inspecting the mark more closely. "That really is bad, you know. But I still can't figure out what he hit you with."

"Feels like an invisible cannonball."

"I thought you said it didn't hurt."

"I said I wasn't too hurt to go to bed with you."

Melanie blushed but covered with a quick, "In that case you should be sexually active on your deathbed."

"Which won't be for a good long time, I hope." He flinched as her fingers probed the purpling skin. "Watch it, Mel. It does hurt there."

Sighing, she brushed at his hair. "You're a mess, you know that?"

"I'm hungry."

"Do you want me to fix you some dinner?"

"It's not that kind of hunger."

He managed to look like a wounded boy, but not enough of a boy to make her forget the man.

She withdrew her hand from his face and sat back on her heels. "Maybe I'll fix you some food anyway. It'll take your mind off your animal urges."

His slow, knowing smile almost did her in. "Coward," he accused. "Didn't you learn anything in the jungle, Mel? Life's a succession of animal urges."

She kept her distance, but he'd pretty much stripped away her composure. "What about feelings, Damien?" she shot back in a slightly sullen tone. "Maybe baboons have emotions, maybe they don't, but I know I do, and I don't want them stomped on by a gorgeous Brazilian with too much

Latin American charm in his blood for either his good or mine.''

"Why?" Damien questioned, his black eyes intent on hers.

"We've been through this before. You know why."

He opened his mouth, then closed it, leaning forward with a swiftness that belied his injuries. "I wouldn't hurt you, Mel," he promised. Then before she could elude him, his mouth closed on hers with a bruising hunger she thought she could taste.

A start of surprise rippled through her, followed closely by alarm. She couldn't let him kiss her. She was on the edge of her emotions with him as it was. If she gave in to the wanting she'd be doomed.

His tongue slid between her lips, another act she felt powerless to defend. How could you fight what you wanted so much?

"Let go, Mel," he said against her mouth. "Don't think, just do it. Kiss me back."

"No."

She felt him smile, felt his breath come into her. She heard him murmur something and caught the word *amo*, Portuguese for love. But no, he wouldn't say that to her.

For a brief moment, however, she allowed herself to touch his face with her fingers, to taste and explore him, to draw his lower lip into her mouth, let the demands of her body have their moment.

But, this was such a dangerous thing to do....

Slowly, reluctantly, her reason returned. Her defenses began to build.

"No," she said again and this time she put her hands on his chest, pushing his beautiful body away. "You'll go back to Brazil and I'll be here, and I don't want that."

"I..." He looked like he wanted to deny it, but he didn't. Oh, but his mouth still tempted her. His lips were wet, his breathing a little uneven. All she had to do was think: to hell with tomorrow. One small thought and she could drive her fears away, make love with this gorgeous man.

She got to her feet instead, a little shaky but she managed, rubbing her damp palms on the legs of her jeans and shoving the hair from her hot cheeks.

He followed her up, pulling her close against him before she could escape. "Don't go, Mel," he murmured into her hair. "We'll start the night again, okay?"

Confused and vaguely mistrustful, she said, "You want me to stay?"

"For a while."

She didn't believe him or her own instincts that told her she should. Lifting her head, she gave him a suspicious look. "Why?"

He smiled. "Well, since you won't let me have my way with you, I'll settle for talk."

"About Rook?" A stray shiver swept through her. "I think I'd rather go south and visit my mother."

"Why don't you go to the phone instead?" he suggested. "Call Rolf and have him tell the private investigator to start checking on one Rachel Taggart, missing since about 1947. In the meantime, I'll drive up to the house and see about finding us something other than hot dogs for dinner."

Melanie relaxed. "I have a better idea," she said, wriggling away from him, because distance was the safest thing for her right now. "You call Rolf, I'll go up to the house. And don't worry," she added, forestalling his objection. "I'll take your car, and I promise I'll be careful."

"Very careful," Damien told her, catching her hand and bringing it to his lips. "He may call it a game, but I wouldn't trust Rook to play by any rules except his own."

THERE WERE LIGHTS burning inside Nev's Sausalito house when Melanie arrived and the smell of cigarette smoke hanging in a room that was usually all sea and spice.

"Regan," she sighed, letting herself quietly into the kitchen. "I hope you're here too, Rolf."

But she wasn't about to check. A run-in with Regan McCall with or without her husband was the very last thing Melanie needed tonight. Her nerves were already frazzled, her emotions all tangled in knots. It was like the mixed-up Pushmi-Pullyu of storybook fame between her and Damien. One minute she'd be ready to jump on him and he would tell her not to touch him, the next he'd be kissing her and she'd be resisting him. It made no sense and yet it did, because they both knew how any relationship they had would inevitably end.

"Stop it!" Melanie said out loud to herself in an exasperated whisper. "Get what you came for, and stop thinking about him."

She was starting for the refrigerator when the kitchen door swung open and a pair of high heels clicked across the plank floor. They stopped abruptly, and Regan's angry voice declared, "How dare you walk in here like you owned the place. What are you doing, spying on me?"

Melanie spared her only a brief glance. "Knock it off, Regan. I'm in a bad mood."

"So am I. What are you doing here?"

"Getting food. Why are you here?"

"I—wanted to be alone." There was the slightest hitch in her voice, easy to miss unless you happened to be anticipating it as Melanie suddenly was.

She swung away from the fridge, her eyes wide with disbelief. "You little bitch. You brought him here, didn't you?"

Jerkily, Regan lit a cigarette, a slim something-or-other. "Who?" she demanded coldly.

"Whoever you're having an affair with."

She expected Regan to deny it, which of course she did, but so loudly that Melanie's suspicions rose even more.

She advanced on the smaller woman. "Why are you blocking the kitchen door, Regan?" she asked. "Is he still here? If I go upstairs will I find him?"

For a pretty woman Regan's expression could get extremely ugly. "I don't suppose it would do any good for me to appeal to you in the name of sisterhood?"

"What?" Melanie almost started to laugh. "Are you crazy? Be your soul sister? I'd rather adopt an ape."

"You probably did as a kid," Regan snapped.

From the front of the house, Melanie heard a door slam shut. Disgust lent an edge of mockery to her voice. "Oh, he's brave, Regan. Fast, too. He got dressed and out of here in under a minute. But why would he be afraid of me, I wonder?" She drew closer. "Is it because I'd know him? Because he works at Romac?" She came to a halt, leaning against one of the polished oak cupboards. "Busy place, Romac. Lots of stuff happening there these days. Your lover's wandering around, the grapevine's going crazy—and then there's Rook."

Regan tapped her tiny foot. She'd put up with all of this in fuming silence. Now she demanded, "What in bloody hell's a rook?"

"Not a what, Regan, a who. You know, he wants to destroy Romac and us with it."

"Us?"

"Neville's heirs."

Regan rested her shoulder on the door frame and smiled. "So, there've been more threats, have there?"

"You don't sound as if you care."

She swept a dramatic arm around the room. "Why should I? None of this belongs to me."

"It belongs to Rolf." Melanie found it hard to keep her absolute hatred for this woman from showing in her face. "Or do you see it as community property? If he dies, you get his share."

Regan gnashed her teeth. "But I don't, remember? If Rolf dies, you and Damien get his share of all that Nev left him. I only get what belonged to us before the old crock kicked off."

"You put it so nicely," Melanie murmured.

"I can put it any bloody way I like. If Rolf wants me to stay with him, he's going to have to do a whole lot better financially for me than he has so far. Maybe you bartered beads and cocoa beans in the jungle, but up here we prefer cash."

Melanie set her teeth. She was going to hit Regan in a minute. "Rolf has plenty of money."

Regan stalked from the doorway to fling her cigarette stub in the sink. "Rolf has a bad case of hit-me-upitis, Melanie."

This conversation was more irritating than profitable. "What's that?" Melanie asked.

"It's a disease." With her hands, Regan outlined the scenario, like a movie director. "Picture a street corner and a pathetic woman with a bell. Now most people might toss a dollar or two in her little plastic bucket. But Rolf, no, he throws in hundreds."

"Well, that's miserly of him," Melanie said sarcastically. "Tell me, Regan, would you rather he pulled out a gun and robbed the woman?"

"Oh right, I suppose you'd be thrilled if your husband doled out money to every hard luck case that plunked its butt on your doorstep. Friends, charities, it's all the same to Rolf. 'Got a buck?' someone asks and up he jumps. 'Here, take ten or twenty. Whatever you need. Hell, take my wallet.'"

Melanie made a motion of disgust. "Don't you ever feel mean, Regan, or guilty, or anything?"

"No."

Melanie sighed, tipping her head back to relieve the tension in her muscles. "Why am I talking to you? This is ridiculous. Rolf's not broke, and you're not suffering."

"I never said Rolf was broke."

"Then what's your problem?"

"I want a Ferrari. I want a Thoroughbred horse and a big estate in England."

"Nice to see you're not greedy."

Regan glared at her. "I like things, Melanie. It's not a crime."

"So your lover's rich, then, is he?"

"Let's just say I didn't marry Rolf for his sexual prowess, shall we?" Regan said with a certain bitter smugness. "If I'd wanted good in bed I'd have gone after Damien."

Melanie almost went for her throat. What did Regan know of Damien in bed?

Regan's cigarette lighter clicked, her eyes narrowing to cunning slits. "Oh, I got you there, didn't I?"

I'm going to blacken both your eyes, Melanie thought. "Nice try," she said. "But I'm not buying. Besides, what makes you think I don't already know what Damien's like?"

Regan laughed. "Well, if that isn't the pot calling the kettle black. It's okay for you to have a lover, but not me."

Melanie couldn't believe this. "I'm not married, Regan."

"Yeah, well, trust me, marriage isn't all it's cracked up to be." Regan took a short puff on her cigarette. "So someone named Rook has made my Rolfie a target for destruction, has he? I wonder why Rolf didn't tell me about that."

"Maybe he was afraid you'd cheer for Rook."

Staring coldly, Regan arched a delicate brow and said, "Rah, rah, Rook."

THEY'D GONE TO SEE Samuel Taggart! Rook paced his carpeted floor in a fury. After he'd warned them not to, they'd driven straight out to Monterey.

"You're going to pay for this, both of you."

He withdrew a fat leather case from his dresser drawer and opened it. Tonight was the night, he decided, and Melanie would be the first to receive his special treat.

He studied the contents of the case. He had to be calm about this, he had to do this right or it wouldn't work. There was a delicate balance that needed to be struck here.

Well, he'd just have to make sure he hit it, wouldn't he? And when he did...

"Oh, Melanie," he whispered softly. "What a trip you're going to take."

Chapter Thirteen

I won't think about him, Melanie told herself as she unlocked the door of her house after dinner with Damien. *I won't think about any of it. No Damien, no Rook, no death.*

The words became a chant in her head. Wearily she collected her mail from the box and pushed the door open. The scent of flowers and green leaves greeted her. She didn't like the jungle, but she loved things that grew, any plant at all as long as it was lush.

It was a damp, misty night, strangely silent on her wooded street. For a moment she paused, her eyes taking in the darkness and the wisps of fog that blew like thin ghosts through the trees, elusive as Rook seemed to be.

A tiny rustle of leaves caught her attention when she would have turned away. A cat, or the wind? she wondered uneasily. Except there was no wind tonight.

Fighting another shiver, she tightened her grip on the mail and started in. Then she caught the rustle again, closer this time and spun to face it.

"Who's there?" she demanded, her tone sharper than usual.

Did she see a shadow fall across the lawn? It was gone in the next second, and taking a deep breath, Melanie backed nervously across the threshold. There were no strange cars on her street and nothing stirring now. She was letting her confrontation with Regan get to her, that's all.

Releasing a deep breath, she started to close the door. Yet, in the time it took to make that small motion, a long shadow suddenly fell across the porch.

"Hello, Melanie," a man's voice said.

Her head came up. She hesitated. She knew that voice. Cautiously she asked, "What are you doing here?"

"I came for a visit."

"This late?" Her mouth felt dry, her heart was beginning to pound.

His smile was bland, and suddenly it seemed he was standing right in front of her. "Sorry if I scared you," Rook said. "It was necessary."

Melanie had no idea where the thought came from, but she knew instinctively that she had to run.

She straightened with a horrified gasp, realizing she wasn't going to escape.

He reached for her as she shoved with both hands on the door. But it wouldn't close. He'd wedged his foot in, and now he was pushing back.

Her eyes went swiftly down to the toe of his shoe. With a grunt she brought her boot heel down onto it, spiking him. She heard his growl of pain and in desperation threw all her weight against the door.

He must have anticipated this because he shouldered his way in before she could get the latch in place or spike him again.

"Oh, no, you don't," he told her, sounding determined and strained and oddly amused. "Come here, you little wildcat. I have plans for you tonight."

She would have screamed, except there was no one around to hear. And no dog to sink its teeth into his leg. All she could do was run through the house and hope to escape out the back way.

She spun from the threshold before his hands could catch her, the mail scattering like leaves on the floor. She felt his gloved fingers on her jacket, but she tore herself free and started for the kitchen.

She might have made it halfway there, but it was hard to be sure with no lights. In any case, he grabbed her roughly, his hand twining in her hair and yanking her back against him.

"Kick me just once, Melanie," he warned, his breath hot and sickening on her neck, "and I'll slit your throat."

She pulled on his wrist. "I can't breathe."

Laughing softly, he kissed her cheek, his lips moist and rubbery. "It doesn't matter," he said. "Now, be a good girl and count sheep for me."

"Count sheep!" She couldn't stop herself, she kicked his ankle. "Are you crazy? Let me go."

Another laugh. "Oh, Melanie, you're such an uncooperative little thing." His voice dropped to a resentful whisper. "You shouldn't have gone to see Samuel today."

She felt something prick her neck, then Rook was blowing on her skin. "I told you not to do it," he said, "but you went anyway. That was very stupid of you. I don't like it when people don't listen to me."

Melanie heard him through a funny sort of fog. Why was the floor beneath her rocking?

"Are you counting for me, Melanie?"

"No." Maybe it wasn't the floor that moved, but her.

More laughter came into her ear, a strange sound to emerge from the throat of a killer. *Why are you doing this, Rook...?*

"Sleep," he crooned, shifting his grip so that his arms were clamped about her waist.

Her head dropped forward. "I bet you don't even have a knife."

"Oh, much better than that, lovely lady." Rook's words were a cloud on the ceiling, showering down on her. "I have a magic mushroom. And I've just given you a bit."

Melanie wanted to fight him, or at least hit him where men were the most susceptible. But it was as if her muscles had seized up, or maybe they'd left her body. She was limp in Rook's arms, a rag doll being floated through the darkness.

It seemed an awfully big expanse of darkness, long and narrow, like a tunnel.

"Backward," she heard Rook whisper. "Ten, twenty, thirty—count the years, Melanie. Think hard, pretend you're there. What's it like, Melanie? The Circle of Five, can you see it? There's a table with five men sitting around it. You know them, don't you?"

From the darkness, a picture began to take shape. "Kelly's Place," she said, and was surprised by the strength of her voice. How clear it sounded. But it couldn't be coming from her, because she was traveling through a black tunnel with Rook....

SHE HIT THE FLOOR with a thump that rattled her teeth.

"Where am I?" she asked out loud, too startled by the sudden jolt to immediately move.

"If you don't know, sugar, best you should lay off the bottle."

The remark came in passing from a woman in a tight-fitting flowered dress with two glasses of sparkling wine in her hands. She sauntered by, sparing Melanie only a brief glance, then disappeared through a shabby door.

Dazed, Melanie looked around. She was sitting on her backside at the head of a long hallway. Noise seeping through a somewhat larger door to her left indicated a party or maybe just a lot of people in a big room. The air smelled like cigar smoke and stale beer, the woman's hair hadn't looked quite right and...

"I'm getting out of here," Melanie decided, scrambling to her feet.

The large door opened and a second woman, this one with blond hair, blue eyes and bright red lips appeared. A cloud of smoke came with her. She was young, maybe twenty. Her eyes lit up when she saw Melanie.

"Are you new, too?" she asked. She looked Melanie up and down. "Funny clothes. You better change before Rita sees you."

Melanie hid her confusion under a smile. "Who's Rita?"

The girl laughed. "Wow, you are new. Are you gassed?"

"I—" Melanie fingered her neck uncertainly. Hadn't something happened? "I don't think so."

"Well, anyway, you better come with me. You can borrow one of my dresses for tonight." She gave her gum a little snap and Melanie a push. "Boy, you're really dopey."

"I beg your pardon?"

The girl pushed again. "Out to lunch. Come on."

"Out to lunch, huh? Well, maybe that's the answer." Melanie tapped her tooth with her thumbnail, still lagging. Her eyes moved about the corridor. "What's your name?"

"Genie. You?"

"Melanie. Uh, Genie, what is this place?"

"Huh?"

"You know, where are we?"

Genie sighed. "Gassed." She tugged Melanie through yet another door, into a tiny wooden room with a bed, a vanity and very little else. "Here." She blew dust out of a glass, then poured some wine. "Have some hair of the dog."

"Roma Wine." Melanie frowned at the label. "But that's old." Her frown deepened and she spied a pack of cigarettes on the dresser. "Philip Morris cigarettes?"

"Sure, 'Call for Philip Morris.'" The girl wrinkled her nose. "Don't you have radio where you come from?"

Melanie opened her mouth, hesitated, then said tentatively, "I'm from San Francisco."

"Nice city." Genie went to the closet. "I'd like to go there someday."

"This is a dream, that's what it is." Melanie pressed her fingers to her temples. "I'll wake up and it'll all be gone."

"Yeah, that's what I used to think," Genie said. She shoved a black dress with tiny blue and pink flowers and a plunging neckline at Melanie. "But you take what you can get, right? Besides, Rita's not so bad and if he's not in a temper, neither's Kelly."

Melanie's head came up. "Kelly?" She glanced away. "I've heard that name before."

"I guess so. He owns the place."

"One block from the train station," Melanie murmured. Her thoughts were cloudy and all twisted up. Something in her head about a man telling her to count sheep. She shook the confusion away and asked, "Is this Kelly's Place, Genie? Are we in Chicago?"

"Boy, you are a wreck." Genie poofed her hair up, then checked the clock. "Oops, I gotta go. Put on the dress fast, Melanie. I need the room."

Shocked and confused, Melanie still had the presence of mind to ask, "How old are you?"

"Twenty-three," Genie said, already on her way out the door.

"Really?"

The girl winked. "I got the papers to prove it. Now make it snappy with the dress, huh? Then vamoose out to the front of the house. There's some big spenders out there. I gotta do my regular Friday nighters, but you're pretty, I bet you'll get lucky. Oh, but push up your bust a bit, honey. What you got you should flaunt, right?"

"Right. No, wait." Melanie clutched the girl's arm, getting decidedly panicky now. If this was a dream it was the most real dream she'd ever had. "*Is* this Kelly's Place in Chicago?"

"Well, sure it is."

Melanie licked her dry lips, her mind filling suddenly with dread. "What year is it, Genie?"

"Silly." Genie laughed, smacking her hand. "It's 1936. February, 1936."

"HI THERE, DOLL." A fat man with a beard and bad breath tucked an arm around Melanie's waist. "You looking for me?"

"Get your arm off me," she said through her teeth.

His grip merely tightened. "That's not a good attitude, doll. Do you know who I am?"

"I don't care if you're—" she thought quickly "—Franklin Roosevelt, I don't like being grabbed."

His laugh was rough. "Well, little lady, we'll just see what Rita and Kelly have to say about that."

"Be my guest." Melanie shoved on his massive chest. Only *she* would have a dream where she played a hooker who got Attila the Hun for a john.

Because this was definitely a dream. She'd established that for certain when Genie had told her the date. It was reasonable. Her mind had been on the Depression a lot lately. Kelly's Place, Chicago, a bar fronting for a brothel, it all fit. Now if she could just remember those other nagging things, like whose voice it was she kept hearing in her ear and why she kept thinking about rag dolls, and poison darts, and sheep. And Rook. Yes, there was something she should recall about him, too.

"He's going to make big trouble for you," a man on her left observed. "That's Charlie Morrow you just turned down. Unofficially, he and his boys were involved in the St. Valentine's Day Massacre."

Melanie wiped at her arms, hating the sensation of filth that clung to them. "Then he should be in jail."

The man chuckled. "You must be very naive," he remarked.

"I'm from out of town," she told him, glancing up for the first time. He had blond hair and big dark eyes, and she gave a tiny gasp. "Hey, I know you! You're Samuel Taggart."

He seemed puzzled. "Have we met?"

"Well, no, not exactly." She hugged her arms across her low neckline. "I sort of know two of your business partners."

His eyes sparkled. "I would assume that one of those partners is Tom Rossi. Is that right?"

"How do you know that?"

He lowered his gaze a trifle. "If you'll pardon my saying so, Tom's the only one of my partners who would 'know' a woman of your type."

Melanie's hand longed to slap his face. "I see," she said quietly.

"There he is now," Samuel went on, nodding at a faded velvet settee beneath a draped curtain. "He's with Lila tonight."

"What?" Melanie snatched her head around, then groaned in disappointment. "Ah, Grandpa Tom."

"Pardon me?"

"Nothing."

She couldn't look—but it didn't matter anyway, she reminded herself. This was all a bad dream. Still, as long as she was having it . . .

"Tell me, Mr. Taggart, why do you and your partners meet here?"

He smiled, accepting the beer he was handed by a passing Lila clone. "Why not?"

"But it's a . . ."

"House?"

"Exactly." She glanced at the gaudy furnishings that surrounded a cluster of green felt tables. "And considering that this is supposed to be a bar fronting for that house, i doesn't do a very good job. I'm surprised the police haven' closed the place down."

He seemed amused. "My dear girl, the police from th local precinct come here nightly. They're valued customers."

"The police consort with gangsters?"

"Well, where—if you'll excuse the expression—sex i concerned, we're all basically the same animal."

She rolled her eyes. "You and Damien would get alon very well."

"Who?"

"A man I know. Never mind. Where are the rest of you partners?"

"In the back room."

Melanie's brows went up.

"We're having a meeting tonight," Samuel explained. H shook his head at her. "You're certainly an odd woma What did you say your name was?"

She shouldn't have felt obligated to lie, because after all a dream couldn't hurt her? Yet it seemed so strangely real....

"I'm Brandy," she said. "Er, when is this meeting of yours?"

"Now." A young, dashing Neville strode over from the bar, and stopping next to Samuel said, "You go on in, Sam. I'll bring Tom." He eyed Melanie up and down, and although she stiffened inside, she knew he couldn't possibly recognize her. "You look strong and healthy," he remarked. "No flab on you."

She managed a bland expression. "Why, thank you, sir."

"Mmm. Well, if you're not busy, why don't you get five beers and bring them to our room. Go on, Sam," he said to his loitering partner. "I'll get Tom away from Lila."

Samuel nodded at Melanie, and left while Neville weeded his way through bodies and crowded tables to where Tom sat with Lila. The woman was all over him, not unreasonable when you considered it was her job, but Melanie couldn't look. A shudder ran through her. Poor Grandma Isabelle. What was it about the Rossi/McCall families that they inspired so little fidelity? Or was lack of fidelity a common family problem and she just didn't want to see it?

"It won't happen to me," she declared, turning for the bar. But then she remembered Neville hadn't said what kind of beer he wanted, so she had to go back.

Thankfully, Lila had been dismissed. Nev and Tom stood by the curtain, alone, talking. Whatever they discussed, however, it didn't appear to be sitting well with Tom.

Melanie couldn't stop herself, she snuck closer, creeping over to the curtain and partially behind it, out of sight unless someone like Charlie Morrow came along and grabbed her again.

"It's not right, Nev," Tom was saying. "And I also don't think it's a good idea. They're getting wise to us, I'm sure of it."

Nev gave a quiet snort. "One thing's sure, you're getting cold feet. They'll go for it all the way. Who wouldn't? It's a great investment. Main-West Power and Light. Who'd turn that down? We all need power and light."

"And what do we tell them when the deal falls through and they lose their investment?"

"Pipe down, Tom."

And damn him, he did. As hard as she strained, Melanie could only catch snatches after that. Something about a racket and funneling money and a scam that would strengthen both their bank accounts.

"This isn't any necessary con, Neville," Melanie whispered, leaning back against the papered wall. "It's dirty and you're loving every minute of it. And you just know Tom'll stay in with you, don't you, because deep down he's every bit as greedy as you are. You're bastards, both of you."

She forced herself to step around the curtain then, and with her head bent, asked Nev about the beer. She collected the bottles swiftly and, silently calling both men every nasty name she could think of, carried the tray to where the bartender directed her.

"Hey, Melanie." Genie lolled in the doorway of her room in a flimsy peignoir with holes in the sleeves. "Looks like you did okay, huh?"

Melanie glanced at her tray. "That's what it looks like, all right," she agreed. "Genie, who's Charlie Morrow?"

"He's a creep. You should stay away from him."

"Too late."

Genie's eyes widened. "What did you do?" She gasped. "You didn't turn him down, did you?"

"Well, sort of."

"Oh no." Genie's eyes got suddenly huge. Grabbing Melanie's tray, she pushed her into her vacant room. "Run," she snapped. "It's Kelly and Charlie."

Melanie started to argue but Genie whispered, "Run," again with such urgency that she thought better of it.

She stopped only long enough to tear off the dress and drag on her jeans, shirt and jacket. The voices outside were loud and abusive. There was a crash of glass, a scream and then more voices, Nev's and Tom's among them.

"Ohhh..." Melanie had the window open above the snow-filled back alley, but she couldn't do it. That had been Genie screaming. Who knew what that creepy gangster might have done to her.

She raced back across the room, grabbed the empty Roma wine bottle and yanked open the door.

"That's her," a red-faced Charlie roared. "That's the slut that rolled me."

Melanie stopped short. "Rolled you! What are you talking about, I never rolled you."

"Brandy, I think you should get out of here." That was Samuel's voice. He had her by the hand.

"Go," Genie pleaded, through a smoke haze.

"What's going on here?" Nev demanded, but it seemed a distant question. In fact the whole scene felt strangely far away now, as if it was either fading out or she was being drawn above it.

"That's enough, I think," a man's voice said, a familiar voice, though she couldn't for the life of her place it.

The hand on her wrist remained, fingers locked tight about her bone.

"Let go, Samuel," she told him, feeling suddenly weighted and tired. "You're hurting me."

"Not Samuel," the voice replied in amusement. "Count forward now, Melanie."

The tunnel formed around her once more, only this time she moved through it in the opposite direction.

"What a weird dream," she murmured as something stronger than the darkness pressed in on her. "You old crooks."

Soft laughter penetrated the tumbling shadows. She saw Tom's face, then Nev's, then Samuel's. And then she saw nothing at all.

OUT OF THE BLACKNESS a face very slowly began to emerge. Melanie recognized the narrow features, the dark eyes and the long curling hair even before she fully surfaced. And she saw another man with him, hovering over her, telling her to wake up. He was blond and she recognized him as well.

But there was a third face, right on the fringe of her consciousness, a man whose features she couldn't seem to grasp. They were smudged, like a pencil drawing partly erased. The harder she tried to bring them into focus the more blurred they became. Only his black raincoat was clear to her, and the name he went by: Rook.

"Melanie, are you okay? Wake up, huh?"

That was Rolf, but he wasn't the one holding her hand, bending over her and stroking her hair.

"Mel?"

Now Damien spoke. Where had he been when all hell had broken loose at Kelly's Place?

It returned in a rush, the whole bizarre scene. She surged up with a panicky, "Kelly—and that horrible gangster!"

She searched the room, but couldn't find either of them. But then this wasn't a bordello in Chicago, was it?

"Where am I?" she asked, pushing at the hair that had fallen in her eyes. "Why am I wearing this dress—oh, I'm not." She frowned. "Where's Genie, and Samuel?" Her gaze came to rest on the two mystified men before her. "What are you doing here?"

Damien glanced at his brother, then back at her. "You didn't answer your phone, Mel, so we came over to see if you were okay." He paused, staring at her. "Are you?"

"I'm not sure." She took in the living room of her A-frame. Not a velvet settee in sight. "I'm in San Francisco, right? Yes, of course I am. I came home last night and Genie was here. No, that's not right, she was in Chicago. But the doorbell rang or something. I remember someone being at the door, and then I dropped the mail." She drew her brows together, struggling to sort it out. "But that can't be right, either, because I'm sure the doorbell didn't ring. Someone grabbed me, though, some dark man who wanted me to count sheep before I slept with him."

"Uh, Mel," Rolf said, clearing his throat, "maybe we'd better get you to a doctor. I think you must have hit your head."

"No, I didn't," she insisted. "Something pricked my neck. And then I had this dream, I guess. Except it didn't feel like a dream. I was in Chicago, and it was 1936, February, 1936, and the Circle of Five was meeting at Kelly's Place, and Tom was there with a hooker named Lila." She grabbed Damien's hand. "And there was this other man."

"The horrible gangster?" he asked.

"No, someone at my door." Lightly she bit her nail. "I can't remember his face, but I recognized him."

Rolf sat on the edge of the sofa behind Damien. "Is this part of the dream, Mel?"

"I don't think so. He came to the door or something right after I got home, and he said . . ."

"What?" Rolf prompted when she halted.

She searched her mind. "I can't remember." Her eyes came to rest on Damien's wary face. "But it was Rook, I'm sure of it, and he did—something to me." She released a heavy breath. "This all sounds crazy, doesn't it?"

"Mixed-up," Damien agreed.

She found herself staring at his mouth, wishing idly that he would kiss her. Then it hit her how he was dressed and her brow furrowed. "You're wearing a Romac uniform. I didn't know you were doing a commercial flight."

His thumb gently brushed her chin. "Neither did I. I got called to do it this morning. It's one of your charters."

To recall which of her Elite charters departed today required more thought than Melanie had energy to fuel. "Madrid?" she tried.

"London." He studied her closely. God, she must look a fright. "Maybe I should give it to someone else."

Melanie dropped her head onto his good shoulder, unable to look at him anymore in his navy blue Romac uniform. What a lucky charter group to get a gorgeous Latin American pilot. "It's better that you go," she said. "Maybe

I'll have this dream thing figured out by the time you get back."

"You sure, Mel?" he asked, while behind him Rolf paced, a troubled expression on his handsome face.

"Positive." She raised her head, her eyes sliding to Rolf whose features had metamorphosed from troubled to unsure. "What is it, Rolf?"

He regarded them both, then extended his hand. "I found these on the floor, Mel. More pages from Nev's diary. They're dated February, 1936."

Chapter Fourteen

"The pages were mixed in with my mail," Melanie told Rolf Sunday night over a Greek dinner in Ghirardelli Square. "I read them, and then I had the dream. Simple as that." *And I don't believe a tenth of what I'm saying,* she added to herself.

But she shrank from that last thought as she had since she'd woken up fully dressed on her sofa yesterday morning. It was a dream, it had to be. Likely drug induced. She remembered that tiny prick on her neck, and the world seeming to go out of phase for a time.

But who was Genie? Why dream about her, or a man named Charlie Morrow? Nev made no mention of those names in his diary.

"So that's how they ran their cons," Rolf said, glancing again through the journal pages. "They got their partners to invest in phony companies when in fact that money was going straight into their bank accounts. It's a miracle this never hit the fan."

"Ways and means," Melanie said with a sigh. "Nev knew how to make people keep their mouths shut. Plus he handpicked his marks. He and Tom knew what they were doing all the way."

She played with her appetizer. Damien wouldn't be back from London until tomorrow, Regan was off doing who knew what with who knew whom and it was cold and damp and foggy outside. What a depressing time this was—and stop thinking that word, she ordered herself in frustration. It was a dream, that's all, a very colorful, very weird dream.

"He must have drugged me," she murmured. "I'm sure he came to the house. I remember him being there. Rook, in a black raincoat and gloves." The blank spots in her mind made her muscles tense. "God, it's so irritating, Rolf. I just can't remember his face. But I recognized him, I know I did."

"It'll come to you, Mel," he consoled, playing with his wineglass. "Don't try so hard."

She sighed, surveying Rolf across the candlelit table. Even with the lights muted to emphasize the already spectacular view of the Bay, she could see that he was distracted, upset by more than their latest gift of diary pages from Rook.

Regan, she thought, but didn't have a clue what to say to him about that. She wasn't going to tell him about their run-in at the Sausalito house on Friday night.

Reaching out, Melanie fingered the white carnation in the middle of the table. "Has your private investigator come up with anything new?"

"What? Oh, uh, yes, as a matter of fact he has. Actually, that's why I called you about dinner. I wanted to tell you."

"Something good, I hope."

He smiled, apparently relieved to have his mind taken off his marital problems. "Encouraging anyway. Herschel's and Rupert's relatives are scattered all over the U.S., but as far as Hopkins could tell, they're all busy with their own lives."

"What about Samuel's family?"

"Well, the son this woman Sonia told you about lives as claimed in Cleveland. He's your average real estate broker, about ready to retire."

"And his two grandchildren?"

"Also in Cleveland, both quite average. But Samuel's missing daughter, Rachel, now that's a different story. Hopkins can't find much of anything on her. He knows she went to Hollywood in August of 1947 and got a job at one of those five-and-dime stores. I gather she wanted to be an actress and was hoping to get discovered.''

''And did she?''

''Only by some lighting guy at MGM.''

''That figures.''

''Hopkins couldn't come up with a name on him. Apparently, though, the woman got pregnant at some point and had a son.''

''Really?'' Melanie slid the flower to one side. ''Do you have a name on her son?''

''No such luck. Hopkins is checking the hospitals, but he figures Rachel, being unmarried, might have given birth under a false name. Also, he doesn't have an exact year of the son's birth. Somewhere between 1952 and 1957 is the best he can do so far. The information he's managed to dig up is pretty sketchy, vague recollections by people she worked with. And then after 1959, nothing, no trace of the woman or her son.''

''So you don't know if they're even still alive.''

''Not yet, but Hopkins is working on it. Maybe he'll get lucky.''

Melanie sat back in her chair, taking in the ghostly night fog and the lighted points and cables of the bridge only faintly visible tonight, and only as the wind blew.

''Maybe *we'll* get lucky,'' she said, changing the emphasis. ''I know Rook, Rolf. He works for Romac or Cable Car. I can see everything except his face and his hair. And I can hear his voice, but not distinctly.''

''But you don't remember what he said to you, except for the part about counting sheep?''

She smiled a little. ''Well, yes, there was that. And there was one other thing. He was angry that Damien and I had gone to see Samuel Taggart, more upset I think over that than our visit to Herschel and Rupert.''

''You figure that's important?''

''I think it might be. I also think your private detective should look very hard for Samuel's missing daughter, Rachel, and her son.''

Rolf nodded. "The unknown child," he mused. "Possibly our cunning Rook."

"MORNING MS. ROSSI," the Romac watchman greeted. "Seven a.m.'s a bit early for you, isn't it?"

"It's too early," Melanie agreed. "But I wasn't in on Friday so I thought I'd better force myself today." She caught a glimpse of a business suit rounding the smoked glass elevator shaft. "Was that Morgan Voss?"

"Yes, ma'am."

"God, Harry, you sound like Sidney."

"I beg your pardon?"

"Nothing." She recalled Lucy Farmer's tale about seeing Morgan in the accounting department. "Does Mr. Voss often come in this early?"

"He has done a few times these past couple weeks. Ever since Mr. Neville died."

"Well now, isn't that interesting." Melanie smiled, unbelting her coat. "Thank you, Harry."

So Morgan had been coming in early recently, had he? Not out of any sense of dedication to his work, of that Melanie was certain. For what reason then?

She lingered in the lobby, watching as the only elevator in use sped upward. She counted the floors: fifty, sixty, seventy, eighty. It stopped at eighty-one, the Romac accounting level, and stayed there.

"Oh, you're up to something, Morgan," she whispered. "And I'm going to find out what it is."

She stepped into a waiting elevator, drawing a plan of the eighty-first floor in her head. It was a straightforward design, all offices branching out from the central shaft, the senior ones to the left and up three or four stairs. The whole place was carpeted. It shouldn't be too difficult to sneak around.

When the doors slid open, she dumped her coat, purse and briefcase at the reception desk, then stood absolutely still and listened. There was movement far to the left, not much but enough to guide her. She crept up the stairs, then down a broad corridor to Jonny's domain.

It was all glass and polished brass up here, an airy motif that made spying as tricky as it was simple. If she could see in, then Morgan could see out, and she didn't want him to be warned of her arrival. Lies would get her nowhere.

Silence closed like a heavy cloak around her. She could actually hear the ticking of her watch. But then she pushed through a glass door and it was Morgan she heard, making sounds deep in his throat. The monster was annoyed.

He was visible to her now, as well. He stood at a computer console behind a desk crammed full of miniature cactus plants and assorted paperback books. Melanie couldn't read the brass nameplate, but she'd bet it was Lucy Farmer's desk.

Her eyes never leaving Morgan, she stepped into the shadow of a light wood column. First she'd watch him, then she'd...

The thought broke off as the door swished open beside her. Melanie ducked deeper into the shadow, though it might not have mattered. The man who entered stared directly at Morgan, his mouth open in astonishment. From Melanie's vantage point it was hard to say which of the two men was more surprised.

Morgan's severe features hardened. "Tucker!" he exclaimed. "What are you doing up here?"

Tucker blinked at him. "I'm...I work here."

"Not up here you don't," Morgan snapped.

Tucker seemed to collect his wits. "Well, neither do you."

"That's beside the point."

"I don't think it is," Melanie murmured as Tucker ventured farther into the room.

"I do the crossover accounts for Romac and Cable Car on Monday," Tucker explained.

"At seven in the morning?"

Tucker's face went red, his fists balled at his sides. Even so, Melanie caught the insolence in his response. "I'm not accountable to you, Morgan. And I could ask you the same question. You're Rolf's assistant, not Jonny's."

Morgan's glare brought a chill to Melanie's skin. It was like watching Frankenstein work himself into a rage. But for once, Tucker didn't appear cowed.

She waited out a string of empty seconds. For a confrontation this was decidedly unproductive. Didn't either of these men want to fling a specific accusation?

"I'm leaving," Tucker suddenly announced, which was Melanie's cue to step out from behind the column.

"No, I don't think so," she said, sounding a great deal calmer than she felt. Still, she was closer to the door than they were, and infinitely faster. "Why don't you both just stay put and tell me what you're doing in accounting before hours." Her fingers closed about a silver letter opener. She leaned on the desk, playing with the sharp tip. "You first, Morgan."

He straightened from the computer. "I have nothing to say to you."

"Fine, shall I call Rolf and you make your explanations to him?"

Tucker snickered, and her eyes slid to him.

"Don't laugh, Tucker, you're next. And just out of curiosity, how old are you?"

"What?"

"Tell me your age."

"I'm thirty-eight, why?"

Melanie looked at Morgan. "Is that true?"

"I have no idea."

"Oh, I think you do, but I'll accept his answer for now. Why are you here, Tucker?"

"I do the crossover accounts," he repeated through thinned lips.

"Not anymore you don't," Melanie told him.

His mouth dropped open. "But you can't just take away my job."

She pushed away from the desk. "I can do anything I want to, Tucker. I can fire you if I choose to, or Morgan, or anyone else."

"Only Rolf could fire me," Morgan said stiffly.

"And you don't think I could get him to do it?" Melanie retorted. "Why are you here, Morgan?"

He stared at her, but didn't respond.

"Okay, if that's your attitude, then I'll just make a new rule. Neither of you is to come near the accounting level ever again. You got that?"

Morgan didn't move. Tucker muttered something unflattering under his breath. It didn't sound very nice, so Melanie turned her attention to him.

"One more thing, Tucker. Where were you born?"

He glared from under his fringe of bangs. "Oakland."

"Is your mother still alive?"

That earned her a hissed breath from Morgan, but nothing else.

Tucker's nostrils flared. "No, she isn't. Is there anything else?"

Melanie studied closely the pair of faces before her, although probably not for the reasons they thought. In her mind she pictured a black raincoat and gloves, and then that face with the smeared features. Was Rook one of these men? Could Tucker be Rachel's son? Were those two things even connected?

The answers simply weren't there. With a sigh and a shake of her head, she said, "No," to Tucker's question. "You can both go."

But Morgan wasn't ready to be dismissed. Lifting his head, he gazed at the far wall as a prophet might. "'Rook takes king, old man,'" he quoted in an eerie monotone. "'The legacy you leave is Death—to all those you love.' You'd do well to remember the warnings, Melanie. 'Revenge is sweet. Bittersweet.'"

DAMIEN TOYED WITH the idea of picking up a copilot and flying the Lear jet to Brazil. Addison was around here somewhere, back from a long haul to Montreal. Maybe he wouldn't mind a round trip.

As if paged, the other pilot strode out of Operations, in a rush it seemed to leave the airport.

He grinned at Damien. "Just the man I wanted to see. You got your car here?"

"What's wrong with yours?"

"I loaned it to Jonny. I need to get to Romac downtown so I can get it back."

"Why?"

"Oh God, not again." Addison eased himself out of the passenger flow. "I have a date. She's very beautiful and extremely impatient. It's four o'clock now. If we hurry I can get my car back before Jonny takes it on another joyride to the house of whatever woman he's been seeing."

Damien studied him through his lashes. "Mind if I ask another question?"

"Yes, but go ahead."

"Do you play chess?"

Addison shrugged. "Sure. You want a game?"

"Not especially. Do you own a black raincoat?"

"Weird," Addison murmured, eyeing a leggy blonde that strolled past. "Yes, I do. Anything else?"

"Where were you Friday night?"

Now Addie's gaze narrowed. "Why?"

"Call it curiosity."

"How about I call it none of your damned business." The glint in his eyes deepened to anger. "I work for you, Damien, but what I do after hours is my business, not yours, so lay off."

Damien accepted the verbal punches in silence. He had a right to pry and Addison had a right to be irritated. "You still want a ride home?" he asked quietly, which earned him a grimace and finally a grudging smile.

"I don't believe this. Look, what happened Friday night that I'm supposed to have done, which I didn't? Couldn't be another plane, or I'd have heard about it."

"Not a plane. More like a threat."

"A threat?" The glint reappeared, suspicion laced with something darker. "What kind of threat? Against who?"

"Never mind."

"That's a lousy answer, Damien."

"I know." Damien combed his fingers through his hair, frustrated by too many things to be polite. A frown invaded his features. "Tell me one more thing, Addie, in chess can a rook take a king?"

"Sure." The mistrust faded but didn't entirely vanish. "Anything can take anything. Rook, pawn, knight, king, whatever, as long as it's properly positioned."

"Have you ever played with anyone at Romac?"

"Yes. Damien, what are you driving at?"

"Does Jonny play?"

"Not that I know of."

That didn't tell him much, Damien reflected, but then maybe he wasn't asking the right questions. Addison was hiding something. Jonny was hiding something as well, and so was Morgan. Maybe those two men knew chess, maybe they didn't. And whether or not any of that was even relevant to Rook, he couldn't say. He couldn't think, either, but that had less to do with Rook than Melanie. All of which had him glancing unhappily at the runway beyond the airport windows.

He had a choice, it seemed. Brazil or Melanie.

"Are we leaving now?" Addie asked in a doubtful tone.

Turning from the window, Damien nodded. "My car's in the lot."

'YOU'VE GOT A MILLION messages, ma'am," Sidney said, poking his head into Melanie's office as he prepared to leave for the day. "Two important ones from Lucy Farmer in accounting."

Melanie looked up from a file that was too complicated for her to be reviewing at 6:22 at night. She double-checked her watch when she saw the time. "My God, is it really that late, Sidney? Why are you still here?"

"I'm ambitious," he said straight-faced.

She hid a smile. "What did Lucy Farmer want?"

"She said you should call her, but she'll be long gone by now." He tugged on his jacket. "Is it true what I heard about you demoting Tucker Smith?"

Melanie stretched her arms out in front of her. "I'd hardly call it a demotion, and where did you hear this?"

"The men's room, where else?" He handed her a wad of papers. "Your other messages. There was nothing else urgent from accounting." He sent her a curious look. "Why the emphasis on that area? Is something going on down there?"

"Not that I know of," Melanie lied. "Do you know if Jonny's still around?"

"He left at noon."

"Again? Are you sure?"

"Positive. Susan in reservations has a crush on him and I have a crush on her. She lost her glow at 12:10 when he walked out the door."

"What about Rolf?"

"Gone. If you'll pardon me, ma'am, you should get out more."

"To the ladies' room?"

He grinned. "You'd be better informed. Mr. McCall left at five-forty with Mrs. McCall, who they say resembled Vesuvius when she marched into his office five minutes earlier."

"I wonder why?" Melanie mused.

"Do you want me to go to the bathroom and see if I can find out?"

Melanie refused to laugh. "No, thank you," she said carefully. "You've stayed long enough."

"If you're sure." He started for the door while she dumped her problem file into the top desk drawer.

Tomorrow, she thought, but was interrupted by Sidney's indignant, "Wait a minute, sir, you can't go in there."

She looked up, expecting Morgan. She was startled and oddly excited to see Damien in the doorway.

He looked in a bad temper, but gorgeous in his Romac uniform with his tie pulled away from his throat and his long hair spilling over the collar of his jacket.

"It's all right, Sidney," she told her assistant. "You're too new to know, but this is Damien McCall, Rolf's brother."

"Oh. Well, in that case..."

Damien spared him a brief glance—no smile, Melanie noticed. She waited until Sidney had gone, then, drawing her defenses, asked, "What's wrong?" A feeling of panic suddenly clawed at her stomach. "You didn't have a problem with your flight, did you?"

"No, only with the traffic in from the airport."

He pushed damp tendrils of hair from his face, then made an impatient gesture. "Where's Rolf?"

He was definitely grouchy. Melanie felt a smile forming on her lips. "With Regan. I don't know where they went."

He swore in Portuguese, then looked straight at her. "Are you all right?"

She perched on the edge of her desk, her palms damp for reasons she preferred not to analyze. "I'm fine, but I don't think you are." She lowered her gaze to the floor and said quietly, "You wanted to go home to Brazil, didn't you? You didn't want to come back here."

She caught the flicker of contrition in his eyes. He shook his head slowly and released a heavy breath. "Not really, no."

"You hate it that much?"

His bad mood seemed to dissolve. "It isn't hate, Mel," he said, sounding closer than before. "I don't know what you'd call it. Resentment maybe. I feel like I'm never here by choice."

He was too close now. She sensed his eyes on her, felt them running over her body, stripping away the knitted silk of her teal dress and every one of her rigorous defenses.

Oh, but who was she kidding? She was the one shredding those defenses, willing him to tempt her straight into bed. Her mind had been on him for days, her body hungry for his touch. And how many more feeble excuses could she dream up about how it would inevitably end?

She forced her head up to find him standing a scant two feet away. With her fingers she touched his chest, a little tentatively, but she wanted him to be aware of her.

His eyes were shielded, black and irresistible in the cold fluorescent light.

"Mel..." he began, then lowered his lashes and shook his head. "It's wrong," was all he said. "For both of us." Yet even as he said those things, he was taking her hand, pulling her up from the desk and into his arms.

His mouth was hot on hers, impatient and demanding. And this time she did respond, with a candor she would have expected to surprise him. It didn't seem to do anything except arouse him even more.

She felt the heat and hard length of him against her hips, his tongue exploring her mouth, roaming over her teeth and lips while his hand slid to her breast.

She couldn't breathe but it was nothing like when Rook had grabbed her.

For a frightened instant, her mind slowed its spinning. When had Rook grabbed her?

The thought slipped easily away under the pressure of Damien's kiss. Let Rook wait. She wasn't going to lose this moment for anything.

But she wasn't going to make love to Damien on her office floor, either.

She dragged her mouth from his with difficulty. "Not here," she said in a shaky voice.

He groaned, dropping his forehead onto hers but not releasing her hips. "All the way to the *Emily-Mac,* Mel? I can't wait that long."

"You could if you had to, I think, but you don't." Taking his face in her hands, she turned his head toward the wall. "Did you ever see the *Towering Inferno,*" she asked in his ear, loving the feel of his hair against her lips.

"Mel ..."

"Nev did," she went on, tugging on his wrists. "He liked the layout of the offices and the private rooms that adjoined them. So he had the Romac Building designed with those same connecting rooms." With her hips, she bumped open a hidden door. "This is mine. It's got a bed and a fridge and a view of the city. And a lock even Rook couldn't get past."

Amusement curved Damien's lips as his eyes touched on her aquarium full of coral and tropical fish and finally on the twinkling night skyline.

"*Eu te amo,* Melanie," he murmured into her hair.

A ripple of shock ran through her at that, but questions could wait. She wanted him, needed him, and for that she couldn't wait.

Closing her eyes, she swayed into him, shivering slightly as he caught her in his arms again and set his mouth on hers. Behind him she heard the door click firmly shut. There was no turning back now.

Chapter Fifteen

Rook smiled at the nervous little creature before him. Lucy Farmer from accounting was just a little too clever for her own good. He must deal with her.

She let him into her cluttered second-floor apartment with no problem. But then why should there be one? He'd been concerned about her quick mind for some time now—and made a point of flirting with her, which she'd eaten up.

"I have coffee or something stronger," she said brightly, removing her glasses with a surreptitious movement and dropping them on a table. "Which do you prefer?"

He smiled again. "I'm not thirsty." He sat on the sofa, reaching for her hand with his gloved one. "I thought maybe we could...talk."

She swallowed a giggle and he cringed. He didn't like women much, and this was going to be a painful extraction. If only he could drug her, but that was too risky.

She settled in beside him, wiggling suggestively against his thigh. "I didn't know you liked me that way," she said, then gave a little sigh. "I didn't know anyone did. In the washroom they say that Ms. Rossi's the big catch. She's very rich, you know, and very pretty."

Rook forced his fingers to her hair. "You're very pretty, too, Lucy. How well do you know Melanie?"

"Oh, not well. I talked to her the week before last about—" she blushed "—well, about something. And I tried to talk to her again today, but she was busy, so I left

messages, two with her assistant, Sidney. Do you know
Sidney?'' She wrinkled her nose. ''He's got an attitude.''

''I'm sure,'' Rook murmured. ''Why did you want to talk
to Melanie?''

''Well...'' She hesitated, squirming a little. ''I don't think
I should say anything to you.''

Rook inclined his head, capturing her earlobe with his
teeth. ''Why not?''

A tiny gasp of pleasure broke from her lips. ''Well, it's
kind of...'' He trailed his mouth down her neck. ''Well, all
right, I guess it'd be okay, I mean seeing as who you are and
all. I found a sort of problem in the books.'' She bit her lip
a little guiltily. ''Are you sure you want to know about
this?''

''Absolutely.'' His gloved hand moved to her breast. ''Tell
me about the books.''

''Ooh,'' Lucy moaned. ''I shouldn't be doing this with
you.''

He kissed her mouth. ''Don't be ridiculous. What's
wrong with the books?''

She trembled, pressing herself against him. ''Someone's
been skimming,'' she whispered.

He raised his head in feigned shock. ''Really? Do you
know who?''

''Oh no,'' she denied hastily. ''I mean it could be anyone, couldn't it?''

''So why go to Melanie?''

''Because I...'' More guilt flashed in her eyes. ''Well, I'd
sort of like to get upstairs and I thought that if I went right
to her with what I found, maybe she'd help me out, I mean,
they say she's awfully nice, you know, approachable.''

Rook smiled. ''She is. Both those things, though I'm still
not sure she's the one you should have told about this.''

Lucy sent him a shy grin. ''Well, now I've told you,
haven't I?''

''Not exactly.'' With one gloved finger he traced the
rounded line of her chin. ''You haven't told me what you
found.''

Now she did giggle. Leaning over, she whispered in his ear, a child confiding her most delicious secret.

"I see," he said when she drew back. "You certainly are a smart little thing."

"Oh, not really. I just don't think computers are everything."

"No, I don't suppose they are." Humming softly, Rook slid his hand into his pocket.

"What's that song?" she asked, then peered at his arm. "What are you doing? Come to think of it, why don't you take off your gloves?"

"I prefer to keep them on. I'm not doing anything, and it's the birthday song."

She laughed and kissed his cheek. "I never noticed it before, but I think maybe you're a little weird."

"Not weird," he corrected with a bland smile. "Rook."

"What?" Her eyes widened as his hand came out of his pocket. "My God, what's that?"

"It's a garotte," he told her calmly. "Old-fashioned but effective. Stops mice from squeaking."

Before she could scream, he had the slender wire wrapped about her neck. "Goodbye, little mouse," he whispered.

DAMIEN WAS ON THE VERGE of losing his control with Melanie. His mouth bruised hers and he pulled her forward so that her breasts were crushed against his chest. He felt their firmness and the lush softness hidden beneath that. He felt dizzy and hard and tormented—and so ready for her that he didn't think he could hold out long enough to shed his clothes.

Still, he expected objections as he laid her on the bed with its covering of sea green satin. One of them had to be reasonable, and he couldn't see it being him, not in his present state of arousal.

He said words to her in Portuguese, tender obscenities that she probably understood. He spoke them into her mouth even as he kissed her, and it seemed she did understand, because her hands grew bolder with each second that passed.

"No, don't stop," she whispered suddenly, clutching at his shoulders when he lifted his head to breathe. "I want this time, even if it's all we can have."

"I'm not going to stop," he murmured back, rolling away just enough so he could gather her breasts into his palms.

The heat of his body blended with hers. He had no time for grace. I love you he'd said, and he meant it. Love and want and need to have.

He hadn't been able to think clearly for so many days now that he couldn't remember the last time his thoughts had been all his. He got hard thinking about her and no one except Melanie could satisfy that purely male ache.

His fingers found the zipper of her dress. "No lights," she'd pleaded when he closed the door. "I want the darkness, Damien, the night."

He didn't understand why, but it didn't really matter. The city glowed beyond a wall of floor-to-ceiling windows and the aquarium contained tiny blue and green beams of its own. Maybe he could even see her better this way. Certainly he could see that she wanted him.

Her hips moved under him, in a motion that was both gentle and urgent. He felt the heat of her as her hands slid along his sides, tugging the shirt from his waistband. He pulled her dress off with more haste than deftness and tossed it aside. Then his mouth found her breast, the diamond hardness of her nipple, through the filmy material of her bra, and with his tongue he dampened the fabric, suckling her with something so close to desperation that it frightened him.

She moaned in her throat as he raised his head and blew lightly on the wet spot. Then his mouth closed hungrily on the peak again.

Oh God, to hear her and see her, to touch and breathe in the scent of her. He groaned. It had to be now.

Somehow he managed to unfasten her bra. Her soft flesh spilled into his hands and he kissed the hot curve beneath her breast, loving the taste of her skin.

She worked almost feverishly at his zipper, a barrier she seemed anxious to be rid of. When it was gone, her fingers closed on him, hard as he liked it, and a little rough.

No more time, his body declared. But he bought a little, sliding his lips across her flat stomach then down to the heat between her legs.

She let him do it, let his mouth explore while a thousand sensations rocked her. Then her hips arched and she convulsed around him, her body shocky and soft and still so ready.

"Damien . . ."

She ran her fingers through his damp hair, pulling him back up to where she could reach him. He wanted to look, but she touched him in such a way that his teeth ground together and he was pushed so close to the edge of his self-restraint that suddenly he couldn't see anything.

He slid his hands beneath her, urgent himself now, kneading her firm round bottom while she tore at his shirt. *Fine, rip it off, but say you love me, Mel.*

She found his mouth with hers, her hands closing about him once again, guiding him. "I love you, Damien," she said softly. *"Eu tu amo."*

And really that was the last thing he heard, the last words they spoke. It was all sensation after that, pure sensation, her heart pounding against him, her hips rising up to meet his fierce thrusts.

No more control, he just held on and drove into her until there was nothing left and he was too exhausted and shuddery to form a consistent thought.

He collapsed on top of her with a groan, perspiring, his hair wet, his breath coming in spasms. He slid his fingers up into her hair, feeling the heat of her, the fragile vertebrae of her neck and the silkiness of her moist skin.

Her heart beat under his ear, slowing now, though her arms were still tight around him, her hands stroking his back.

He couldn't force himself to move, but he heard her whisper, felt her lips moving against the top of his head.

"Why couldn't it be simple?" she asked softly. "Why can't love be enough?"

He moved then, he didn't know how, gathering her into him and wrapping himself around her warm body. "Because," he murmured in her ear, smiling just a little in spite of himself.

He was glad to feel her lips curve against his cheek. "Bad reason, Damien." Her smile became a tender kiss. *"Mas foi óptima."* But it was great.

"HERSCHEL!" Rupert had scuttled across the hall in his bare feet to his friend's room. "Wake up. Tell me what he said."

Herschel snored on, so Rupert tried again.

"Sounds like a buzz saw," he grumbled. "Wake up, Hersch."

"What?" Groggily the other man surfaced. "What's wrong? Is the lodge on fire?"

Rupert sat down on the bed. "No, but you said Rook called. I want to know what he said. Did you ask him about that bomb Tom's granddaughter told us about?"

Herschel had to put his teeth in, but when he did he glared. "You woke me up for that?" He hesitated. "What bomb?"

"The one Rook made that we didn't know about." Rupert's lined face grew anxious. "I don't like it. I don't want people getting blown up. Money, he said when he came to us. He'd get us the money Nev and Tom gypped us out of."

"And he's been doing it too, hasn't he?" Herschel challenged. He stuck his bare feet into his slippers, put on his robe then picked up his cane and shuffled his skinny body to the door.

"Where're you going?" Rupert asked.

"My feet are asleep. I have to walk." He flapped a bony hand. "The bomb didn't go off and Rook said he didn't mess with the planes."

Rupert frowned. The word sabotage rang a bell, but only a dim one. He hated it when his memory faltered like this. "What planes?" he asked.

"Don't know, don't care. He said no one's going to get hurt and I believe him."

"Well, I don't." Rupert remembered then. "Think about it, Herschel. What do we know about this Rook?"

"We know he's getting us our money back, some of it anyway," Herschel snapped. "What else do we need to know?"

"But where did he come from? Why is he doing this for us?"

"Could be he's kin to one of us, Sam maybe." Herschel tap-tapped into the game room, careful not to alert the fussy desk monitor. "It doesn't matter. Put it out of your mind." He cackled. "That shouldn't be hard for either of us to do."

The floor heater warmed Rupert's icy feet. "I don't want anyone getting hurt," he insisted. "Maybe we should call the girl."

"No!" Herschel stabbed the air with his cane. "You leave it be. No one'll get hurt, Rook promised. Now you just sit down and we'll have us a game of checkers, and hope like hell that Nurse Fuzz doesn't catch us."

"Hope like hell that Rook is telling the truth," Rupert added. He shuffled over to the table. "I don't trust him, Hersch. There's something funny about him. I think he wants more than money."

"Forget it," Herschel told him.

But Rupert knew this was one thing he'd never be able to forget, especially if he was right.

DAMIEN THANKED GOD for long nights and slow sex and Melanie's boldness with his body. But he thanked God most of all for her, because she could have demanded just about anything from him, promises that would have made them both miserable in the end. She could have, and yet she didn't.

She didn't even cry and that amazed him. No tears when they dressed and went out for midnight seafood and pizza in the Mission District, or later as they strolled through Chinatown and he bought her a jade dragon with rubies for eyes and razor-sharp claws.

"What a romantic you are," she teased, but she probably knew it was his way of symbolizing their night together. A beautiful fantasy, something you dreamed up that could never be.

Of course that thought was hardly in his head when he bought her the statue. All he could think of was Melanie and how much he wished this one night could go on forever.

He'd had his flight bag in the car with his jeans and T-shirt and jacket inside. She had a change of clothes in the office very similar to his. They didn't look executive or upscale or even trendy as they prowled through the clubs and coffeehouses of North Beach—where the beatniks used to hang out—although they were both too young to remember that era.

They went to Fisherman's Wharf as well and she told him about the Dickens Fair put on there every Christmas season. For a second, he felt uncomfortable, but she explained.

"No, Damien, I don't expect you to be here for it. I was thinking of Tom and how he used to compare himself and Nev to Scrooge and Marley." She sighed. "I wish I could stop thinking about that dream I had. I wish I could remember Rook's face. I don't know why I can't. But you know what's even scarier? He knows I saw his face. So why isn't he worried? Well, there's only one answer to that. It's because he knows I can't remember."

"Drugs will do that, Mel," Damien said, stroking her hair. He didn't want to talk right now. Could you make love on the wharf in the middle of the night without anyone noticing?

Melanie must have sensed his fixation. "No, I won't do it here," she said, batting at his hand that wanted to slide up under her shirt. "Let's go to my place and we'll make a fire and put the plants all around and pretend for just a little while that we're in the tropics."

"All the way to Tiburon, Mel?"

"Well, maybe not all the way..."

They went to his car and drove to Golden Gate Park. He couldn't believe it but they actually made love in the back seat. It was cramped and hard and thoroughly uncomfortable, and he loved it.

Melanie winced afterward. "It's got to be easier when you're younger."

"It is," Damien said, then grinned when she pinned him to the leather seat. "No sex, Mel," he said. "Just a lot of heavy necking. I was a very careful teenager."

And he was an equally careful man. He always had protection, which seemed to relieve Melanie greatly.

"I don't want to be pregnant right now," she confided when they reached her home. "Maybe I never want that."

"No kids?" Damien was faintly shocked. "Why not?"

"Oh, I like them," she said. "I only question the wisdom of having them. I mean, look at us, targets for revenge. And look at Samuel Taggart's kids. At least two of them were consumed by hatred."

"Sonia seemed fine."

"She was also very pregnant," Melanie recalled, her tone thoughtful. "I wonder if she's had the baby."

"We could phone tomorrow."

"Or drive down to Monterey and see for ourselves."

Damien grabbed her waist, burying his face in her neck as she unlocked the door. "And have Rook pay you another visit? Not a chance."

"Maybe this time he'd visit you."

"He'd have to follow me to Detroit to do it."

She leaned back into him. "That's right, I forgot. You have a flight tomorrow afternoon. Commercial?"

"Cargo." He pushed her gently through the door. "And don't worry, I'll be careful. Now, come on. I'll start a fire while you rearrange the plants. I want to make out in the jungle."

MELANIE THOUGHT IT WAS a parrot screaming high up in a palm tree that dragged her out of a deep and wonderful sleep the next morning, but it was only the telephone and she had the receiver in her hand before she remembered that her answering machine was on.

"Melanie?" Rolf's voice on the other end was unnaturally strained. "Mel, we've got a problem, a big one. Is Damien there? And for God's sake, don't lie."

She kicked Damien's shin behind her. "Yes," she said, then kicked him again when he settled in more firmly against her. "What is it, Rolf, what's wrong?"

"It's that woman from accounting, Lucy Farmer."

Melanie sat up in the bed, her brain coming instantly awake. "What about her?"

Rolf took a deep breath. "She's dead, Mel."

"What?" Her voice was a disbelieving whisper. "Dead now? What happened to her?"

"The police say she was strangled. A girlfriend found her body in her apartment this morning. Her place was a mess. They think it was a robbery."

"But who'd want to rob her?" A distant recollection cut its way through Melanie's shock. "She left messages for me, Rolf. Two of them yesterday at the office."

"What about?"

"She didn't say, only that she had to talk to me and that it was important." Her voice caught slightly. "I didn't think it was life or death important."

"Oh now, don't start blaming yourself. Maybe the police were right."

"No," she said firmly. "People like Lucy don't get robbed and strangled out of the blue, or if they do, they don't also work for people who happen to be on a homicidal maniac's hit list." Melanie felt her throat tightening, but she refused to cry. "Lucy worked in accounting, Rolf. There has to be a connection there somewhere."

"I know." He sounded weary and indescribably sad. "I'm at the office now. Tell Damien what's happened, then get over here as fast as you can. The police are on their way."

Melanie glanced over and was surprised to find Damien already zipping up his jeans. His features were dark and somber. He'd heard; he knew. Closing her eyes, she pictured Lucy Farmer's innocent face.

"Oh Rook, you won't get away with this," she swore under her breath, then she replied softly to Rolf, "We're on our way, too."

She returned the phone to its cradle with a controlled motion. "It's too big a coincidence," she murmured, and would have slid from the bed except that she noticed her message light flashing. "I wonder—no." But she pressed the play button anyway.

Damien was in the bathroom, so he couldn't hear. But Melanie could. And what she heard didn't make her feel any better. When Damien came out she sent him a look of abject misery.

"Lucy found something wrong with the Romac accounts," she told him, then reached over and played the message again.

Chapter Sixteen

"Uh, Ms. Rossi, this is Lucy Farmer. I don't like to bother you at home but I thought you'd want to know about this. I found a—well, I guess you'd call it a discrepancy in the Romac accounts. I think maybe someone's been fixing the figures. Maybe you don't know this, but I have a computer brain when it comes to numbers. It's weird, but it has its advantages. I mean, unlike a computer, a brain won't usually pack up on you. I can't really get specific on the phone, and I'm kind of in a hurry right now, but maybe tomorrow at work I could talk to you. It's not that I don't like Mr. McCall, you understand. I mean, I wouldn't want you to think that. It's just that sometime I get tongue-tied around good-looking men and Mr. McCall sure is good-looking. Anyway, um, that's about all I have to say. Good night, Ms. Rossi."

There was dead silence in Rolf's office after Melanie played Lucy Farmer's message. They'd have to turn this tape over to the police, she knew, but she'd wanted Rolf to hear it first.

Shoulders slumped, he sank his face into his hands. "I don't believe this." He appealed first to her and then to Damien who'd hardly spoken a word since hearing the tape for the first time. "Is it Rook?"

"It has to be him," Melanie said. "He wants to destroy Romac and us with it. Embezzling is as good a method as any—assuming that's what he's doing."

Damien wandered over to the glass wall with its floor-to-ceiling sweep of burgundy draperies. "We need Jonny," he said, his tone one of deliberate dispassion. "And while we're waiting for him, you might want to get Tucker and Morgan in here."

Rolf flipped on his intercom. "Tracy, send in Mr. Voss and call down to the Cable Car Foods accounting office. I want Tucker Smith up here immediately." He glanced at his brother. "I take it Mel told you about her run-in with them yesterday morning. Morgan was screwing around at Lucy Farmer's computer."

"I know."

The door whooshed open and Morgan strode stiffly in, his expression stony and unpromising. "You wanted to see me, sir?"

Rolf stood, fingers splayed on the top of his walnut desk. "One of our employees in accounting is dead, Morgan. Lucy Farmer. Melanie saw you at her computer yesterday morning. I want to know what you were doing there."

Morgan didn't bat an eye. "I got off on the wrong floor. I would have carried on but I thought I saw someone, so I decided I should have a look."

Melanie snatched her head around. He was lying—but why? "There was no one else up there, Morgan. Not until Tucker came in." She narrowed her eyes. "Or are you suggesting that it was Tucker you saw?"

He didn't look at her. "Tucker came in later," he said in an uncommonly quiet voice. "It wasn't him I saw."

"Then who?" she demanded.

"I don't know."

Rising slowly to her feet, Melanie faced him. "Why are you lying, Morgan? Is it to protect yourself?" She folded her arms across her chest. "Or is it Tucker you're protecting?"

Damien closed in from the other side. "Why did you get him a job here, Morgan?" he questioned softly. "You don't do favors for anyone that I've ever seen. Why for Tucker?"

"My reasons were personal," Morgan replied evenly. "There's nothing wrong with doing someone a favor, is there? And Tucker's certainly adequate in his job."

Was that a tiny quaver Melanie detected in his response? It was hard to tell, but something about him wasn't right. He looked strangely deflated.

Rolf came around his desk. "Morgan, I'm sorry, but I think there's more to this than you're telling us."

The man stared straight ahead. "I'm sorry, too," he said. "I've told you everything I can and it's all true. I'm afraid there's nothing more I can say to you."

Oh, yes, there was, Melanie thought, but she caught the warning shake of Damien's head and swallowed her protest. Badgering Morgan was pointless. He wouldn't budge. And they were straying into personal territory. Except for the part about what had happened in accounting yesterday morning. He was definitely lying about that.

For a moment Rolf studied his assistant, then he nodded. "Not right now," he agreed. "You can go, but not far. The police are downstairs with Jonny right now. They'll want to talk to us when they're through."

Morgan politely nodded and gave Melanie a look she couldn't quite read. It was either contrition or contempt. Before she could decide which, he turned and walked out.

Seconds later Rolf's intercom buzzed.

"Tucker Smith's here, sir," his secretary announced. "Shall I send him in?"

"Might as well," Damien said with a shrug. "We probably shouldn't have let them pass each other out there, but if they're working together, I imagine they'll already have their stories straight."

It seemed they did, unless, as Damien suggested, Morgan had said something to Tucker outside.

"Yes, of course I was there," Tucker admitted. "But I came in after Morgan. I thought I saw someone, too."

"Too?" Melanie asked. "So you have talked to Morgan about this."

"No, of course not," Tucker denied hastily.

"You don't lie worth a damn, Tucker," Damien noted from the window. "What's going on between you and Morgan?"

"Nothing."

His voice was too loud, but was that real or contrived? Melanie wondered.

"Look, I don't know what you people are driving at, but I had nothing to do with that woman's death."

"Who said you did?" Damien challenged.

"No one said it." Now he seemed offended. "But it sounds like you're implying as much."

"And you're lying," Melanie shot back.

"This is getting us nowhere." Rolf sighed. "Go back downstairs, Tucker." He touched his call button. "Tracy, have Mr. Morelli contact me when the police are finished with him."

Glancing at his watch, Damien pushed off from the window. "It's twelve-thirty. I have to get to the airport."

It startled Melanie a little when he kissed her neck, although Rolf scarcely seemed to notice.

"Jonny should have caught any tampering," he said in a puzzled tone. "I wonder how he missed it?"

"Jonny hasn't been around much, Rolf," Melanie reminded him.

"And Addison knows chess," Damien murmured.

She slid him a suspicious look. "What does that mean?"

Sighing, he pressed his lips to her forehead. "It means we still don't know who Rook is."

THIS WAS THE WORST, most depressing day of her life, Melanie decided after an hour spent with the police. Lucy Farmer was dead, Damien would be halfway to Michigan by now, who knew what Rook was up to and every time she passed Regan, which was far too many times that day, she got a dirty look.

She also passed Addison a few times, an oddity in itself, since he seldom came downtown and one made doubly annoying by the fact that twice she found him flirting with the office staff. The second time was with Rolf's secretary, and Melanie wanted to kick him. How could he be so callous?

"Don't you have a flight or something, Addison?" she demanded, slapping a file onto the secretary's desk.

"No, and don't yell at me, Mel. I came to get my car from Jonny which I got here too late to pick up yesterday and which cost me an indecently good time last night."

Her eyes flicked to Rolf's closed office door. "Jonny's busy."

"So I heard." He levered his lanky frame from the edge of the desk. "Look, I'm sorry, Mel. I heard about the woman downstairs." He felt about in his pockets, pulled out his cigarettes, then grimaced. "Bet I can't smoke here, can I?"

"No." She studied him, searching for Rook, but found only Addie. This memory block was getting really irritating. "Damien says you know chess."

He rolled his eyes. "Oh, not again. What is it with you people and chess?"

"How good are you?"

"Not as good as Boris Spassky. Is it important?"

She shook the question away with no idea why she'd even asked it. "Probably not. Just something Damien mentioned."

"What did Damien mention?" A rumpled Rolf emerged from his office, rolling down his shirt sleeves.

"Chess." Melanie peered at the man behind him. "You look awful, Jonny. Did you find what you were hunting for?"

He nodded. "Finally."

One of Addie's shaggy brows went up. "What were you looking for?"

"Gremlins." The answer came from Regan who strolled in with her coat over her arm. "I'm leaving now, Rolf. I have my massage therapy and then a hair appointment. After that I'm getting fitted for a new gown. French, of course."

"Of course," Melanie murmured. She couldn't help wondering from whom Regan received her massage therapy. Rolf should sic his private investigator on her for a while. But then again, maybe Rolf wasn't ready to face the whole ugly truth.

Addie stuck an unlit cigarette between his lips. "Keys," he said to Jonny who immediately looked chagrined.

"Sorry." Jonny dug through his pockets and tossed the keys to the other man.

"So was I," Addie murmured ruefully.

He followed Regan out the door, which left only Jonny for Melanie to stare at. "Were the accounting discrepancies hard to find?" she asked.

"Pretty hard," Jonny said without inflection. "But that's no excuse. I should have caught them."

Rolf shrugged. "Well, they're caught now, that's the main thing. Mel, can I talk to you?"

"Of course." Her eyes were still on Jonny, whose handsome features she couldn't seem to read.

"I'm really sorry," he said again. "I'll keep a closer watch from now on. I feel bad about Lucy, though. I can't help thinking the two things must be connected, the skimming and her death."

"That's for the police to decide." Rolf held his hand out to Melanie. "Go have lunch, Jonny, then get that printout for me, okay?"

"Will do."

"What printout?" Melanie asked when Rolf closed his office door.

"A copy of the tampered figures. I want to study it tonight. I can't imagine Regan being around."

Melanie squirmed a little but covered her discomfort. "What about your private detective? Has he learned anything more about Rachel Taggart?"

"Only what I said before. She had a son—and a grudge."

"Or so Sonia claims."

Rolf gnawed on his lower lip. "Did she ever explain where that grudge came from? I mean, Samuel doesn't appear to have one."

"Sonia says that's just how it is in her family. Everyone knows the story. She mentioned a Great-aunt Millie, Samuel's sister, who prefers it as bedtime reading to *Cinderella*. Maybe Aunt Millie's the one who poisons minds." Melanie shrugged. "All I know is that Sonia's not spiteful, even though her mother apparently was."

"And Rachel," Rolf added.

Melanie nodded. "The answers have to be in there somewhere, Rolf." Her eyes found his. "And we've got to find them, before somebody else gets killed."

SNOW WOULDN'T HAVE surprised Damien when he returned to San Francisco late the next night. Actually it was early morning, after 2:00 a.m. and cold enough that the gangplank of the *Emily-Mac* had a thin coating of ice on it.

This couldn't be normal even for the Bay area, although the fog was certainly typical, a light frosting tonight, little more than a misty veil.

He pulled up his collar against the chill and told himself for the hundredth time since leaving Detroit that he would not wake up Melanie at this hour and that it was better he didn't, anyway. He needed to think, really think for a change. There had to be a way to work things out between them. For the life of him, though, he didn't know what that was.

He hopped onto the deck and started at once for the cabin. Then he saw the white envelope with the red rook drawn on it taped to the door and felt his teeth begin to grind.

"Not tonight," he growled, but he snatched the envelope free, anyway, and stuffed it in his back jeans pocket. "Damn you, Rook, whoever the hell you are."

Weariness pulled at him, deepening his frustration. There was so much running through his head, thoughts of Melanie and Lucy Farmer, the Circle of Five, little red chess pieces, three old men, Rolf and Regan and a faceless Rook. He couldn't sort through the layers, couldn't concentrate on any one specific thing, and that wasn't like him. His was not an undisciplined mind. It shouldn't be this difficult to separate it all out.

"Damien."

He had his hand on the door when he heard the voice. It seemed to emanate from the water on the starboard side of the boat, and yet it felt much closer than that.

He moved toward the wheelhouse. "Who is it?"

"You don't recognize my voice? I'm disappointed."

Damien squinted into the mist. "You sound more pleased than disappointed to me."

"Well, maybe that's because—" an arm snaked out of the gloom to wrap itself around Damien's throat and the voice came into his ear "—we're not close enough." Something sharp jabbed his spine in a warning. "One move, Damien, one twitch and you're dead. I know all about your trip down the Amazon. You were tough for a kid who got a silver spoon shoved into his mouth when he was nine. Instinct tells me you're no different today."

Damien shut off his emotions; it was the only way. He did recognize the voice, he had from the start, but that reaction, too, he shoved back. He kept his own voice impassive, cold.

"What do you want—Rook?"

The hot breath on his neck made his skin crawl. It felt uncomfortably close to a caress. He twisted away slightly.

Rook laughed, a silky sound that echoed in the damp night air. "Many things," he replied. "But first you're going to do something for me."

Shifting the knife to the hand that was wrapped around his prisoner's throat, he used his other to push the hair from Damien's neck. Damien felt a tiny pinprick, then Rook breath blowing on his skin.

"You're going to count backward for me by ten. And—" his grip tightened, the knife blade pressing dangerously hard against Damien's carotid artery "—you're n going to fight me. I will kill you, Damien, don't think I won't. Remember Lucy Farmer...."

Right then and for whatever reason, Damien couldn't remember much of anything. The cold was numbing his muscles, or was it a drug, something that attacked his mind while it paralyzed his body?

"Count," Rook whispered in his ear, but Damien refused to obey.

He should have fought, he reflected, only dimly aware that Rook's hold on him had shifted. At least he would have died fighting. Who knew how it would end this way?

The deck seemed to spin out from under his feet.

"See the years fly by," Rook whispered, his tone that of a visionary. "Keep going, Damien, farther back."

Although Damien's mind resisted the images, they crept in anyway. Around him the mist deepened to black. He saw nothing except word pictures somersaulting through his head.

"Bastard," he managed to croak and for a moment felt the blade slide across his throat.

"No." Rook eased the blade away. "I won't kill you now."

"You should," Damien murmured, too limp now to make any of his muscles work. "Because I swear I'm going to kill you."

It wasn't laughter in his ear this time, it was a low growl and then he was thrust forward, away from Rook's tense body, down to the wet black surface of the *Emily-Mac*'s deck.

Chapter Seventeen

He landed facedown in the snow, very hard. The black curtain of night remained, but this was not the *Emily-Mac*.

"Are you hurt, mister?"

Through his confusion Damien felt someone tugging on his arm, a woman.

"Boy, you really took a header, huh?" She dumped several parcels onto the snowy sidewalk next to him. Sidewalk? "Come on, I'll help you, but you gotta be willing."

His vision cleared slowly, the buzz in his head resolving itself into the wail of a siren. He pushed up from the snow, dazed and weak, the way he felt when he had the flu.

"Where am I?" he asked, too bemused to really look.

"Oh brother, I've heard that before. What were you drinking?"

Whoever she was she had a cheerful voice. Damien climbed to his feet, pushed the snow-wet hair from his face and struggled to bring her into focus. He saw blond hair under a knitted scarf, a brown fur-trimmed coat and galoshes.

Her blue eyes peered up at him, brightly curious. She seemed oblivious to the blowing snow and the fat, round Ford that was crawling by.

"It's like something out of a gangster movie," Damien murmured, swaying unsteadily. He drew his brows together in a frown. "What is this place? And who are you?"

"I'm Genie Bakowsky, soon to be Genie Kelly. See?" She pulled off a knitted mitten and wriggled her fingers at him. "Donny Kelly, he's my boss, or he used to be, he said we should get married and blow this town in the new year. Maybe we'll go to New York he said and he'll let Rita have the house, I mean the bar, because you shouldn't be partners with people these days. Kelly says they'll play you for a sucker every time, sure as you're standing here."

Damien disguised a shiver. The wind was cutting through him. "Where am I standing, Genie?" he asked, wishing he could remember where he'd heard that name before. Not at Romac, he didn't think. Something to do with Melanie.

Genie laughed. Even blurred by snow she looked more like a girl than a woman. "You know, someone else asked me that once. She wore funny clothes like you, only she being a woman, that made it even more strange. I mean guys can wear blue jeans and it was okay for me on the farm, but ladies don't do it, especially not in the city."

Damien's mind was clearing, but not fast enough. Another car rolled past, a big black whale with huge fenders and poor headlights. Turning from the street, he took Genie by the arms. Who was the woman? he wanted to demand, but he couldn't bring himself to do it. Something told him he didn't want to know.

"Where are we?" he asked instead, giving her a shake that was probably a little rough.

She regarded him through uncertain eyes. "Wabash Avenue?"

He released her, searching his fuzzy mind, then staring at her in disbelief. "Chicago?"

"That's right." She brightened again. "Boy, you gave me a scare. I thought you might be going to say what planet? You know, like you thought you were Flash Gordon or something. People do sometimes who get hold of a bad bottle."

Damien's eyes narrowed, the wind blowing his collar against his cheek. "What year is this, Genie?"

She laughed. "It's like I'm hearing a ghost."

She bent and started collecting the parcels. After a moment's hesitation and another mistrustful look at a passing car, Damien crouched down to help her.

"What year?" he asked again.

She released a tolerant breath, as if dealing with a child. "Well, I'll tell you, but then you have to come with me and get warmed up. Those clothes you're wearing wouldn't keep a fly warm. You'll catch cold for sure."

"Genie..."

"It's 1937. December nineteenth, 1937, and this is the second time in two years someone's asked me that same question."

Damien's stomach muscles tightened, although he couldn't have said why. None of this could possibly be real. "The second time?" he echoed distantly.

"Yeah, the first was that girl I told you about. She said her name was Melanie."

"IN HERE."

Genie pulled him through a door and into a stuffy, hot room. There was a lot of smoke, and a lot of people to go with it. Only one of the green felt tables was empty but Genie dragged him firmly past it.

"Can't sit there. That's reserved."

Damien stopped. "For who?"

Genie wagged a finger at him. "No last names, but Kelly calls them Tom and Neville. Now come on and I'll get you a drink, maybe try to find some of Kelly's clothes." She eyed him up and down. "They'll probably be too big, though. You're not one bit fat."

"Thanks."

Her admiring gaze fixed on his face. "But you sure are a looker." She touched the wet curls plastered to his jacket collar. "How come your hair's so long and soft? I mean, there's no greasy stuff in it."

"I'm an actor," Damien replied, not really paying much attention by then. Thankfully the lie just came. "I'm doing a period play on Broadway."

Two men sat down at the empty table, Samuel and Tom, if he wasn't mistaken, but a lot younger now. "Genie." He drew her around to face him. "Who are those men?"

She pushed a glass into his hand. "Oh, you don't want to get mixed up with them." Her voice saddened, dropping in volume. "I shouldn't be telling you this, but there are five of them altogether and Kelly says two of them rooked the other three."

A small shock went through Damien. "Rooked?"

"You know, cheated them. It's no big deal, it's done all the time, but I kind of feel badly about this one because the way I see it, all these guys are pretty nice. But it's like Kelly says, you can't trust anyone these days, even the coppers." She placed her palms on Damien's shoulders and propelled him into a corner. "Now you stay put by the door here and don't let Margie see you. She likes actors, but she's rough in bed. She'll wear you out fast, and you look like you could use some food. I'll be right back, okay?"

Damien heard her from what seemed a great distance. His attention was fastened on the table where now four of the Circle partners sat, all of them except for Neville. They had suspicious looks on their faces, but only Tom's was laced with misery.

Damien took a drink from his glass and almost choked on it. Whiskey, strong enough to make his eyes water. But he finished it anyway, to fight the cold in his bones and the fuzzy sensation in his head.

This was a dream, all right, he decided, but not an ordinary one. He remembered a small prick on his neck and Rook's voice. However, the face, the identity of the man on the *Emily-Mac* escaped him. Which was exactly what McInnie had said, wasn't it? And the name Genie, she'd mentioned that, too, and Kelly. It couldn't be mere coincidence that he was now dreaming of the same people and place. It had to have been induced, undoubtedly with drugs.

He squinted through the smoke at Herschel's thin face. Oh, he was angry all right. His fist was pounding on the table.

Damien edged closer. There was a group of people standing a few feet away from the Circle of Five. Using them as a shield he strained to hear the conversation.

"Nev'll be here in a minute," Tom was saying in a subdued voice. "All I can tell you is the deal fell through. I'm sorry, but we lost a bundle, too."

"But our businesses," Rupert objected. "We can't stay afloat after three straight financial losses. That's what this partnership was all about, you told us. We'd help one another at times like this."

Tom nodded. God, he did look miserable. "Well, initially that was the idea. But you have to appreciate, Rupert, that we're no better off than you are at this point."

"Now why don't I believe that?" Herschel remarked, giving a cynical snort.

"Because you wouldn't believe your own mother," a snow-covered Nev said, joining them. "Sorry, boys, bu Tom speaks the truth. We lost our shirts on the freigh deal."

Samuel, who'd been observing all of this, finally broke hi silence. "And you can't bail us out and we certainly can' help one another, so it looks like we're all going under. Un less of course you feel that you and Tom can squeeze by."

Nev didn't flinch. "Could be," he said. "We'll have t see."

"So the partnership's dissolved then," Herschel state with a bang of his hand. "We lose our businesses, our shir and all our money."

Nev spread his hands. Tom continued to look unhappy "That's about the size of it. I'm sorry, but Tom and I ju: can't help you out this time."

"No more token loans to string us along." Samu laughed. "Oh, Nev, you played us all real good, didn't you I assume you have the dissolution papers with you."

"Tomorrow," Nev told him in his banker's tone, ve: certain. "Tom'll bring them by in the afternoon...."

"Hey there, honey."

A woman's freckled arms suddenly wound themselves around Damien's neck, startling him.

"You are gorgeous. I want you."

Damien started to say no thanks, but her mouth cut him off. He disengaged himself from her clinging lips, then reached up and removed her arms.

"I'm broke," he said, because that would have to be the most effective deterrent to her.

"On the house," she replied instantly. "I've never seen anything like you before. Beautiful hair and face, and no gut." She rubbed his stomach. "I bet you're Italian."

He drew back, grimacing. "Brazilian-American and I'm waiting for Genie."

"Uh-uh. Genie's out. Kelly'll kill you if you touch her. Come on, the rooms are this way. My name's Margie, by the way."

"The rough one," Damien murmured, dragging his feet.

"Beg pardon?"

"Nothing. Look, Margie, I'm really not interested...."

He was cut off by the hand that clamped down on his shoulder, then hauled him forcibly around. The man glaring at him was heavyset, with a beard and breath that smelled like two-week-old Scotch.

"Oh now, Charlie, don't go making a big fuss." Margie poked at his arm. "You'll get yours. I have half an hour before you, and I want this one."

"So do I," Charlie said dangerously. His fingers dug into Damien's flesh. "I think we'll just take a little walk, huh? Maybe out to the alley."

Damien knocked the hand away. Fear of bullies had never been in his repertoire of emotions. He wouldn't have survived even his short time on the Salvadoran streets if it had.

"Fine," he agreed, a bit impatiently. He wanted to get back to the unraveling of the Circle of Five. "But here, inside."

The man showed yellow teeth, then brought a clenched am-hand over his shoulder.

"No!" Margie's scream got everyone's attention, mild though that was. They went on about their business while Damien ducked the punch and brought his own fist up hard into Charlie's stomach. One "Oomph," as the man doubled, then a crack on the jaw that bruised Damien's knuckles and down he went.

"Oh-oh. Now you're in trouble."

Margie's warning came too late. Before Damien could react, two very large men had hold of him from behind.

Genie's, "Hey, what's going on here?" didn't help. Neither did the kick Damien landed in the crotch of the man on his left. But they did have everyone's full attention now.

A fist slammed into Damien's throat, momentarily blinding him. He could imagine the onlookers placing their bets, not on who would win, but on how long it would take Charlie's henchmen to beat the crap out of him.

"Bastards," he swore.

Somehow he broke the hammerlock. Shaking off the effects of the blow he caught the bigger man under the chin. It cut off his oxygen long enough for Damien to shove the other one's head into the bar.

It was a stall tactic at best. These guys were pros and now Charlie was coming around.

"Three against one," a voice whispered in his ear. "should let them have you."

Rook!

The name snaked through Damien's head, the name and a rolling cloud of smoke.

His eyes stung and his throat throbbed where he'd been punched. He squinted into the mass and saw Genie pulling on Margie's arm. He also saw the Circle of Five partners ignoring it all—except for Samuel, which seemed rather odd. He watched in thoughtful silence, staring at Damien face as if...

The smoke thickened, growing darker and more dense. dragged at his limbs, like invisible fingers clinging to him. The bar began to fade out, one movie scene melting into another, or in this case the fusing of dream scenes.

But contrived, he managed to remind himself. Rook had set this up deliberately, he must have. Rook, whose voice echoed in his head, yet with no substance, no timbre beyond the fact that it belonged to a man. And his features were washed-out, smudged as Melanie had said.

"A dream," Rook's voice revealed. "Yes, Damien, that's what it is. Relax, and I'll bring you back." The voice came closer, words whispered against his ear. "I couldn't let Charlie Morrow hurt you. That pleasure is mine, my gift to myself."

Damien's mind was drifting badly now, the blackness wrapping itself around his body. But he heard it even so: Rook humming the birthday song.

HE WOKE UP ON the aft deck of the *Emily-Muc*, alone and surrounded by fog. His head throbbed, and he was soaking wet and cold.

Groaning, he rolled onto his back. A dream, he thought, like Melanie's, engendered by Rook whose face was a complete blur to him.

He had to get to Tiburon, he knew that, but he couldn't seem to make himself move. He felt like all the energy had been stripped from his body.

He could still think, more or less. And what he thought was that Rook had turned inevitably deadly. He'd killed Lucy Farmer and now he'd revealed the truth about Nev and Tom's scam. Yes, they were swindlers. They'd screwed their three partners totally, then gone on to thrive because of it. That it had happened during the Depression was an excuse, a poor reason for scamming people, but Damien couldn't believe they'd have done it in a less desperate time.

He exhaled heavily. "Maybe they would have," he said out loud, climbing to his knees. "Maybe they did. Who the hell knows?"

Rook knows, his brain whispered, but it was an answer lost in what his eyes suddenly discovered on the deck.

He stared at the torn envelope and white papers for a long time, then tipped his head back, to relieve the tension in his neck muscles. "The diary pages," he murmured. His breath got lost in the wet shroud of the fog. He felt his back pocket—gone—then glanced down. "December 19, 1937. I don't believe this."

His fingers stiff from the cold, he retrieved the pages before the wind could blow them into the Bay. It was then he noticed the skinned knuckles on his right hand.

MELANIE SLIPPED INTO the Romac hangar at eight o'clock on the morning of October twenty-seventh, the day after the discovery of Lucy Farmer's strangled body. She still shuddered every time she thought of it. *Damn Rook to hell for his viciousness*.

Somehow, though, she shoved the memory aside. Mr Hiroshi's Halloween flight departed this afternoon. Sidney had seen to the decorative details; now she must make the final check. *Life goes on,* she reflected with weary cynicism.

She climbed the endless access stairs to the forward hatch and stepped inside, avoiding the hanging spiders out of habit, then stopped in the process of removing her raincoat and sniffed the air.

"Cigarettes," she muttered in disgust. "I told them not to smoke in here."

"It doesn't sound like they listened."

"Damien!" She twisted her head around, her face momentarily lighting up. But she tempered the spurt of happiness with the knowledge that he'd be gone for good very soon.

She tossed her raincoat over one of the seats. "Why are you here?"

He approached from the far aisle, looking tired and tousled and absolutely adorable. "Waiting for you." With his hands in his jacket pockets he kissed her thoroughly, then made a small gesture with his head.

Melanie saw nothing out of the ordinary, only yards of black cloth and powdered cobwebs. She'd rather he kissed her again. "Mysteries first thing in the morning?" she asked.

He offered no explanation. He merely led her through a batch of pumpkins carved with dragon faces to the plane's midsection, then nodded at a silver tray.

"Cigarette stubs," she said. "I know, I smelled the smoke. Decorators do that sometimes."

Curling his fingers around her wrist, Damien pulled her to a crouch beside him. "Decorators didn't do this, Mel." He picked up two of the stubs, a Camel and something ultra-slim. "Regan," he said, dropping the slim in her palm. "And Addison."

Startled, Melanie recoiled from the thing. "Well no, maybe not," she protested automatically. "You can't be sure."

"No?" He nodded through a porthole. "Take a good look at the couple on the far side of the hangar."

Melanie didn't want to do it, but she forced her eyes to look. She cringed inside when she located the pair. It was them all right, Regan and Addie, and their body language said it all. Unless Regan made a habit of being groped in corners by Romac pilots, Addison Brown was the man with whom she was having her affair.

"But why?" Melanie wondered out loud. "He's nice enough, but Rolf's better."

"Not to Regan." Damien called her an insulting name in his native language then brought the shade down.

On her knees, Melanie stared at him, still disbelieving. "So what do we do now, about Addie, I mean? I don't think it's fair to fire him." She frowned. "Or is it? And Rolf." She lifted her eyes to the blacked-out ceiling. "What do we say to Rolf?"

"I don't know." Damien was silent for a moment, then he dipped his head. "Mel, that dream you had the night before I left for London, do you remember it?"

"Nightmare," she corrected. Her fingers itched to ease the shade up. What a twit Regan was. "What about it?"

"Did it feel almost—" his features darkened as he searched for the word "—choreographed?"

She considered the idea. "I suppose. Sort of, yes. It made sense, if you know what I mean. Usually dreams jump all over the place, but this one was more like a play."

"Like someone was directing your thoughts in sleep?" Damien suggested.

"Yes. Why do you ask?"

"Because I had the same dream." He shrugged. "Similar anyway. My time frame was different, but it was Chicago and there was a hooker, actually an ex-hooker, named Genie."

"Really?" Melanie felt absurdly relieved. "She got out?"

"In a way." A tiny smile curved the corners of Damien's lips. "I have her engaged to Donny Kelly."

"The owner of the house."

"It's a bar, according to Genie."

"I was there, Damien, in the back rooms. I almost had Charlie Morrow for a john. It's a bordello."

"Anyway," he went on, his eyes straying to the shade, "I also met a man named Charlie, probably your horrible gangster. He wasn't especially friendly."

"He wouldn't be with you." Melanie regarded his narrow, beautiful face through her lashes. "How many of the 'ladies' came on to you?"

Damien's smile widened just a little. It still contained a trace of melancholy, no doubt due to what he'd seen in the hangar. "Only one," he told her. "Someone named Margie. Genie said I didn't look up to handling her."

Irrational pangs of jealousy aside, Melanie was tempted to laugh. But then she thought of Rolf, Regan and Rook and released a sad breath instead.

"I think you could have handled her," was all she said, then with her fingers she touched his right hand. "What did you do to yourself?"

"I put my fist in someone's face."

Again she almost laughed, but it was more pleasurable to bring his hand to her mouth and kiss the bruised skin.

"Addie's, I hope."

His smile grew vague. "Not quite. One of Charlie Morrow's henchmen."

Melanie froze, her blood turning to ice, her heart suddenly pounding loudly in her ears. "That isn't possible, Damien."

He looked at her, his eyes dark and unreadable. "I know."

Chapter Eighteen

"Boston!" Addison scowled at Damien. "You're making me take an Elite Charter to Boston instead of the New Orleans flight? Why? It's snowing in Boston."

Damien forced a smile. "And you've got a hot date in New Orleans, right?"

"Exactly." Addie ran his fingers through his mop of brown hair. "This feels like a punishment of some sort. Did I screw up and I don't know it?"

Damien could look as innocent as a child when he wanted to. He faced Addie, his expression blank. "Not that I'm aware of. You'd know if you screwed up. You're too smart not to realize when you've made a mistake." He handed the revised flight roster to Morgan Voss outside Rolf's office and said again, "Boston. Maybe you can get another date there."

Now the glint Damien had been waiting for appeared in Addie's eyes. "I see," was all he would say in front of Morgan. "And after that, what?"

"Just do Boston," Damien told him wearily, in no mood for clever word games.

The pilot hesitated, then finally shrugged. Tugging on the bill of his hat, he raised a meaningful brow. "You might want to hear my side of things, Damien," he remarked calmly. "And remember the old saying."

"It takes two, I know, Addie."

"Hi, Addie." Rolf strode in then and Damien winced inwardly as his brother gave the other man's arm a good-natured tap. "Lousy day out there."

"Lousy day in here," Damien muttered under his breath. "Have a good flight, Addie," he said, and with a wordless nod the pilot left.

The moment he was gone, Morgan stood. "Tucker tells me you've passed him over for the vacancy at Romac accounting. May I ask why?"

"He's not good enough," Damien replied. Bluntness was about all that worked with Morgan.

"You're sure of that, are you?" Morgan challenged. "You're not just being petty?"

"We're not petty people," Rolf told him patiently "You know that, Morgan."

A stab of guilt passed through Damien's stomach, but it didn't last. Addie deserved worse than a flight to Boston for screwing around with Regan. For bad taste alone he should have his head examined.

"Just out of curiosity," Damien asked, "what is Tucker to you?"

Morgan's response was quick, maybe too quick. "He's the son of a friend of mine."

"That's all?"

"Would you like to see his birth certificate?"

"I'd like to know what you two were doing in the accounting department at seven o'clock last Monday morning."

"I explained that."

"The hell you did. Melanie said—"

"I know what Melanie said, but she's mistaken. I saw someone up there, and I went to check. That's all there is to it."

Damien's sore fist clenched. Just one swing, he thought, one good slam with all his weight behind it.

Rolf leaned an arm on his right shoulder, pressing down firmly. "Not worth it," he whispered. Out loud he said quite seriously, "Melanie's your boss, Morgan. Remember that.

One word from her and you're gone. Do you under-stand?"

He was shocked, that much was obvious to Damien.

All he said, however, was, "I understand." Then he sat and resumed his paperwork.

They went into Rolf's office where Damien immediately inquired, "Where's Regan?"

"Downstairs. Why?"

"No more trips to Nassau?"

Rolf looked up sharply. "She wants to fly out tonight. How did you know?"

Damien moved a shoulder. "I didn't." God, he felt guilty, as if he was siding with her in some ridiculous way. Who knew? Maybe he was. He probably should have sent Addie to Nome. "Any news of Rachel Taggart?"

"Not a word. It's like she and her son dropped off the face of the earth."

"It might be good if they had. What about the accounts?"

"Well, we know how much we lost, but I couldn't tell you where it went."

Damien hoisted himself onto Rolf's desk. "I have theory, but no proof."

"Shoot."

"Call Mel first."

Rolf smiled and punched a button on his telephone. Five minutes later Melanie had joined them, gorgeous in black wool pants, boots and a deep rose sweater. She looked smugly satisfied, but refused to say why.

"Talk," she said, dropping into a chair in front of Damien and nudging his denim-covered shin with her toe. "I have a Hong Kong charter with a problem, and Sidney hasn't quite grasped the art of Chinese etiquette. What's the theory of yours?"

"It's about the Circle of Five."

"A little more specific, please."

"We figure Rook wanted us to know what Nev and Tom did, right?"

"That they conned their partners, yes."

"We also figure that Rook works for Romac."

"Or Cable Car Foods," Rolf put in.

"He didn't appreciate us visiting Rupert and Herschel, and he was furious about Samuel."

"Extremely," Melanie agreed. "What's your point, Damien?"

"He wants to destroy Romac, which would be where most of the money they conned from their partners would have gone. But what do you end up with except emotional satisfaction if you simply destroy something? It doesn't get the partners' money back, does it?"

Melanie rested her head against the chair back, eyes closed. "So he dipped into the accounts and got what he could for the ex-Circle partners first."

"Which was a considerable sum, although it won't break us," Rolf said.

Damien combed back his hair with his fingers. "I doubt if he was finished."

Melanie raised her eyes to his face. "Lucy?"

"Lucy," Damien repeated. "She caught on, he caught her and killed her."

Rolf tapped his fingers on his blotter. "So then Rook must be an accountant."

"Or he has an accomplice with accounting knowledge," Melanie suggested.

"In which case he could still be anyone." Rolf slumped back in his chair, his gaze sliding over the rain-streaked window. "Gloomy day." He paused then added, "I feel like he's toying with us, you know, leading us around by the nose. And I wasn't going to mention this because we all know how Nev and Tom held on during the thirties, but maybe you should know. I got more diary pages last night. They were dated April, 1938 and they told all about Romac the early years. No money problems there."

Damien exchanged a resigned look with Melanie while Rolf went on staring blindly out the window.

"It's funny, though," he continued. "I mean, I read the pages, but then it was like I fell asleep and dreamed about it, the way you did, Mel, except that I know I read the pages first."

She tipped her head to one side. "Did you meet Rook?"

"Not that I remember." He blew out a frustrated breath. "Oh hell, I might as well admit it. I polished off half a bottle of brandy last night about eight o'clock, right after I read the diary pages. The only thing that sticks in my mind is that dream and it's a foggy bunch of pictures at that."

"Do you remember anyone in it?" Melanie asked softly.

"Not really." He rubbed his eyes, bloodshot, Damien noticed for the first time. "There was this big guy with a beard, I think. Nev and Tom were there, counting their money so to speak. And there was a woman. She'd just gotten back from her honeymoon and she was chatting it up with a bunch of other women."

Damien hopped from the desk, wrapped his fingers around Melanie's wrists and pulled her to her feet.

"What was the woman's name, Rolf?" he asked. But he knew the answer before it came.

"Genie. Why?"

"Because I had a dream last night, too," he said solemnly. "So we've seen it all now, it seems. We know in detail what Nev and Tom did."

"The only thing we don't know," Melanie inserted, "is exactly what Rook intends to do about it, and when."

"OKAY, MEL, why the smug look when you came into Rolf's office?"

Damien had to wait all through the afternoon to ask her that question. He did it now after office hours and after Chinese take-out dropped onto her file-strewn desk.

She pushed away from her work. "Bribing me with food, huh?"

"It seemed appropriate. It's after seven, you know. I've been out to the airport twice since we talked to Rolf." He shoved a stack of folders aside and sat cross-legged on the desk in front of the steaming cartons. "Why smug, Mel?"

She smiled, playing idly with her long hair. "You sent Addie to Boston."

"I know."

"So did Regan when I bumped into her downstairs. She looked like Thor on a rampage. There she was all secretly booked to Nassau via New Orleans and you stick her lover with a New England charter. Our only other flight to Boston had already departed by the time she got the bad news and even for a hot fling Regan won't pay to hitch a ride on another carrier."

Grinning, Damien located the egg rolls. "Did she know what happened?"

"Oh, I think so."

He glanced up. "Did you tell her?"

"I didn't know you'd spoken to Addie at that point, although I figured you might have been responsible for the switch. No, I just kept my mouth shut, smiled and walked away." She reached for the rice. "I think the smile did it. Regan called me a few names before I got to the elevator."

"Bet that smarted."

"She called you worse ones. By now she'll probably be sharpening her verbal claws on Rolf."

Damien shrugged, unconcerned. "I doubt it. Rolf's in accounting. He was with Jonny the last time I saw him."

Melanie abandoned her chopsticks and picked up a plastic fork. "Doing what?"

"Balancing the books, I imagine." The egg roll didn't taste right. Damien made a face and tossed it back in the box. "This stuff's lousy. Let's go to Ernie's Cellar."

She looked at him, her eyes a lovely shade of green in the glow from the city behind her. The rain made a palette of the glittering night skyline. "Okay, I'll go," she agreed. "But only if Rolf comes along."

Damien caught her hand before she could pull away. "*Eu amo*, Mel," he murmured wistfully. "But that won't make it work, will it?"

"Not in any language." He saw her shoulders hunch, but she didn't remove her hand from his. She did falter slightly, though. "Maybe I shouldn't go with you."

Now, to make her unhappy was something Damien didn't want to do. "Yes, you should," he said firmly, kissing her hand and smiling at her. "Get your coat and we'll go find Rolf. Jonny, too, if he's still around."

He unfolded his legs and slid from the desk, determined to distract her even if it wasn't with the most pleasant subject.

He waited by the door while she collected a short wool jacket to match her pants, then said, "Did you ever find out why Jonny lied about the flood in his basement?"

"No." She tugged her hair free of the rolled jacket collar.

Mission accomplished, Damien thought with relief. "I don't know why he's been leaving early, either, or why he didn't catch the double entries in the Romac books."

Damien opened the door, his features solemn. "There's an answer, Mel, but it's not a nice one."

"That Jonny's Rook?" She jammed her hands in her pockets. "I thought about that. I don't believe it. Tucker maybe, except he's not really clever enough. And Morgan—I don't know, he just doesn't seem like Rook material. Even Addie strikes me as farfetched, although in my wildest dreams I wouldn't have suspected him of having an affair with Regan, so who knows who's telling the truth about anything?"

Damien couldn't resist. He slid his fingers up under her hair, holding her still while he lowered his mouth to hers. "I tell the truth, Mel."

"I know." Her body melted softly into his, her lips were warm on his cheek. "And just once I wish you wouldn't."

SAMUEL'S BEDSIDE CLOCK ticked loudly, like a bomb, to his mind. Except that now the ticks had become words: It must be tonight. It must be tonight.

He wanted to clap his hands over his ears, but of course he couldn't. He wanted to tear the old Circle of Five picture from the wall. He wanted to talk to Sonia, his sweet, beloved granddaughter—but none of those things was possible. *Oh, child, how could this have happened?*

The footsteps came. He'd known they would. Where was his housekeeper, Jessie? Had the man hurt her?

"Hello, Samuel." Rook's voice greeted him from the doorway. He wore black tonight, pants, a turtleneck sweater and gloves, always gloves. He looked dangerous, determined.

It must be tonight....

"I'm sorry I'm late." The bedsprings creaked beneath his weight. "I had to talk to Herschel and Rupert. Well, Rupert mainly. He doesn't want me to hurt them. I lied. I told him I wouldn't."

Go away, Samuel ordered in his mind. *Be a nightmare, something I dreamed up on my deathbed. Oh, Sonia, please come. Please see. Don't let this happen!*

Soft leather brushed Samuel's forehead. "You seem agitated," Rook said in a soothing voice. "Don't be. I won't harm you. I'm doing this *for* you. Soon it'll all be over and we can begin again." He smiled. "You understand that, don't you? You know what lies ahead?"

Sonia...

Rook leaned closer. "If you're wondering, your housekeeper's fine. She's sound asleep on the living-room sofa. I won't harm her, either. I'm not a killer by nature, you must believe that. Lucy Farmer would have exposed me. In a way she did anyway, I suppose. You see, I didn't know about the message she left on Melanie's home answering machine. Still, I bought an extra night by disposing of her. I got the three of you quite a lot of money, something for you to leave our heirs."

Samuel's eyes became accusing. Rook saw the look and sighed.

"No, I'm not thinking of myself. I don't need that money. It's for you and Mother."

Samuel's body gave a convulsive jerk. Oh, to be able to move, to whisper a single word to this person.

You're no heir to me, he thought. *Don't you see? We set ourselves up to be conned. Nev and Tom saw their opportunity and they took it. What happened to us was our fault as much as theirs. Please don't kill their heirs.*

Rook didn't hear the silent plea. His eyes moved to the clock. "A few more hours," he said with the ghost of a smile. "You relax and let me handle this. I have to leave for a while, but I'll be back. It ends tonight, Samuel. I promise."

Humming, he rose from the bed. Samuel closed his tired eyes. He wished he could close his mind to the truth. More than that, he wished he could close his ears to Rook's smug rendition of the birthday song.

Chapter Nineteen

"It's awfully dark down here," Melanie observed in a doubtful tone. "Are you sure Rolf's still around?"

"Not at all," Damien said, evidently trying to remember where the power panel was. "Must be at the relay station. Wait here, Mel. I'll be back in a minute."

"Sure," she grumbled. "Leave me in the shadows with a crazy Rook around."

But Damien was long gone, and once her eyes adjusted it wasn't so bad. That was one advantage of wall-to-wall windows. They let the lights of the city in, making it possible at least to distinguish familiar shapes.

Too restless to stand still, Melanie left the elevator bank and started groping her way toward accounting. If Rolf was here, he'd have the lights on, unless he was deep in thought about Regan, in which case he might be sitting in the dark.

The accounting offices loomed ahead, unlit, she noticed with a sigh. Nevertheless, she pushed through the double doors and called softly, "Rolf? Are you here?"

No answer.

"Not here," she concluded, shoving her hands into her pockets and turning with a light shiver.

Why a shiver? she wondered uneasily. She'd never practiced Damien's Salvadoran *candomblé*. Even if she had, she was too tired and worn out emotionally to be in tune with her senses.

Except for her hearing!

A tiny shuffle behind her caught her attention before she could slip back through the doors. She swung around, not sure whether to be nervous or not. Forget that, should she run for the elevators?

She paused on the threshold. "Rolf?" she tried again, very very softly.

Silence only.

But then something swished deep inside the offices. There was someone here, and in all probability it wasn't Rolf.

Jonny maybe?

She was starting to whisper his name when she felt a movement behind her. A pair of hands wrapped themselves around her arms and a familiar voice said in her ear, "This isn't the elevator bank, Mel. What are you doing here?"

Her knees almost gave out on her. "Damien," she gasped, then she remembered the swishing noise and she pointed toward the rear of the office area. "I heard something," she whispered. "Back there."

"Not Rolf?"

"I called. He didn't answer."

Damien's palms rubbed her arms, but his eyes were on the darkest of the shadows. "Go wait by the elevators, Mel."

"No. I'm coming with you."

"You're a pain."

"I'm a partner." She peered into the darkness. "Do you think it's Rook?"

"Maybe." He pressed a hand against her hip. "Stay behind me."

"So you can get shot first?"

"This Rook doesn't shoot bullets, remember? They're more like invisible torpedoes that hit but don't penetrate."

They'd reached the back section of accounting now. Three corridors branched out from here. Melanie slowed, undecided. "This one, I think," she murmured after a moment's hesitation.

Damien didn't answer, and when she reached out to touch him, her hand found only air. She couldn't very well call him, either, not with an unknown person lurking in the shadows.

"Damn you, Damien," she whispered in exasperation. Her heart felt like a steel hammer in her chest. For all she knew, Damien could be calling her. With her blood pounding in her head she'd never hear him.

She shifted her weight from foot to foot, her senses alert, her eyes searching for even a pinpoint of light. But back here the windows were heavily curtained.

A tiny scrape broke the stillness to her right. Damien? His name stuck in her throat. Fists balled in her pockets, she inched forward, using reason to conquer fear. Rook couldn't have known they'd come here looking for Rolf, so he couldn't be planning to kill them, right?

On the other hand, when presented with the opportunity...

A shudder tore through her body. Her teeth chattered and not from the cold. But maybe it wasn't Rook.

Far ahead, she thought she detected a voice. Well, surely Rook wouldn't be having a chat with anyone—unless he and Damien had had a coming together.

Her feet dragged on the carpet, but she refused to retreat. Not until she found Damien.

The voice grew slightly louder, unintelligible words spoken at intervals and in very hushed tones.

Whose voice was it?

Melanie strained to locate the source and at the same time not stumble into a wall. Big brass plant pots lined the corridor, easy to trip over but good for hiding behind if someone were to suddenly rush out.

The murmurs continued. She still couldn't identify the speaker. Then suddenly the voice stopped and she heard a click. A telephone receiver being replaced?

Her fingers closed on the nearest door frame. This was the office, she was sure of it. Drawing a deep breath, she listened for a minute, then peered around the edge.

Did she imagine that the adjoining door was just being closed? She didn't think so.

Seconds later as she was creeping forward to check that door, she heard a loud crash. The sound of running feet followed, then a grunt and finally another crash.

No bullets, she noted gratefully. And now she could shout, because the noise had come from the outer offices, as if someone were trying to escape.

"Damien!"

She ran in that direction, maybe a foolish thing to do, but what if he was hurt?

It took her only a few seconds to establish that he wasn't. She collided with him full stride in the reception area. Only his hands grabbing her waist prevented her from being flung over one of the outer desks.

"Was that you making all that noise?" he asked, inspecting her carefully for bruises as he spoke.

She made a forestalling motion. "I'm fine. No, I thought it was you. Were you chasing someone?"

"Not really. I heard a sound in the hallway so I followed it. Then I heard the crashes and that's about it. I ran into you."

Melanie saw a bamboo plant stand lying on its side. "He must have known you were after him and knocked that over." Her muscles tightened. "Shouldn't we be chasing him?"

"He'll be long gone by now, Mel." Damien started for a phone, raking his hair from his forehead in mild annoyance. "I'll call Harry downstairs and tell him to watch the elevators."

Melanie started back for the area where she'd heard the sounds. "I'll check the office he was in. Maybe he left a clue."

Two minutes later she was sitting at the desk, her feet propped up on the top, the lights blazing overhead. "No clues," she said when Damien came in. "Maybe fingerprints on the phone, but I doubt that."

"So do I." Damien prowled the room. "Harry didn't see anyone."

Dropping her feet, Melanie leaned forward. "The phone," she repeated thoughtfully. "Damien, there's a redial button. I'm almost positive I heard him talking on the telephone when I was out in the hall."

"Try it," Damien suggested, coming up behind her.

Using a tissue—just in case there were fingerprints—she picked up the receiver and pressed the redial. Four rings and a woman's voice answered.

"Hello, this is Sonia Benson, and you've reached the home of Samuel Taggart. There's no one available to take your call at the moment. However, if you'll leave your message at the beep..."

The tape rolled on to completion, but Melanie didn't hear it. With the receiver held slightly away from her ear, she looked up at Damien.

"Whoever he was, he called Samuel."

Damien's dark brows lifted. "Whoever he was, Mel?"

"You think it was Rook."

It was a statement, not a question, and he made a seesaw motion with his hand. "Could be, although Rook doesn't strike me as a clumsy person."

"Or a person who'd leave anything to chance." Melanie frowned in confusion. "But if it's a setup, how did he know where to be? I mean, how could he possibly have known we'd come down here?"

"How does Rook know anything?" Damien returned in a considering voice. "This is not an ordinary man."

"A psychic, Damien? Telepathic? Is that what you're suggesting?"

A hint of a smile formed on his lips. "Actually, I was thinking of something a little less metaphysical."

Melanie swung around sharply as his meaning penetrated. "A bug!" she exclaimed. "He bugged my office! This was a setup." She stood, her fingers curled at her sides. Absurd though it was, she felt more violated than worried. "So what do we do now? Drive to Samuel's place?"

Damien rested his forehead against the back of her head. "That seems to be what Rook wants us to do—assuming this was all a setup."

"I think it was." Melanie shuddered deeply. "Rook lures pawns, Damien. I feel like we're playing right into a trap."

"We probably are."

"That's not very comforting."

"It hasn't been from the start, Mel." He lifted his head. "But it's Rook's game, as he told us. All we can do is play it and hope he's got a weak spot."

"And if he hasn't?"

Damien turned her around. There was no deception in his face or in his response. "If he hasn't," he said calmly, "he'll kill us."

ROLF WAS STEPPING out of his car when they reached the underground parking lot and Damien's Jaguar.

"You drive. You know the coast better than I do," Damien said to Melanie. Then he grabbed his brother's arm and shoved him into the back seat.

Rolf looked dazed, displaced. He had a take-out deli sandwich and a beer in his hand. "I thought I was going upstairs to do some work," he said as Melanie gunned the engine. "Apparently I was wrong. Would someone like to explain?"

"We're going to Samuel Taggart's," Damien told him.

"At eight-thirty at night?"

Damien filled him in, finishing with a reflective, "I can think of anything except that Rook wants us there."

"That, or maybe you just caught him off guard," Rolf replied. "He could have been in accounting trying to divert more money."

"Why call Samuel Taggart's place, then?" Melanie asked, her eyes on the wet road. "And why make all that racket when he left? It was like he drew us in, Rolf. A shuffle here, a bump there, and he certainly hung up the phone loud enough."

"Okay, let's say you're right. Shouldn't we call the police?"

"What if we're wrong?" Damien said softly. He twisted around in the seat to face his brother. "Besides, do you think the police would be willing to barge into an old man's house because we pressed a redial button and got his answering machine?"

"I see your point."

Melanie drove right on the edge, barely missing crashing each gear. Damien still found that strangely arousing, an odd reaction, considering what might be waiting for them in Monterey.

"You know," Rolf remarked at length, "it's barely possible that Rook wanted you out of the building so he could slip into the Romac accounts one last time, clean us out, so to speak."

Damien reached back a hand for a piece of the sandwich. "He couldn't do that in a single night."

"He could if he was good enough, or had good help."

"Jonny?" Damien asked, taking a bite.

"Or Tucker. He's not great but given a string of uninterrupted hours, he could do some serious damage."

The speed Melanie was driving, they'd be down to Monterey and back before he could do much more than access the relevant files. Damien refused to look at the blurred scenery.

"Do you want to go back?" he asked Rolf. "We can let you out. You could grab a cab and be at the office in ten or fifteen minutes."

Rolf thought about it for a moment, studying Damien closely. "No, I'll stay with you two. Nev always said you had good instincts." He paused. "I, uh, don't suppose they're telling you anything more, are they?"

"Like who Rook could be? Sorry, no."

"But you think this is all part of some grand plan?"

"Game," Damien corrected. "I have a feeling that to Rook, this is all a life-size game of chess. We lose, we die."

Rolf sank gloomily back in his seat. "Match to Rook."

IT WAS PITCH BLACK on the stretch of uneven road leading
to Samuel Taggart's front door. A heavy mist shrouded the
dead oak trees, giving them the appearance of Halloween
spooks. Melanie had had her foot to the floor most of the
way down, but now that they were here, she wanted quite
badly to turn back.

"Cut the engine," Damien told her as they approached
the lonely old house. "And the headlights."

She did both things at once, easing the car off the road.
"Now what?"

"What do you think?"

Her fingers dug into the steering wheel. "Actually, I was
trying not to."

Rolf leaned over the seat. "Maybe you should wait here,
Mel."

She sighed. "I wasn't trying that hard. Come on, let's get
this over with."

The mist seemed to be everywhere. It floated between
branches, clung to power poles and more than once it completely obliterated the two weak lights that burned in Samuel's house.

Melanie held tight to Damien's jacket as they walked. It
was too quiet, she thought. It never got this quiet in San
Francisco or in the jungle, either, for that matter. There
should at least be a dog howling in the hills.

"This reminds me of my dream," Rolf said in a low voice.
"Everything was covered in fog—" He broke off abruptly.
"What was that?"

Damien stopped, causing Melanie to bang against him.
"What was what?"

Melanie peered into the filmy layers. "I don't see anything."

"Well, I did," Rolf insisted. "Something moved, over
there to the left."

The house was to their left. Melanie's fingers dug deep
into Damien's jacket. She sidled closer. "Maybe it was a
rabbit or something. We're pretty far out of the city, you
know."

Rolf didn't seem convinced, although it was difficult to judge expressions in this weird, practically nonexistent light. It wasn't quite as hard to judge sounds, and Melanie picked up on one a moment later.

"It sounds like grass rustling," she whispered to Damien. "Can you hear it?"

He nodded, slowing again. Yes, definitely, something was moving, charging toward them. Melanie held her breath as it shot through the ditch and ran straight across the road not two feet in front of them, its tail flying behind like a plume.

Amusement tinged Damien's voice. "What a mass of nerves we all are. It was a squirrel."

Melanie preferred being scared and alive to being nerveless and dead. She kept her eyes trained on the darkness to her left and her cold fingers fastened to Damien. It was still too quiet out here. She didn't trust this much silence.

The driveway, a narrow strip of muddy ruts, led straight to the house. But it had its drawbacks even so. More dead oaks lined the sides, with patches of overgrown bushes in between.

Manderlay, Melanie thought, but it wasn't really like that, only that forbidding on this misty night.

"When the lights are blocked out, the place looks deserted," Rolf remarked. "Maybe we should..."

From the darkness a gunshot suddenly rang out, shocking Rolf into silence and sending the three of them diving for cover.

Rolf must have gone one direction while she and Damien went the other, because there was no sign of him when Melanie scrambled into the shelter of an old marble fountain.

A stream of questions raced through her terrified brain. Who'd fired the shot? Where had it come from? Was Rolf hurt?

Damien was crouched down beside her, his hand on her neck. "I think it came from behind us," he murmured. "Do you see Rolf?"

She shook her head, then did a double take. "Look!" She grabbed his wrist and pointed. "Behind that tree! There's a man."

"Where? Never mind, I see him." Damien squinted into the long shadow. "It's not Rolf."

"Not unless Rolf was packing a rifle we didn't know about," Melanie agreed, feeling strangely breathless.

The figure eased out from the blackened trunk, not quite visible to Melanie's straining eyes. With the rifle barrel he poked at a prickly bush.

"Come on, all of you," a familiar voice ordered. "Up and out where I can see you."

Melanie's heart gave a lurch. "It's Tucker," she whispered. She stared at his outline. "I can't believe it's Tucker."

"I can," Damien said in disgust.

"Come out now," Tucker warned, "or I'll start shooting every which way."

"Christ, he thinks he's Clint Eastwood," Damien muttered under his breath.

"I'll do it," Tucker shouted. As proof he fired two shots dangerously close to the fountain.

"Funny thing, Tucker," Rolf's voice called out from some hidden spot across the driveway. "But we just don't trust you. How do we know you won't shoot us the minute we step out?"

Tucker swiveled instantly. "You'll have to risk it," he sneered.

Beside her Melanie felt Damien's muscles tighten. That could mean only one thing, but before she could open her mouth to protest, he was gone, across the muddy drive and launching all his weight at Tucker's unsuspecting back.

A loud grunt burst from the man's throat. The rifle flew from his hands as he went down, facedown into a patch of weeds.

Melanie didn't hesitate. Using her terror to propel her, she ran to where the rifle had landed and grabbed it. She could hear Tucker's ongoing grunts, then his whiny pleas a

Damien dragged him to his feet and shoved him chest first against a tree trunk.

With his arm impossibly twisted behind his back and his cheek pressed into the rough bark, Tucker panted and said, "Stop it, Damien. You'll break my arm."

"Or maybe I'll shoot you first," Melanie threatened, lifting the rifle to her shoulder. She hadn't settled to calm yet, only relieved—and angry. *How dare this little weasel try to kill them!*

With his body, Damien held Tucker in place. "She'll do it, you know," he warned. "We primitives who grew up in the wilds of South America tend to be barbaric."

"Cold blooded," Melanie added, prodding his shoulder with the barrel. "Like you. Where's Rolf?"

"How should I know? Damien, for God's sake, let me go."

"Are you Rook?" he asked, then when Tucker didn't answer, he gave his arm a jerk.

"I—arghh—no!"

"Just his minion, huh?" Damien shook the man. "Who's he?"

"I can't..."

"Okay." Giving Tucker's arm one last twist, Damien stepped back. "Shoot him, Mel."

"What?" Tucker spun around, still plastered to the trunk. He looked shocked, but no more so than Melanie felt. "You can't shoot me. That's murder."

"We'll call it self-defense. Who's Rook?"

Tucker blinked in fear. "Mel, you wouldn't!"

She squeezed the trigger. She did know how to shoot—a basic jungle lesson as Damien had said—but she was still grateful when she heard the bullet impact in nothing more fleshy than tree bark.

Damien didn't bat an eyelash. "Who's Rook?" he repeated, his expression completely empty of emotion.

Tucker opened his mouth. He was going to answer. Even with the thickening mist Melanie could see the defeated light in his eyes. But then another shot rang out, and he dropped in slow motion to his knees.

Damien swore, and spun swiftly around. Melanie could only stare. She hadn't fired that shot.

Tucker's eyes went wide, and his hand came out to clutch at the air. Then very slowly his facial muscles slackened. His jaw fell open, and his eyes, already shocky, glassed over. He made a bubbling sound in his throat, swayed for an endless moment, then from his knees toppled lifeless to the ground.

"MEL, DAMIEN!" Rolf's voice whispered to them from the bushes. "Where are you? What's going on?"

"We're right behind you," Damien rasped, "and stay down. Tucker's not Rook."

"So I heard." He grimaced. "My foot was caught in a hole. I only now worked it free."

"Is anything broken?" Melanie whispered.

"I don't think so. Tucker?"

"Dead," Damien told him. "Rook must have shot him."

Rolf frowned. "Why? To keep his identity a secret for another five minutes?"

"More likely to keep private any secrets they might have had," Melanie said. She sounded scared, Damien noticed, but in control. "What do we do now? Wait?"

Damien looked around. "For a minute, anyway. I have no idea where that last shot came from."

"Well, maybe..." Rolf started to say, but once again he was cut off, this time by that mechanical voice they knew so well.

"You're within my gun sights, all of you," it said. "Melanie, put the rifle down. Now stand up, the three of you and go to the house. Use the driveway. Step one foot off it and I'll kill you as I did Tucker Smith. When you reach the house, go upstairs to Samuel's bedroom. You know where it is." The voice mocked them openly with that. "You have three minutes, starting now."

SONIA LISTENED to her own voice on her grandfather's answering machine, then hung up the telephone for the twentieth time that night.

"Where are you, Jessie?" she asked her empty kitchen.

She glanced at her watch. Ten-thirty. Her husband would be home any minute now after a night of taking stock in his store. The baby was due anytime, so she shouldn't be thinking of anything except packing to go to the hospital. But she couldn't help it. She'd been calling for three hours straight. Jessie never left the machine on that long, and even if she had this one time, she would have realized her mistake when she heard Sonia telling her to pick up the receiver.

No, something was definitely wrong.

With an effort Sonia worked herself to her feet, put on her coat and located her car keys.

"Please don't come tonight," she begged the baby. Then she wrote out a brief note for her husband.

Chapter Twenty

The house was listening to them, Melanie swore it was. O[f]
course that could be her nerves talking, or the fear that wa[s]
making her limbs shake and her skin ice-cold from the in[-]
side out.

"He's watching us," Damien said, taking it all in as the[y]
entered: the dried and faded wallpaper, the long shadow[s]
and the woman sleeping on the sofa, drugged, no doub[t.]
"He's been doing it from the start, but I can't figure ou[t]
how. It's like he knows almost everything we do in ad[-]
vance."

He, being Rook, the still featureless blur in Melanie'[s]
mind. Why couldn't she remember that face? She'd seen i[t.]
Why the big blank spot in her memory?

Telepathy, she would have said to Damien, but she didn[']
believe that. Rook was something else, uncommonly clever[.]

Whoever Rook was, he was almost certainly insane, an[d]
insanity could take on any number of forms, or so she'[d]
heard from various media sources. A person might appea[r]
perfectly fine one minute, then turn around and kill his be[st]
friend the next.

A shiver crawled through her. Now *there* was a horrib[le]
thought.

They mounted the creaking stairs single file, first D[a-]
mien, then Melanie, then Rolf. The house was absolute[ly]
still. Only the ticking of the grandfather clock in the low[er]
hallway broke the silence.

She saw the door to Samuel's room at the far end of the corridor. Light spilled weakly through the crack.

"Ready?" Damien asked.

She nodded and heard Rolf's murmur of agreement behind her. Oh, but she didn't want to do this. She didn't want Rook to be real.

They stepped through the door in turn. Melanie saw Samuel lying there, his heavy-lidded eyes on their faces as they entered.

Everything was as it had been before: the old-fashioned iron bed, the rocking chair beside it, the nightstand and the small hanging picture of the Circle of Five.

Better days, she thought with a pang. Or so three of them had believed.

It seemed then that Samuel's hand twitched. His fingers curled, all but one, and it looked to be pointing. At least it was trying to point.

The skin on the back of Melanie's neck prickled. The claw finger had come up an inch off the covers. It *was* pointing—to something or someone behind them.

It was inevitable, the click that signaled the closing of a trap. Their escape was blocked. Rook had sealed them in here. Now all they had to do was dredge up the courage to look.

It had never been so hard for Melanie to do anything in her life, but she forced herself to turn.

And there he was, a man in black pants and a black turtleneck leaning against the door, a big lazy smile on his face.

"Surprised?" he asked, then he laughed, "Yes, I can see you are. But this is it, the truth. I'm Rook, and you're all going to die."

"BUT THAT'S . . ." Melanie started to exclaim.

"Crazy?" Rook finished with a slow, evil grin. He took a menacing step toward her and Melanie felt Damien's muscles tighten. His smile widened. "No, Mel, I'm not crazy, not at all. I don't hear voices in my head or have vi-

sions or think I'm someone else when the moon is full.
Everything I've done, I've done for a reason." His eyes
flicked to Damien, a statue in front of him. "Everything,"
he said softly.

Melanie still couldn't believe this. "I don't understand,"
she said in a strained voice. "Who are you?"

"Oh, come on, Mel," he crooned. "You don't need
glasses. You can see me well enough." When she didn't respond he dropped the teasing tone and shrugged. "No sense
of humor, any of you. And no answers, either. But then I
had it planned that way. You couldn't be anything except
confused." His gaze moved from one face to another, his
own features distorting slightly in the shadowy light. "Call
me what you want to call me, all of you. I am Rook."

No, Melanie wanted to shout at him. *Not Rook. You're
one of our pilots. You're Addison Brown!*

It was almost as if Rook had read her mind. A humorless
smile curved his lips. "So transparent, Mel," he said softly.

Beside her, Damien tipped his head slightly as he studied
Addie's face. "How did you do it?" he asked. "You're
supposed to be—"

"In Boston?" Addie supplied. He laughed. "Obviously
I didn't go, did I?"

Monster, Melanie thought with venom. And then quite
suddenly it all fit. She'd said to Damien that Rook hadn't
gone after Rolf, but he had. He'd done it through Regan.
He'd had an affair with her because that was the most effective way of hurting Rolf.

In her mind she called him every disgusting name she
could think of, then she edged closer to Damien whose impassive stare hadn't left Addie's face.

"Why did you do it?" she found the courage to ask,
wondering obscurely where he'd put his gun. There was a
leather case by his left hand, but no gun.

"Revenge," he said simply, returning to lean on the door.
"I wanted to get Samuel and his friends a little of their
money back. The reasons for that of course you already
know."

"Because Nev and Tom conned them," Rolf said. "But I still don't understand. Our people saw you get on that Boston flight."

"I did." Rook smiled. "Then I turned around and got off again. I developed a sudden malady. Brogan took my place. You see, we don't always tell you everything." His smile taunted. "Like for example, why your wife was in such a snit this afternoon and why she suddenly decided not to fly to Nassau after your loving brother here took me off the New Orleans flight. Not that I could have gone to New Orleans anyway."

Rolf's features hardened, his fists clenching at his sides.

"Careful," Addie warned. "I'm just itching to get this over with, punish all of you as I see fit."

"Then why don't you?" Damien challenged. "Drug us or shoot us or drown us, whatever you intend to do."

Addie laughed. "What a nasty memory you have, Damien. You don't enjoy being dumped in the Bay, do you? Tell me, did you like my Lucifer's hammer?"

Damien's eyes narrowed. "Your what?"

"That's what I call the little weapon I hit you with. It's my own invention. It has a technical name, but you'd never understand the concept." Again he chuckled. "Tucker couldn't even pronounce the word, but then Tucker was an idiot. He almost let that cretin Morgan catch on to what he was doing in accounting." He sighed, picking up the leather case and leaving the door. "I should have tried to get Jonny on my side. I could have stripped you of a lot more funds, but unfortunately Jonny's not one of the family grudge bearers."

Mistrustfully, Melanie echoed, "Family! You mean you and Jonny are related?"

Giving them a wide berth, Rook crossed to the bed and laid a hand on Samuel's lined forehead. Samuel didn't appear to appreciate the gesture. His hand jerked about convulsively on the covers.

"We're second cousins or something," Rook revealed in an obscure tone. "I'm not exactly sure of the relationship. Anyway, Jonny doesn't know about it."

Confused and suspicious, Melanie now looked at Damien who merely continued to watch Rook.

"Why doesn't he know?" she asked cautiously.

"Because I never told him." Addie made a dismissing motion. "Forget it, Melanie. It's beyond you, all of you."

"What is?" Rolf demanded.

"The whole thing. My plan, or game if you prefer."

Melanie's suspicion deepened, to say nothing of the chill in her bones. "Are you Rachel's son?"

"Nope. Jonny is."

"What?" Rolf sounded shocked. "Did Nev know that?"

"Of course." Addie's movements grew mildly agitated as he took a small kerosene lamp from inside the nightstand and lit it. "Jonny told him the whole truth when he applied for the job. Nev couldn't believe that all Jonny wanted was a job, but that was the sum total. So maybe old Neville had a twinge of conscience at last, or maybe he just knew a stroke of good fortune when he saw one. Jonny's a whiz with numbers. Lucky for me his mother got sick or Tucker never would have pulled off his computerized juggling act."

Damien's eyes remained steadily on Addie's face. "Lucky?" he questioned, "or predetermined? What did you do, Addie, drug her, too?"

Addie waved a hand. "She'll be fine," he said. "I wouldn't permanently damage a relative, unlike some people."

His tone held a trace of snappishness now. Melanie watched as he adjusted the lantern's orange flame.

"Why are you doing that?" she asked, not trusting him an inch.

He sent her a dark look. "In case the power goes out."

"But why would it do that?"

"Because there's a storm coming."

"Are you cra—" She swallowed the word and substituted a hasty, "There isn't supposed to be a storm tonight."

"You know," he said, straightening and advancing on her, "you're one of the few women I don't mind." He halted at the end of the bed. "In case you're interested, Rolf, Regan's a bitch, both in bed and out."

Rolf would have lunged at him if Addie hadn't suddenly produced a knife from under Samuel's quilt.

"Old-fashioned but effective," he said with a shrug. "Now back off, all of you, over by the window."

"Planning to push us out, Addie?" Damien inquired.

"Nothing that simple." He took a step closer. "I think you'll be last, though, Damien." He pressed the tip of the blade to Damien's heart and smiled. "Because I like you best."

If he wanted a reaction, he didn't get one, not from Damien, anyway, and beyond cringing inside, Melanie refused the bait as well. Rolf made a small sound, but it was Samuel's choked cry that diverted Rook's attention.

He backed away to pat the old man's twitching hand. "Don't be upset," he murmured. "It's almost over."

Damien studied him. "What are you to Samuel, exactly?"

Addie gave a short laugh. "I'm his great-grandson."

"But Jonny doesn't know it," Rolf ascertained. "Is that right?"

"I told you, Jonny doesn't hold a grudge, and believe me, Rachel did everything she could to get him to develop one. There was no point in my telling Jonny anything. He couldn't even lie well when he needed time off to take care of his poor sick mother."

"Why didn't he tell us about her?" Melanie asked, her fingers curling about the windowsill. She might be imagining things but she thought she heard thunder in the distance.

Addie shrugged. "He probably didn't want you to know about his connection to the Circle of Five. For Nev to know was all right, but you're his friends. And who knows, maybe he was sick of the whole thing. Maybe he wanted to keep his job there on his own merit, not because of any sense of obligation you might have felt."

"Starting with a clean slate," Rolf translated.

"Something like that." Addie's eyes traveled to the window. "Lightning," he said with an enigmatic grin. "And the mist is starting to clear." He arched a brow at Melanie. "Still think there won't be a storm?"

She was so numb and cold she could hardly feel her fingers. "How could you possibly know what the weather forecasters didn't predict?"

He smiled, a secret and vaguely unsettling smile. "Rheumatism," he answered with a completely straight face. "It acts up whenever it's going to rain."

"Look, Addie," Rolf tried, then he paused. "Is Addison Brown even your real name?"

"Nope. Only the initials are mine. Damien, why are you staring at me like that?"

"Like what?"

"Don't get smart. What are you looking at?"

"I'm trying to figure you out."

"What's to figure?"

"Well, for one thing," Melanie said, "you're remarkably clever. How do you do what you do?"

"You mean the—" he chuckled "—the dreams?"

"Yes."

His eyes took on an eerie glow, his tone deepened. "Maybe they weren't dreams, Mel."

"What does that mean?"

"Think about it."

"Did you drug us? Is that why we couldn't remember your face afterward?"

"Could be."

"Why call yourself Rook?" Damien asked, since Addie obviously wasn't going to give Melanie any straight answers.

"It's my nickname, always has been. Any more questions?"

Too many to sort through, Melanie thought uneasily. She didn't much like the way Addie, or whatever his real name was, held that knife. And what was Samuel trying so desperately to accomplish with his crippled hand? There couldn't possibly be anything shocking left to point out.

"I, um, think Samuel's upset," she said, in the vague hope that Rook might become distracted.

Addie's gaze didn't waver. "He doesn't understand it all, yet. I haven't had time to explain. His granddaughter's here most of the day and that makes things difficult."

"Why?" Damien asked.

"Because," Addie shot back. His eyes gleamed. "Your favorite answer, I think, Damien." Again he picked up the leather case. "Now, over to the wall by the top of the bed. We're going to do this one at a time."

"Do what?" A chill of dread slithered down Melanie's spine. "Stab us, shoot us, what?"

He smiled but didn't answer. How could anyone smile with such total menace?

She forced her feet to move, couldn't really feel them, though. Oh God, she should have gone to Brazil with Damien. She'd go there now in a minute. She'd go anywhere he asked her to.

But he'd never have another chance to ask, would he? Rook was going to kill them and that would be the end of it.

No! She stiffened her back. It didn't have to be like that. There must be something the three of them could do to fight him.

She knew Damien would not quietly accept his fate. Neither would Rolf, so all they had to do was turn as one and make a lunge for Rook's throat.

Beside them Samuel made a horrible sound, as if he was choking. His hand danced frantically on the quilt.

"Shh," Rook said to him, bending a little over the foot of the bed. "I won't do it here if it bothers you that much."

"I'll count to three," Damien said softly. "Then we'll go for him."

Melanie nodded, but her eyes were on Samuel. Was he indicating the wall? She looked sideways at the picture hanging there, the framed photo of the Circle of Five partners seated around a table at Kelly's Place. She could see it clearly from where she stood.

It must have been the desperation in her mind that made her scan the crowd of onlookers behind the Circle. Then suddenly she stopped. There, behind Samuel, who was that?

She blinked not believing it. But the woman was real, her features were unmistakable even surrounded by smoke. "Genie," she whispered in astonishment. "It can't be."

But it was. The surprise that Melanie felt at this discovery, however, was nothing compared to the shock that hit her in the next second.

Beside Genie stood a man, a tall, lean man with a mop of brown hair and a lazy smile on his lips. She recognized him instantly. It was the same man who stood behind them in this room tonight!

"Rook!" The name fell from her lips. Her voice was a mere thread of sound, inaudible above the approaching thunder and the wind that had gathered force beyond the windows. She was hallucinating, she had to be.

Damien had started to count, she understood that much if little else. And Addie was still talking to Samuel, telling him to please calm down. But how could anyone be calm when faced with such an impossible discovery? Had Samuel seen it, too? Is that why he was so distressed?

"Two," Damien said.

"Relax," Addie entreated the old man. "You'll hurt yourself. Samuel, please. I'll take them to the—what's that?"

Addie's head snapped up sharply as a pair of headlights suddenly swept the room. Damien stopped counting. His fingers closed on Melanie's wrist. And then it seemed that the room, the scene, the moment and everything in it, took on a new and vaguely unearthly aspect, something dark and slow and menacing, and maybe not quite real.

"Run, Mel," Damien whispered to her.

But she couldn't seem to move, not her feet, anyway. She was only dimly aware of her hand reaching up to slip the picture from the wall and tuck it into her jacket pocket.

"Don't move, any of you," Addie ordered. He ran to the window, looked out, then pounded on the sill in a rage. "Damn her! What's she doing here!"

Melanie caught the spasmodic movement out of the corner of her eye. It had nothing to do with Rook or storms or headlights that shouldn't be there. It was Samuel's hand and it flew out wildly, knocking the kerosene lamp from the nightstand and sending it crashing across the carpeted floor to the curtains in a splash of oily flame.

"No!"

Addie spun from the sill, like an animal on the verge of attack. The knife sailed toward them, only narrowly missing Melanie's head.

The flames spread rapidly, catching on the dry carpet fibres and the curtains.

"The bed!" Melanie gasped as smoke from the synthetic material began to fill the room.

"Get Samuel," Damien said, giving her a push. "Then get out of here."

"But what about—?"

"Go!"

And this time, she didn't argue. She saw Damien through the growing flames. He had Addie already, or Addie had him. At any rate they were fighting and as much as Melanie wanted to be with him, Samuel was an invalid. He couldn't get out of here by himself. Coughing, Melanie's hand stripped the blankets from his wasted body.

Rolf reached past her. "I can't get to Damien," he shouted. "I'll carry Samuel down. I think the power has gone, but the phones should still work. Find one, Mel, and call the fire department."

"No, I'm staying with Damien."

"You can't."

Melanie hesitated, torn. She couldn't even see the two men anymore; certainly she couldn't reach them through the wall of orange flame.

Swallowing a sob, she turned and raced for the door. Rolf pushed past her with Samuel.

"Don't forget the housekeeper," Melanie shouted after him.

She was relieved to see a telephone on a stand just outside the bedroom. She scrambled for it, dialing 911 with shaking fingers. Using her free hand, she waved at the smoke and prayed that Damien would think to break a window, or just climb out and jump, and to hell with Rook.

"Grandfather!"

Through the tendrils of billowing white smoke, Sonia appeared, but not from the direction Rolf had taken with Samuel. She must have come up a rear staircase.

"Grandfather!" she screamed again, dropping the candle she'd been holding and hurrying toward the room as fast as her pregnant body would let her.

Melanie caught her sleeve and pulled, still talking into the phone. "Rolf's got him," she said during a pause, then she repeated the address to the woman on the other end of the line.

Sonia hovered in the doorway, undecided.

"Rolf took him out," Melanie repeated, pulling harder on her now.

"But there are people in there!"

Melanie had to clench her teeth to talk around her angry tears. "I know. It's Damien and Rook."

"But they'll get—!"

Eyes wide, Sonia doubled over, her hand pressed hard to her swollen stomach. "Oh, my God, not now!"

Melanie gripped her arms tightly. "The baby?"

"Ohh."

Swiping at her tears, Melanie waited until Sonia could straighten. "Come on," she said. "I'll help you downstairs. They're sending an ambulance."

She took one final tearful look into the bedroom, then drew a deep breath and guided Sonia toward the staircase.

The last thing she heard was the sound of splintering wood. Then the roar and crackle of the flames took over, and there was nothing more.

Chapter Twenty-One

Damien landed on the floor of the bedroom adjacent to Samuel's with a painful thump, but at least he was out of the suffocating smoke.

Rook came through right behind him, panting and covered with soot. "It's screwed up, Damien," he growled, "but I can still kill you."

It wasn't an idle threat. Rook had more strength in his body than anyone Damien had ever met. He also had something in his hand that looked like a miniature bazooka. Lucifer's hammer, Damien assumed, twice avoiding its discharge, but only by a fraction of an inch each time.

Already the smoke and flames were pouring into the room, the fire catching on an upholstered chair and crawling toward the curtains.

"Who are you?" Damien asked, his voice little more than a croak.

"I told you," Addie snarled. He kicked away a burning cushion, coughing as he approached. "I'm Samuel's great-grandson, and I want you dead."

Damien circled the bed, but Rook cut him off before he could reach the door. "Did you cause Nev's heart attack?"

"No. That was destined to happen." He aimed the weapon at Damien's chest. "Can't mess with destiny, my friend. Damn!"

His shot, obscured by layers of swirling smoke, missed its target again. Damien ducked. He couldn't see the point of

mpact or anything else for that matter, but he'd bet the wall
was a mess.

He dipped down a bit to avoid the smoke. The room was
hick already. A few more minutes of this and they'd both
suffocate.

He kept moving, wary of the man before him. His fingers searched and found a small object, something hard and
porcelain. Hiding it in his palm, he edged away from the
bed.

"Tell me about the dreams, Addie," he prompted, struggling not to cough. "How did you cause them?"

"Magic," was all Addie would say, except that his name
wasn't Addie, was it, and that was another puzzle.

"Drugs?" Damien pressed.

Addie merely smiled and took aim again. The fire was
directly behind him now, a wall of flame, devouring the
wallpaper at an alarming rate.

Damien tensed and waited. The shot came. With a jerk he
flung his body sideways, rolling onto his shoulder across the
carpet and back to his feet in one motion. Then before Addie had time to respond, he threw the porcelain figure at the
man's hand.

The weapon spun free and tumbled into the flames.
Rubbing his wrist, Addie swore, "I'll kill you, Damien."
Then all of a sudden he stopped and snatched his head
around. "What?"

Damien listened and, confused, repeated, "What?"

Addie let out a defeated breath. "It's too late," he murmured. His head fell back and he started to laugh. "Do you
hear it, Damien? It's too late."

Damien heard the fire and in the distance the wail of sirens, but those things wouldn't bring such an ironic smile to
Rook's lips.

"The clock," Addie said, still laughing. The smoke
seemed to swallow him up, it had to be choking him and yet
he didn't move. He simply closed his eyes and continued to
laugh, softly, ruefully. "The chimes, Damien. Count them.
Three, four, five..."

On his knees, barely able to breathe, his eyes stinging, Damien asked, "What about the chimes, Addie?"

"It's midnight."

"So?"

Addie's smile took on a cynical air. Tongues of flame licked at his heels. But still he refused to move.

"It's over," he said. He stood there, his hands at his sides, his gaze calm on Damien's face. "You've won."

"You're going to get burned, Addie," Damien warned, wiping damp hair and smoke from his eyes. "For Christ's sake, do you want to die?"

"Can't die," Addie told him. Bending over, he scooped up his weapon. "Eleven, twelve," he counted. Then he turned and walked toward the wall of fire. On the rim he paused, twisting his head around. "Sorry I can't stay longer, but I'm out of time."

"What the hell are you talking about?"

Addie's smile widened. "Didn't I tell you, Damien? Today's my birthday."

Too startled and confused to react, Damien could only watch as Rook turned once again and disappeared calmly into the fire.

"I STILL CAN'T BELIEVE it," Damien said five minutes later to Rolf and Melanie. "But that's what happened. He said it was his birthday, then he walked into the fire."

The emergency vehicles were almost there. Melanie could see the flashes of red and blue neon far down the deserted road. The house was an inferno now, a solid wall of flame. Samuel's head rested in Sonia's lap, the housekeeper lay on the grass close beside them.

Melanie put her arms around Damien's neck, too relieved that he was here to really absorb what he was telling her.

But apparently Sonia caught the gist. Breathing carefully between contractions, she said, "He must have been crazy — what did you call him again?"

"Rook," Melanie murmured into Damien's smoky skin. "We don't know his real name, only that it wasn't Addison Brown."

All jackets and coats had been piled on Samuel's supine body to keep him warm. The wind caught wispy tendrils of his white hair, but Sonia smoothed them down and smiled.

"Well, whoever he was, at least he didn't hurt you."

Rolf stared at the house far ahead of where they sat. "I don't think he wanted to hurt any of the Circle partners."

"Only us," Damien said.

Melanie lifted her head. "But why did he kill himself? I don't understand that."

"Neither do I." Damien rubbed his bloodshot eyes. "Maybe he really was crazy."

"Well, at least he told me about a cousin I never knew I had," Sonia offered, then clamped her mouth shut as another contraction started.

"The ambulance is here," Melanie told her, leaving Damien to take her hand. "It's just pulling into the driveway. Are you okay?"

"Fine." The pain eased off and so, slowly, did the strain on her features. She laughed. "I'll tell you, though, it's been a night. What was his name again?"

"You mean Rook?" Melanie asked with a quick glance at the flaming house.

"No, my newfound cousin."

"Jonny Morelli," Damien said. He coughed, then motioned to Rolf. "Tell them two stretchers. And it looks like the housekeeper's been drugged."

"And Rook?" Sonia inquired tentatively.

"Dead," Melanie said, shivering in the wind that seemed to slice right through her. "If he walked into those flames, he must be."

Three ambulance attendants hastened over, lifting first Samuel then Sonia onto separate gurneys.

"How far apart, ma'am?" one of them asked.

Sonia winced. "About three minutes."

Melanie bit her lip. "Do you want me to come with you?"

"No, my husband will be there, and you've done mor
than enough as it is. I'm mostly concerned about Grandfather. That man, for all his noble claims, has done nothing but harm to Samuel."

Damien stood, looking down at her, his arm around
Melanie's shoulders. "I don't think he meant to, Sonia. He
told us he was Samuel's great-grandson."

A grimace of pain pulled Sonia's face, then subsided. Her
expression was one of certainty. "Well, he might have said
that, but it's a lie. Unless Jonny Morelli has a child, Grandfather has no great-grandchildren." She touched her stomach as the attendant finished covering her. Her features
softened to a smile. "At least not yet."

THE HULL OF THE *Emily-Mac* rocked in its moorings,
pounded by the waves of the storm that wasn't supposed to
be taking place.

With a shudder for all he'd seen that night, Damien hung
up the phone and, stretched out on the sofa in his smoky
clothes, waited for Melanie to come out of the galley.

She emerged moments later carrying two cups of coffee
and wearing a puzzled look on her face.

"Why did he lie?" she asked for the fiftieth time that
night, which was now about to brighten into dawn. "Who
was he?"

"A crazy person," Damien suggested, then he cleared his
throat and groaned. "My lungs feel scorched."

"I don't doubt it." Melanie sat cross-legged on the coffee table beside him. "You shouldn't have fought with him.
You could have gotten killed."

"We all could have gotten killed if Samuel hadn't
knocked over that kerosene lamp." Damien's eyes darkened. "It was almost like he did it on purpose. I wonder if
he knows something we don't?"

"Well, if he does he's not likely to tell us. He still can't
talk, although I gather from your conversation with Rolf
that he's okay." She nodded at the phone. "I assume it was
Rolf you were talking to."

Damien smiled a little, reaching out to play with her hand. "It was." He lifted his eyes to her smudged face and beautifully tousled hair. "He's filing for divorce today."

Melanie sent him a slightly guilty glance. "Is he mad that we didn't tell him about Addie, or whoever he really was, and Regan?"

"Mad, no, at least not at us. I don't think he's too thrilled with Regan, and Rook's a moot point."

"Rook's a maddening point, if you ask me," Melanie said with a sigh. She cupped her chin moodily in one palm. "Maybe he meant he was Herschel's or Rupert's great-grandson."

"Nope. Herschel doesn't have any great-grandchildren, and Rupert only has one, a girl who's ten."

"Rolf's P.I. tell him that?"

"Uh-huh."

"What about Tucker? I mean, has Rolf spoken to Morgan yet?"

"A few minutes ago."

"So? Is Morgan Tucker's father?"

Damien couldn't resist a small laugh. "No, Mel. But I bet you want the story."

"If you don't mind."

"Well, what it comes down to is that during the war, World War II that is, Morgan met a woman."

"They had an affair?"

"I guess you could call it that. The problem was that the woman was married, to one of Morgan's old college friends."

"Oh-oh."

"That's right. But as I said, Tucker wasn't Morgan's son. Morgan just felt guilty over the affair, and I gather pretty resentful toward the woman."

"Did his friend ever find out?"

"Apparently not. The favors Morgan did for Tucker he did more for his friend, who's dead by the way, than for Tucker himself."

"You mean that's it?"

Damien arched an amused brow. "You're disappointed?"

"A little." She sobered. "And sad, I guess. It didn't have to be like that for Tucker. I mean, I wish he hadn't died. I also wish he hadn't let Rook use him." She gave a small shrug. "I didn't like him, but I didn't want him dead."

Damien nodded. "I know. In case you're interested, and on a less morbid note, Jonny's mother, Rachel, is fine. Whatever Rook gave her couldn't have been fatal."

"What about Sonia?"

Damien brought Melanie's hand to his mouth. "She had a seven-pound, thirteen-ounce boy at 12:47 this morning."

Melanie smiled. "So now Samuel has a great-grandson."

"Now he does," Damien agreed, kissing her fingertips one at a time.

Melanie laughed, pulling her hand firmly away. "You're distracting me, Damien. I want to get this straight."

He sighed, stretching his sore arms above his head. "I think it's as straight as it's going to get, Mel."

"But the dreams . . ." she started to say, then straightened as a thought suddenly hit her. "The picture!" she exclaimed. "Damien, he was in the picture."

Damien frowned, not understanding. "Who?"

"Rook." She picked up her jacket and began hunting through the pockets. "And Genie, too. But it was seeing Rook that shocked me most." She held the coat upside down and shook it. "Where is it? I know I took it off the wall." She groaned. "Oh, it must have fallen out."

Coming up on one elbow, Damien plucked the jacket from her hands. "Forget it, Mel," he said. "As strange as it sounds, I believe you. But I don't think we'll get anywhere by dwelling on it. Let's just make sure that Samuel and Rupert and Herschel are given the money that was rightfully theirs to begin with and put cons and dreams and great-grandsons and birthdays out of our minds, okay?"

"Well," she said with reluctance, "all right. But about today being Rook's birthday . . ."

Gently Damien tapped her chin and brought her mouth down onto his. "No birthdays, Mel. Let's talk trip to the jungle and a visit with your mother. We could sail there in the *Emily-Mac*, then go on to Brazil."

She let him pull her on top of him. "Where we'll live happily ever after?" she asked, humorously mistrustful.

"Well, six months' worth, anyway. Maybe we could open a South American branch of Romac."

She kept her mouth just out of reach of his. "And what about the other six months? Romac, San Francisco?"

"I could probably get used to the idea—given the choice."

Melanie kissed his cheek. "But before we sail, we have to help Rolf get things straightened out here, right?"

"Sounds fair." His fingers curled themselves around her neck, pulling her head down. "As long as we're together. *Eu te amo*, Mel."

"I love you too, Damien. Now that Rook's gone, I have a feeling it'll be more than enough. Hey, wait a minute." She pulled back and laughed. "We won!"

"Won what?"

"Well, you said it was all a big chess game to him. And we won. Pawns take Rook."

"Not quite. That doesn't win the game."

"Don't be picky. We won."

"True." He smiled against her lips. "Checkmate, Mel."

Epilogue

Monterey, California
One year later

"Oh, he's beautiful, Sonia, a real sweetheart, and already a whole year old. You and David must be so proud. And Samuel, too."

Sonia beamed at her great-aunt. "We are, Millie, very proud."

She hugged her grandfather's frail shoulders. He lived with them now. He had ever since the night his house had been destroyed in that awful fire, the same night his first and so far only great-grandchild had been born. Andrew Samuel Benson they'd called him. He had Samuel's big brown eyes, and what a bright little thing he was.

Amid a throng of friends and relatives he played on the living-room rug at his first birthday party. There were presents scattered everywhere. But he seemed to prefer one gift above all, returning to it time after time, no matter how hard David tried to get him interested in the stuffed polar bear.

From his wheelchair Samuel watched in silence while Sonia hugged him again and whispered, "Isn't it wonderful, Grandfather? You get to watch him grow."

"I don't believe this kid," David exclaimed, laughing. "He's doing it again. Going straight for the chess set. Look, he keeps grabbing the castle. What is that piece, Aunt Millie?"

"It's the rook," she answered, then proceeded to finish telling the story about Neville and Tom's Circle of Five swindle.

David ignored her and chuckled, scooping his son, chess piece and all, off the floor and kissing his cheek. "Well, I guess that's just what we'll have to call you from now on, huh? Would you like that?"

The baby gurgled happily.

"Okay, that settles it. No more Andy. We'll call you Rook."

"Rook," Sonia repeated, frowning. "Now, why does that sound—?"

She stopped abruptly, the color draining from her face. Something tightened in her chest. Her eyes flew to Samuel's. He was watching her now through a veil of unshed tears.

Stunned, she looked at her small son. "Rook!" she whispered in a horrified voice. "Oh my God, no..."